D1374583

We hope you enjoy this book. Please return or renew it by the due date.

You can renew it at www.norfolk.gov.uk/libraries o by using our free library app.

Otherwise you can phone 0344 800 8020 - please have your library card and PIN ready.

You can sign up for email reminders too.

3|23

NORFOLK ITEM

30129 088 760 864

NORFOLK COUNTY COUNCIL
LIBRARY AND INFORMATION SERVICE

THE BROKEN AFTERNOON

Also by Simon Mason

A Killing in November

THE BROKEN
AFTERNOON

Simon Mason

riverrun

First published in Great Britain in 2023 by

riverrun

An imprint of

Quercus Editions Limited
Carmelite House
50 Victoria Embankment
London EC4Y 0DZ

An Hachette UK company

A CIP catalogue record for this book is available
from the British Library

Hardback 978 1 52941 571 1
Ebook 978 1 52941 572 8

10 9 8 7 6 5 4 3 2 1

Typeset by CC Book Production

Printed and bound in Great Britain by Clays Ltd, Elcograf S.p.A.

Papers used by riverrun are from well-managed forests and other responsible sources.

For Eluned

ONE

Poppy Clarke, four years old, standing in the sun-dazzled gateway of Magpies. Giggling.

Deep in the heart of rich Oxford, Garford Road glowed in the heat, a moneyed hush of rustling copper beech, murmuring voices of girls from the private schools, muted conversations of construction workers at the Edwardian villas under renovation – and Poppy's laughter ringing out bright as summer birdsong as she danced on the spangles of sunshine on the gravel driveway of her nursery school, waiting for her mother at four thirty on a July afternoon.

It was a game, their usual game. She knew where he was, she could see his shadow on the bright pavement. Pausing, she watched carefully as she knew she was supposed to. Her eyes shone. She clapped her hands. She jumped round in a circle, all dimples and ribbons in her red and black pirate costume, the season's craze. Still smiling, she shook her head sternly and wagged her finger. Covered her eyes with her hands, snatched them away, and burst out laughing again.

Briefly, she turned and looked at the nursery building behind her, where her mother was talking to a friend, but there was nothing to see there except a boring empty doorway, so she turned back to the street. She looked shyly, but only pretend-shyly; really she was watching between her fingers in that clever, sly way she had. And soon she was giggling and jumping up and down, until, when beckoned, she skipped forward. And when her mother came out a few moments later she had gone.

TWO

Ten hours later, five miles away, in a poky shed-like office smelling of engine oil and instant coffee, night-watch security guard Ryan Wilkins broke the long hours of his shift by catching the news on repeat. Two o'clock in the morning, night rain creeping with tiny claws across the plastic roof. He turned up the volume and leaned in.

On the screen: his former partner, Detective Inspector Raymond Wilkins, flanked on one side by the new Superintendent and on the other by the Thames Valley Police crest in gilded carpentry, fronting a presser. A little girl gone missing. Her picture appeared, an irresistible advert for the human race with her blonde curls and dimples, her bunched cheeks and shining eyes, appropriately pleased with herself in pirate costume, eye-patch and cutlass, ribbons and sash. Vanished from outside her Oxford nursery while her mother talked for no more than two minutes to her teacher in the lobby. A picture of the nursery appeared too, a snippet of sculpted beech hedge and immaculate lawn – another advert, for parental serenity, priceless at fifteen grand a year.

From which, in broad daylight, a little girl had been snatched. Upper-middle-class England was freaking out. In the echoey conference room journalists shouted questions over each other.

DI Wilkins said they were following a lead but declined to give details, and Ryan turned him off and sat there in the sudden quiet staring out of the window at the rain-crackly darkness of the van compound beyond. He could imagine the situation. A news shout so quick wasn't ideal – things were still too messy – but the timetable of sensational cases was driven by the media. A lead? If real, probably the father; Ray pointedly hadn't mentioned him and the disappearance of very young children was mostly the result of parental disputes. Ray would be good at dealing with that, smooth and tactful. He'd looked good on television too, no denying it. Cameras loved him, tall and black in his uniform; they loved his serious features, educated tone, the way he paused between sentences, the firm shapes he made with his strong hands, the resolute look in his eyes. Handsome Ray. The thinking woman's law enforcement.

Ryan considered his own reflection in the window. Skinny white kid in nylon uniform, a discount purchase from mywork-wear.com. He looked at his overlarge nose and attention-seeking Adam's apple, quick eyes under scratchy brows, shiny smear of scar tissue down his left cheek, a grimace about to happen, a fidget coming on somewhere – Ryan Earl Wilkins, twenty-seven years old, trailer-park rat boy, one of the youngest ever detective inspectors in the Thames Valley force, dishonourably discharged three months ago, now working nights at Van Central, off the Botley Road. Boom. Hero to zero in three minutes. Or two and a half.

Still, Ryan was never down for long; he always revived, without warning or indeed reason, his optimism an inexplicable part of him, unasked for, like his nose, his fidgets or his beloved son, Ryan Junior, nearly three years old, by far the calmest and most discerning of all the Wilkinses, asleep now at home with his Auntie Jade. Grinning at the thought of him, Ryan was turning on his broken-backed swivel chair to put the kettle on when his eye was caught by a tiny blip in the corner of the security screen. Gone almost before it had happened, but not too quick for Ryan. Things stuck to his eyes. Another quirk.

He stared unblinking at the screen for two minutes more. Nothing. Only the unvarying van compound, an area of grizzling darkness, of rental vans stored between railings, a big box of toys put away at bedtime, a dead zone of silence, complete stillness. Except, just momentarily, a brief tremor in the texture of the shadow of a Ford Transit. A little jolt of interest went through him. He initiated the required security procedure, activating the police response and logging the time, checking the codes for the doors to the offices and workshop. All fine. Everything was nice and smooth – until he tried to switch on the compound flood-lights. Not a glimmer. After a moment he began to rummage in a drawer of his broken-down desk for a flashlight.

Outside, silvery rain was drifting down on a fine breeze scented with diesel, and Ryan followed the beam of his torch across the concrete forecourt to the metal gates, still securely padlocked. As he went, he mentally reviewed the last few hours for signs of anything out of the ordinary he might have missed. There was nothing he could think of. When he'd arrived at ten there had been a van left on the forecourt – usually there was at least

5

one – and he'd driven it inside the compound and parked it and locked it, as per, and given the pen a last look round. Everything had been secure; he'd double-checked the gates. He looked about him now. The compound was surrounded by a two-and-a-half-metre-high palisade fence in galvanised steel, pretty much burglar-proof. Perhaps an animal had got in, one of those muntjac deer from the water meadows at Hogacre. He'd seen them on the pavements among the surrounding warehouses, strange creatures, dog-like, with foreshortened front legs and raised hindquarters, creeping along as if in shame. He scanned the ground ahead as he unlocked the gates and went inside, listening. The vans around him seemed to bulge forward in the torch beam as he waved it slowly to and fro, walking down the narrow channels between them. He came to a halt at the end of a line and waited a few beats, listening again. Nothing but the whisper of rain on van roofs. And then, five metres away, very softly, a scrunch of gravel.

He switched off the light and went quietly back along the row towards the entrance, and a shadow movement on the other side of the line of vans seemed to keep pace with him. At the end he waited a moment, then stepped smartly to the other side.

The figure looming in front of him was big, six six at least, and bulky, head hooded. When Ryan appeared, he flung his arms out and canted forward with a grunt, but Ryan was quicker, shining a light at him with one hand, taking a picture with the other before he could flinch away.

There was a panting pause as they confronted each other, a moment of unexploded-bomb uncertainty when things could still go either way.

Ryan said, 'Go ahead, kill me with a spanner, why don't you? Murder first degree, ten to fifteen in Grendon, no parole, come out in time to waste the rest of your fucking life on street meds.'

More panting.

He tensed himself.

Then the figure spoke, a deep sticky voice. 'Done Grendon already.'

Ryan hesitated; a flutter of recognition went through him. 'Mick Dick?'

The man lowered his hood and showed him his face, trembling. Those familiar puffy cheeks, those bloodshot eyes, lopsided mouth. All distorted now in fear. Terror.

'Mick Dick! What you doing here?'

All the man could do was moan. Passing a big hand across his face, he brought it away shaking. Shook his head, dumbly suffering. He didn't seem able to speak. Something was wrong with him. Ryan stood there shocked, puzzled, trying to remember when he'd seen Mick Dick last: maybe not since school, when they were both sixteen, when Mick was still promising, a boxing heavyweight in the Nationals, trying out for Wantage Town, and Ryan was running wild at the raves and in the clubs.

'What the fuck's the matter with you?'

Still no reply. Moans. Some trembling.

'Jesus Christ, Mick Dick. Didn't even know you were out.'

He'd read about it at the time. Aggravated burglary, minimum five at Grendon, category B facility out in Bucks. Nice lad, Michael Dick, but easily led, always doing favours for the wrong people. Some weakness let the violence in. They said the man he'd attacked during the burglary was in a coma for a fortnight.

Looking at Ryan with his bloodshot eyes, he finally spoke. 'Two months. Trying to get work. Every day, man, knocking on doors.' He moved his tongue around his lips. 'Get something soon. But this. This is fucked up. I can't be here.'

'Yeah, well, don't want to let you down too badly, but you are actually here, and you need to tell me what the fuck you're doing.'

'I'm telling you, Ryan, it's a mistake.'

He was shaking again.

'Listen. You got about five minutes before the bobbleheads get here. You can explain to them if you like.'

There was a faint noise wafted on the breeze: sirens.

Mick Dick was moving his head wildly; he said in a rush, 'Ryan, Ryan, man, can't go back. They put me away for long this time. Got a little girl, four years old, she grow up without me. Ryan!'

'Calm down. I need to know what you're doing here. Say something I can understand.'

'I got nothing, I done nothing, I swear.' He spread his arms. 'Check me out, man. It's just . . .'

'Just what?'

He looked ashamed. 'I got nowhere to stay. She kick me out till I get my shit together.' He gestured hopelessly at the sky. 'It's raining, man.' In his voice nothing but defeat. An ex-con on the street.

'You been sleeping in vans?'

He said in a sullen whisper, 'I done it, other places. There's always one left unlocked. But not here, man, you locked up tight.' He gave Ryan a closer look. 'What you doing here anyway? Thought you went for a police.'

8

'Never mind that. Show me again.'

He put his light on him and Mick Dick turned out his trouser pockets, stood there humble and defenceless as if convicted already. Nothing but his wallet, bunch of keys, papery scraps of rubbish scattering on the ground.

'That's it, that's everything. All I got.'

The sirens were closer now.

'Ryan, man. Got to help me out.' His mouth was loose with fear. Terror, again. 'My little girl, Ashleigh,' he said. Plucking at his lips with his teeth.

Ryan looked at him.

'*You* know,' Mick Dick said softly. 'I can see it.'

'Know what?'

'Know what it's like. Be out of luck.'

Ryan thought of Mick Dick aged sixteen, taking his boxing seriously, doing what he was told, forgetting to think for himself; he thought of handsome Ray on the screen, of himself in the fuggy shed where he spent his nights. There was no sound of the siren now, only the long, rising engine-whine of acceleration coming along the stretch of Ferry Hinksey Road two hundred metres away.

He had thirty seconds to decide. Do the right thing, do the wrong thing.

'Go on then. Fuck off. Don't come back till your luck's changed.'

Mick had already gone. Moved easily for a big lad. Of course, he was practised: slipping in and out of places is what he'd gone down for.

The squad car was on the forecourt and Ryan ambled out to meet them. Two bobbleheads known to him only by sight.

9

'Good news, boys,' he said. 'No need for heroics. Turns out just one of those little deer things got in. Thanks for your time and that. Always nice to have a spin, eh?'

And he watched them drive away.

THREE

At the bottom of the hill below Christchurch College and the cathedral – those grandiose monuments of piety and swag, gorgeously dressed in morning sunshine – St Aldates police station sits drably on the main road, an architectural poor relation, a low-slung building of pale stone, like a wash-house with pretensions. Nearly a hundred years old and considered unfit for purpose for about fifty. The main Thames Valley police work is done elsewhere now, at Cowley and Kidlington, but in the listed building a reduced staff pant on, making do in cramped offices and corner-spaces among inconvenient new air vents and electrical infrastructure. The downstairs has been much knocked about. Behind the public front desk is a tedious maze of walkways between meeting and interview rooms, and, on the floor above, misshapen offices and briefing rooms bodged together over the years. Only on the top floor, around the new open-plan, have some original rooms been preserved, with their period window-seats, fireplaces and stuccoed ceilings, now the desirable offices of the senior ranks, including, at the south-eastern corner,

Superintendent Dave Wallace, hard bastard of the old school with grey buzz cut and inflexible jaw, one month into the job and flinty keen to make his mark.

Seven thirty in the morning, a fine day after overnight rain. Geese on the river throwing out strangulated cries. Smells of coffee, medium roast, Blue Mountain Jamaican.

On Wallace's desk was a copy of a police dossier titled *Diversity, Equality and Inclusion Strategy*, a recent directive mandating new recruitment policies and incidentally providing new criteria by which superintendent-level attainment would be judged. Something had caught Wallace's eye: targets for representation in the detective inspector class of white boys from low socioeconomic backgrounds. Currently, this was the hardest group to reach and, given the usual requirement of a degree and a highly selective training procedure, new recruits from the group were the slowest to arrive. From scratch, it took five to seven years. Consequently, the recognition awarded to superintendents for success was proportionately greater. Quick wins were big wins. And that was why he was reading another report titled *Misconduct Procedure: Thames Valley Police vs DI Ryan Wilkins*. If new recruitment could take seven years, reinstatement could be done in a few weeks. Wallace was nothing if not shrewd. And he'd come up himself from hard times. But first he needed to know how reformable the dishonourably discharged Wilkins was.

He sipped coffee as he read.

Ryan Earl Wilkins, born 5 February 1990, Hinksey Point Trailer Park, Oxford, England. Educated at New Hinksey Primary and Oxford Spires Academy. No formal academic qualifications. Accepted onto the Inspector Level Direct Entry Programme June 2013. Fast-tracked to completion December 2014. Top attainment marks in his group.

Wallace frowned, stopped reading. Acceptance onto the Direct Entry Programme was unusual, particularly without prior qualifications. To complete the course in eighteen months was borderline irregular. He knew of only one other person who had done it. Himself.

He read on.

First career posting: Wiltshire Police, terminated in dismissal after six months for Misconduct. Allegations brought by the Bishop of Salisbury of breaching the following Standards of Professional Behaviour: a) Honesty and Integrity, b) Authority, Respect and Courtesy, c) Discreditable Conduct. Proven. Verdict overturned on appeal.

Second posting: Thames Valley Police, terminated in dismissal after four weeks for Gross Misconduct. Allegations brought by the provost of Barnabas Hall, Oxford, and others, of breaching the following Standards of Professional Behaviour: a) Authority, Respect and Courtesy, b) Discreditable Conduct, c) Equality and Diversity. Proven.

A disaster, a fucking pile-up. Looking grim, he flipped a page.

Family. Ryan Wilkins has one son, Ryan Wilkins Junior, aged two years and nine months at the time of writing. The child's

13

mother, Michelle Toomey, is deceased. The father of Ryan Wilkins, Ryan Wilkins Senior, is currently serving a custodial sentence at Huntercombe Prison, Henley, for the abduction and threat to cause bodily harm to Ryan Wilkins Junior.

Christ almighty. Family fucking saga from hell. Closing the folder, he looked out of the window, along the river where the geese were asserting their pain, past park-like Christchurch Meadow with its ruminating deer, past the university boat houses and booming ring road, towards Hinksey Point Trailer Park crouching out of sight in its hollow of traffic noise and dirt. He was a man of short bursts of forceful thinking and sudden decisions. He liked to do things his own way. His fingers ticked on the desk as he frowned. Then he brusquely pushed the folders to one side and consulted his watch, already impatient for the imminent arrival of the senior investigating officer of the missing girl case, due to deliver his morning report.

Leaning forward above the washbasins in the lavatory on the first floor, DI Raymond Wilkins gave himself a last long, narrow look. He'd been awake since five o'clock when Diane, his wife, had come into the spare room in distress asking for hot flannels and oat milk. Before she became pregnant, he'd never heard of oat milk; now they bought it in bulk and the fridge was stacked with cartons of it next to the multi-packs of pickled gherkins, ice cream and Polish dumplings. He'd never seen Diane sick before either but over the past few months she'd been ill literally most of the time, with persistently high blood pressure, second-trimester gestational diabetes and periods of hyperemesis gravidarum, vomiting so continual that at one point she'd been forced to spend three days in hospital on a nutrient drip. She'd changed in other ways too. Her shape, obviously. Not big to start with, elfin in fact, carrying twins she was all bump, a child clutching a medicine ball, staggering round the house, anxiously looking for somewhere to put it down. She had a look, hunted and furtive, seen by him before only in the eyes of certain first-time offenders, those without anyone to help them, frightened enough by the thought of prison to do something desperate. It was clear that she blamed him for her condition. He had started to feel a little afraid of her.

'I'm here for you,' he told her, over and over. 'Here I am.' But she pushed him away. The truth was, he was good only for hot flannels and oat milk. He was on the outside, at fault. She was irritable and cross. For five weeks straight he'd been sleeping in the spare room.

He peered hard in the mirror. He was blurred around the edges, eyes gritty, skin loosening around the mouth. The glory days of Handsome Ray, when he only had to look at a woman a certain way to see a spark of interest come into her eyes, were gone. He missed them. But a phrase of his father's came to him: *the sun that melts the wax hardens the clay*. He summoned the will to make it good, to be less desirable but dependable, sleepless but unflagging, pushed away but unbudgeable. To be the man his Nigerian father had always wanted him to be in Britain, as, in fact, he had become, Detective Inspector Raymond Wilkins, Balliol College graduate, boxing Blue, currently SIO on one of the country's highest-profile cases.

His phone rang and he glanced at it, frowning. Diane. He looked at his watch, hesitated a moment, then cancelled it.

15

Straightening up in front of the mirror, he turned to the left, to the right, examining himself. He adjusted his Mr P suede trucker jacket, brushed a speck of lint off his Acne Studios dark navy denim jeans. Put his Ray-Bans back on. Even a wreck can dress well. Then he turned and went out, and walked across the open-plan to the Superintendent's office.

The Super didn't like Ray, didn't like his educated tone, his middle-class manners. Ray didn't like the Super either with his hard-man tics and Govan accent. He had a habit of looking at Ray without blinking and asking abrupt questions.

'News on the father?'

'Not yet, sir.'

Poppy's father, Sebastian Clarke, thirty-eight years old, a clever, ambitious man known in north Oxford dining circles for his impatient views of public healthcare, was a senior consultant at the Radcliffe Hospital. He'd separated acrimoniously from Poppy's mother, Rachel, a year earlier, since when they had been in a bitter dispute over custody of their four-year-old daughter. According to Rachel, he'd twice threatened to take Poppy to France, where he had a house. Only a week earlier Rachel had been granted a court order against him until the childcare dispute was resolved. He'd not been seen at the hospital since the morning before and was not replying to calls or messages.

'Place him outside the nursery?'

A car matching the description of Dr Clarke's silver Mercedes had been seen by a witness in Charlbury Road, but they hadn't yet found it in the CCTV: there were no public cameras in the side streets near the nursery; they were waiting for access to the private cameras outside The Dragon and Wychwood schools on Bardwell Road. One of Ray's team, Nadim Khan from Communications and Intelligence, was on it.

'Don't let it take too long.'

'No, sir.'

'Where does he live?'

Since leaving the family home, Dr Clarke had been living in one of the canalside apartments in Jericho. It had been placed under surveillance but there had been no sighting of him there.

'Warrant?'

'We'll get it later this morning.'

'Shouldn't be waiting for these things, Ray.'

'No, sir.'

Geese yelps came through the window while the Super did his staring thing.

'Witnesses? Eyes on the little girl?'

No one had seen anything. Garford Road was a cul-de-sac, a backwater. The roads around it – Charlbury, Bardwell, Linton, Belbroughton, those impeccably mannered avenues of lilac bush and mellowed brick – had been almost deserted, the only people in them a handful of workmen, a dog-walker or two and a few schoolchildren drifting home from after-school clubs. Ray's DS, Livvy Holmes, was tracking them down and taking statements but no one so far had seen or heard anything out of the ordinary. The construction workers had all been interviewed and their vehicles were going through forensic analysis.

'SOR?'

They exchanged a brief, tight look. Neither wanted things to develop in that direction – Operation Silk, the investigation into historic child sexual exploitation in Oxford, was still traumatically vivid in the memories of many at the station – but Ray's team had run a review of the sex offenders' register and pulled out names of men to be interviewed.

'Gut?'

'Feels different.'

'Why?'

He paused. 'She's so young.'

'Some bastards don't know the meaning of too young.'

Ray acknowledged it. 'Still, it's such a quiet, exclusive sort of place, any stranger hanging round is bound to be noticed. And if Poppy had been snatched, there would have been some sort of commotion, someone would have heard something.'

'So you think the father took her?'

Their eyes met again. No blinks from the Super, only a cold, hard examination of Ray, a laser point of purpose, while the geese on the river screamed.

'I hope so,' Ray said at last.

Abruptly Wallace fired off more questions. 'Talking to the Hub? What about CRA? Next steps?'

The Hub was the local intelligence-gathering centre and Ray had been in touch with Maisie Ndiaye there; he was expecting a preliminary view from her later in the day. The Super looked sour: he wasn't a fan of the so-called profilers. The Child Rescue Alert was a system for putting out appeals to the community. The feed had been up and running since the night before with photos and bulletins, and the Twitter response had been unbelievable; the incident room was already finding it hard to keep up. Over a thousand calls had come in, including dozens of sightings of little girls in pirate costumes in Wakefield, Penzance, Carlisle, even Lima, Peru. Hundreds had volunteered to help. As Ray knew, such public interest would be fed by the media. He'd done one national broadcast already, essentially a calming exercise, and would do another later that day. Before then, he would talk to Poppy's mother again – he thought she had more to give in getting to the father – and to the headteacher at Poppy's nursery.

The Super was gazing at him again in that expressionless way. 'Difficult case, Ray,' he said at last.

'Yes, sir.'

'Public interest. Media pressure. Could get a lot worse. How are you holding up?'

Ray nodded. 'Fine.'

'Lonely business leading an investigation like this.'

His gaze went on and on.

'I can handle it, sir.'

'Things all right at home?'

He couldn't suppress a little twitch of surprise. 'Yes, sir.'

'Wife's pregnant.'

'Yes. Twins.'

'Hard. Thing is, Ray, I need you one hundred per cent.'

'Understood, sir.'

'Up to it?'

'Absolutely, sir.'

Another pause.

'So you're going to sort this for me, Ray?'

'Yes, sir.'

'I have your word on that?'

'Yes. Sir.'

A long stare, and at last a small nod. Ray waited a moment longer, then, when the Super picked up the folder on his desk, turned to go.

'By the way. You worked with the other Wilkins.'

Ray turned in surprise. 'Ryan? Yes. Yes, I did.'

'What's he like?'

He stood, flummoxed. 'Well, you know he was . . .'

'Dishonourable discharge, yes.' The Super carried on looking at him.

'Sharp, sir. He sees things.'

No comment.

'Sometimes a bit . . .'

'Yes?'

'Nothing,' he said. 'Just a bit . . . well, uncontrolled, perhaps. Sometimes.'

The Super sighed thoughtfully through his nostrils, looked out of the window again to where the sky ran blue and grey to the horizon, and after a moment Ray withdrew.

FOUR

In the long, empty hours between two and four on a weekday afternoon, the big supermarket out on the ring road has the forlorn, aimless air of an airport at midnight. The few shoppers at that time are the unemployed, the unwell, the elderly – and night-shift workers like Ryan Wilkins, now carrying a basket with young Ryan in tow. He'd changed out of his security guard uniform into grey trackie bottoms, orange Loop jacket and Burberry plaid baseball cap and Ryan Junior was wearing his old blue T-shirt and corduroy trousers with elasticated waist.

At the entrance they went hand in hand past a rack of newspapers, all displaying LITTLE GIRL MISSING headlines and close-up photos of blonde curls and dimples, through to Clothing, Adults, where effortless, affordable beauty lived in life-size photographs at the end of every aisle, and on further to Clothing, Children's, and a change of mood to Fun and Guilt, where all the signs seemed to read *Can You Bear to Look Your Children in the Eye and Tell Them You're Not Buying This For Them?* They entered a zone of pirate merchandise, a grotto of branded toys, books, games and costumes, and little Ryan came to a standstill, gazing in awe at the red and black jackets, ribbons, cutlasses, eye-patches and bootees hanging on the rack.

'Daddy?'

He had a clear treble voice, polite in tone.

Ryan sceptically confronted the rack. 'Don't you think dressing up's for girls?'

'Thomas has got one.'

'Yeah. But you know what Thomas is like.'

'No, I don't.'

'Thing is, Ry . . .' He hesitated.

'What thing?'

'We got no money at the minute. Sorry.'

They moved on to get the things they needed, bacon and sausages, milk and pasta sauces, fish fingers and chicken nuggets. Distracted, Ryan gurned and fidgeted. He hadn't slept well; he couldn't get the memory of Mick Dick at the compound out of his mind. It twisted in him like an itch – not the break-in, which was neither here nor there, but the look on Mick Dick's face, the way his hands had shaken, his shot voice, yellow eyes. That look of terror.

His phone rang. Number withheld.

'Yeah?'

A polite, busy voice announced itself as belonging to the Thames Valley Police, Superintendent's office, said that the purpose of the call was to discuss issues arising from his recent disciplinary hearings, and that—

Ryan interrupted. 'Fuck's sake, don't you think I've had enough of all that shit?'

A small silence at the other end.

'All the bollocks,' Ryan said. 'Why don't you leave me alone? Hang on.' He bent down to his son. 'Daddy's talking on the phone. What is it?'

'You shouldn't say fuck, Daddy. Or shit.'

'Yeah, all right.'

'Or bollocks.'

'Okay, fair enough.'

He addressed himself to his phone again. 'Listen, don't know who you are but you're pissing in the wrong pocket. I'm done with all that. Dropped the appeal and everything. Don't want anything to do with it. Serious. Got nothing on me any more. You got it all already. Can't get blood from a –' he looked around to see if his son was in hearing distance – 'fucking stone,' he said.

The voice in his ear asked him to wait a moment and, muttering to himself, he dawdled down the aisle, taking things off shelves and putting them back, his phone stuck to his ear, waiting. After a minute a different voice – gruffer and deeper – said, 'Wilkins? Wallace. It's very simple. Are you interested, yes or no?'

He stood between Canned Vegetables and World Food. 'Wallace who?'

'Don't jerk my chain, son. It's not a hard question. I've looked at the paperwork. There's a reinstatement argument to be made here. Not saying it's nailed on. There's a process. You might not make it. But the only question you have to answer now doesn't come any simpler. Are you in or out? If you're out, say so and stop wasting my time.'

Ryan was too smart to overthink things. 'In,' he said quickly. 'Sir,' he added, wisely.

'Okay then. I want you here soon as. My PA will be in touch. I'm not hanging about. It happens fast or not at all. All you need to get ready are three things. Smart answers, tremendous desire to serve again and an absolutely impeccable report from your current place of employment. We'll help you with the answers. The other stuff's entirely up to you.'

Then Wallace had gone.

Ryan blew out his cheeks. Shoppers went by, unseen. It was rare that he bothered to analyse his emotions, usually he let them blow through him uninterrupted, but now he dwelt on the feeling. A lightness in his body. Luck, physical as pins and needles. As soon as Wallace had mentioned reinstatement, he'd known with absolute, instinctive certainty how much he wanted to get back to the force, felt the offer of it like a kiss out of the blue. Now he clung to that feeling of lightness.

'Fuck,' he said out loud, grinning to an old woman going slowly past and she gave him the finger as she tottered on.

'Hey, Ry!' he said, looking about. 'Ry?'

He began to look for his son. Scanning up and down the aisles, he went past World Food, past the pick and mix, the Australian Merlot on special offer. He turned into the main drag, still grinning. Between Small Electrical and Breakfast Cereals he had a vision of his son as a new-born. The most beautiful thing he'd ever seen, grey-mauve crumpled mess of wet hair, dumpy, bunched body covered in bruises, though none of that had registered at the time; what he'd seen instead had been blond hair, eyelashes locked in sleep, sipping curl of a mouth. Funny how the brain overrules the eyes. Or was it the heart? He walked all the way round the freezers and back onto the main drag, glancing

24

up and down, expecting to see his son in every deserted aisle, in this one now, or the next one, or the one after that, until at last he found himself back at the newspaper racks with the headlines and pictures of that missing girl with her own blonde curls, her own sip of a mouth. CHILD GONE. HUNT FOR POPPY. ARE OUR CHILDREN SAFE? He stopped grinning then. Frowning, he went back down the aisles, quicker now, feeling his chest tighten. There was no sign of his son anywhere.

This is when it happens, when there's no danger of it happening, on an ordinary day, in a few seconds of utterly normal carelessness. This is how it sinks in, gradually then all at once. Six months earlier, while Ryan was distracted at work, little Ryan had been snatched from his nursery by his alcoholic grandfather, a man Ryan had vowed never to let within sight of his son. Now, racing past Breakfast Cereals and Cosmetics, he felt the same squeezed breathlessness of panic he'd felt then. The supermarket got bigger, the aisles longer; the piped music slowed him down even as he ran, until, in the middle of the store, he forced himself to a stop. He was police; he could find people. All it took was a little self-control.

Changing direction, he headed for Clothing, Children's, and found little Ryan standing next to the pirate costumes.

'I wasn't touching, Daddy.'

Ryan crouched down, panting a little. 'You're so good, you're bad. But you shouldn't go off like that, Ry.'

'Why?'

'Well, 'cause there's people . . .'

'What people?'

He winced and shook his head. 'Don't matter. Tell you some

other time. Got something else to tell you, some good news on the phone just now.'

'Will we have a conversation?' Little Ryan loved conversations.

'That's it. Listen, tell you what.' He took hold of a pirate jacket. 'Let's get some of this stuff anyway.'

Surprise and pleasure came into little Ryan's face like a glow. 'Really, Daddy?'

'Yeah, really.'

'What will Auntie Jade say?'

'Don't think it'll fit Auntie Jade.'

His son looked at it with something like awe, as he might look at the last flower on planet earth.

'Can I touch it?'

He nodded. 'What does it feel like?'

'Dry.'

Little Ryan carried the costume to the checkout. He kept hold of it on the conveyer belt, and on the way to the car, and in the car, and into their house in Kennington, where he took it to show Auntie Jade, who said, 'Well, that's nice, isn't it?' And turned towards the door. '*Ryan!*'

Jade was two years younger than Ryan, shorter but fiercer, her eyes on the alert for offence, her mouth held ready for action. Her hair was scraped back, giving her face a no-nonsense, useful look. She could make someone flinch just by pointing her nose at them. She had a daughter, Mylee, same age as little Ryan, a quiet girl interested in sweets. No partner. Darren was long gone; the joke was, his body would never be found. Ryan had moved in with her after his discharge. For reasons to do with their father, they were unusually close. Their mother, whom they took it in turns to visit, was in a care home. Early onset.

Little Ryan was put in the other room to show Mylee his pirate costume ('You can wear it but it is mine') so Jade could talk confidentially to Ryan.

She pointed her nose at him.

'Did we have a conversation yesterday about money or did I fucking well dream it?'

'All right, point taken. Got some good news, though.'

'Did it involve finding thirty quid in your back pocket?'

He told her what Wallace had said.

'Jam tomorrow, Ryan. When will you ever learn?'

Gradually she calmed down. They moved on to other topics, the rubbish at the back that needed taking to the tip, the bicycle that needed fixing, the washing that needed putting out. Jade reminded Ryan that he had to give the kids their tea while she did her shift at the Co-op.

'By the way,' Jade said before they parted, 'did you hear on the news?'

'About that little girl?'

'No. Body of a man found in North Hinksey Lane this morning, side of the road. Hit and run last night, they think. Not far from the school. I used to take Mylee down there in the pushchair when she was little, do you remember? Kiddie living opposite found him just lying there.'

North Hinksey wasn't far from the Osney industrial estate, where Van Central was, just across the water meadows.

'Some kid out of his head, it'll be. I think they meet in the car park of that club at the end, where it's nice and quiet. Anyway, knocked him down, didn't stop, left him to die.' She looked at him. 'Local guy, they said.'

'Catch his name?'

'Something Dick.'

It stopped him. He felt his hands go cold.

'Not Michael, was it?'

'That's it. Michael Dick. Why, did you know him?'

FIVE

Park Town is Oxford's most exclusive postcode, a bit of Georgian Bath transported to a secluded spot off the Banbury Road in the form of three crescents of stone-fronted townhouses arranged around two elliptical private gardens, all done up with lashings of wrought ironwork. Old money, comfortable and a little cramped. The padlocked gardens are dark, the pavements narrow, the antique houses squashed together like slightly shabby multi-millionaires leaning on each other to avoid falling over. Multi-millionaires, nevertheless. As he walked through, Ray passed a man washing a Porsche so low to the ground he could almost step over it. There was no one else about except workmen emptying wheelbarrows of masonry into skips, renovating houses sold by the super-rich to the even richer. Ray could taste their dust in the air. He stopped briefly to look at the local noticeboard – advertisements for private tutors; description of a missing tortoiseshell cat – and went on; and as he was going through the second garden he got a call: Maisie Ndiaye, operations intelligence analyst from Force Intelligence at Abingdon – 'the Hub'. Like most of the folks at the Hub, she was a data-head, but her background was in clinical psychology and she'd made child abduction one of her specialisms. For over twenty years she'd been the go-to analyst on local abductions.

'Maisie. You've read the stuff?'

'Yes.'

'Think we're looking at a parental?'

'Quite likely. The younger they are, the more likely a parental abduction is. You're in touch with Reunite?'

'Yes.'

'That's good; they have contacts with charities abroad. A majority of children abducted by their parents end up out of the country. Spoken to the mother again?'

'On my way now.'

'You'll be able to get a better sense of things. But Ray . . .'

'Yes?'

'A sizeable number of abductions of the very young aren't by parents. You have to remember that. No one wants to think it, but it could be a stranger.'

'A paedophile?'

'Yes. Trafficking's rare. Ransom even rarer. I'm afraid the abduction would probably be for sexual exploitation.'

'A four-year-old?'

'Don't lose hope, Ray, but if your abductor's a paedophile, your window is very small. Let's talk again later today.'

He stood for a moment in the gloom of the little enclosed garden, breathing in dust and pollen, then went on to the crescent beyond, mounted worn stone steps to a raised pavement, and found the apartment at the end. Solemnly he straightened his jacket, put his Ray-Bans in his top pocket, exhaled.

Rachel Clarke pulled open the door at once, as if she had been waiting behind it for his knock, a young woman of about thirty with pink-tinted hair, her face unnatural with anxiety. He said quickly, 'Nothing yet,' and she stood there a moment, breathing hard, panting almost, before turning and leading him along the hall and up the stairs to a sitting room.

It was an old-fashioned room with a bohemian feel, high-ceilinged, filled with light from two large windows facing the tops of trees in the garden. At one end was a table used as a desk, a mess of art paper, pens and inks, magazines and books. Unmatched sofas and armchairs were draped with rugs, and everywhere, scattered on the floor, covering the furniture, were toys. There was a large decorative feature in stucco on the ceiling where a chandelier had once hung, now empty. She sat at the edge of one sofa and Ray sat at the edge of another, facing her. She had one of those well-bred English faces, long and pale, that seem designed exclusively for lazy, faintly quizzical expressions. Now it was stiff with fear. Her leg twittered up and down.

There was an awkward silence. Before Ray could speak, she said, 'She ate slug pellets once.'

Ray hesitated.

'She was three. She stood over there and she said, "I like those sweeties, Mummy, but they're a bit soapy."' She bit her lip.

After a moment Ray said, 'Do you have access to help? Family? Friends who might come and stay?'

She continued to look at him after he'd finished speaking, as if dazed or waiting for a different question, and at last shook her head.

He said carefully, 'Would it be all right if I asked you one or two more questions?'

Gazing around at the floor where the toys lay scattered, she made no response. Ray noticed that the backs of her hands were covered with red marks.

'I left her,' she said. 'I was talking to a friend inside.'

Ray began to tell her that she shouldn't blame herself but she talked on, as if hearing only her own thoughts. 'She's a happy girl. She likes drawing. She has six favourite toys, Clown, Doctor Poll, Sealy, Singing Teddy, Mostyn and Baby Annabel. She calls lollipops lillilops. When she grows up she wants to work with animals.' She swallowed. 'These are the things to hold on to,' she whispered to herself.

When he made a noise, she looked up at him with a sudden, angry stare as if surprised to find him there. He took a breath and said, 'We have someone who says they think they saw a silver Mercedes in Charlbury Road.'

Her face loosened, her mouth fell open crookedly. 'It's him,' she said. 'He must have taken her. Thank God. Thank you, thank you.' She began to weep.

'We can't corroborate it yet. We haven't finished reviewing the CCTV.'

Nodding, she continued to cry.

'We haven't been able to contact him either. I wanted to pick your brains about that.'

Gradually, she recovered. She said, 'He'll go to France, the house in Bergerac.'

'There's no record of him leaving the country.'

'He'll have found a way. That's what he's like.'

Ray nodded. 'We're working with Interpol, also Reunite – that's a charity specialising in international parental abductions. But I was wondering if there was anywhere nearer he might go?'

'No,' she said impatiently. 'There's nowhere. You've been to his flat?'

'It's been under surveillance for the last twenty-four hours; he's not been there. We have a warrant now so we'll get in, see what we find.' He cleared his throat. 'But is there anyone else he might go to? A relative, a friend?'

She shook her head. 'He's on his own in this.' She looked at him. 'He threatened to do it. He said if I got a court order against him, I'd never see her again. He can't bear not getting his own way.'

'How much contact has he had with Poppy since you separated?'

She gave him a bitter look. 'Much more than before. Suddenly he was Fun Dad – fun with Poppy, games with Poppy, taking Poppy out, buying things for Poppy.' She flushed with anger. 'He'd turn up at any time, demanding to see her. He'd have her for a weekend and not bring her back till the middle of the week. And at the nursery . . .' She breathed hard, trying to calm herself. 'At the nursery,' she went on in a strained voice, 'I'd find him playing games with Poppy on the pavement when I arrived to pick her up, and he'd have promised to take her out for tea somewhere, and we'd have this colossal argument in the street with Poppy dancing round shouting about ice cream. All to punish me.'

Her face had stiffened again and she was crying now with anger. Ray waited.

33

He said, 'May I ask you again about yesterday afternoon? The moment you . . . realised she'd gone. Anything you can remember. Even small details can help us.'

Her leg was still twitching. After a long silence, she said, 'When I came out, the driveway was empty. I went onto the pavement, looked up and down. I saw her cutlass lying there. You know, from her pirate costume. Natalie – she's the nursery teacher – was looking in the gardens. A bird was singing. It was all very quiet, as if nothing had happened.'

'Did you see anyone?'

'No one. The street was empty.'

'No workmen, no one passing by at the end of the road, schoolgirl, parent, childminder?'

'No one.'

'Any car go past?'

'No.'

'Any car parked in Garford Road?'

'No, only the pickups and transits of the workmen. But he wouldn't have parked in Garford Road anyway, it's too hard getting in and out. He would have left the Merc in Charlbury Road.'

Ray nodded as his phone rang. 'Excuse me.'

He walked to the other end of the room talking quietly, and she watched him, picking at her hands.

At last he came back. 'I'm sorry, I have to go.'

'Has something happened?'

'My colleagues have got into Dr Clarke's flat.'

'What is it?' she asked anxiously, her voice rising. 'What have they found?'

He hesitated. 'Some items of a pirate costume dropped on the floor in one of the bedrooms. We can't be sure—'

'It's him,' she said. 'I knew it. The bastard.' She balled her fists and began to cry.

'I'll be in touch again as soon as I can. If he contacts you, let me know straight away.'

She made no response and he turned and went out of the room. As he went down the stairs his phone rang again. This time it was Diane.

'Babe.'

He was out of the door before she spoke, in a whisper, asking Ray to pick up some ginger lollipops for her from the health food shop in Summertown.

He hurried through the little Park Town garden, phone cramped against his ear. 'I'll try. But I have to go now. Okay?'

He could hear her breathing. 'Five times this morning,' she said in the same quiet, almost humbled voice. 'Why? Why am I still getting sick?'

'I don't know, babe.' Ray strode out of the park and onto the pavement, heading towards his car. 'Listen, I've got to go but I'll call you later.'

She was saying something else, he could hear the tiny wash of her voice in his ear, but he cut the call and accelerated across the road.

Leaning against the living-room wall, feet wide apart, head lowered as if to butt against the exposed brickwork, Diane dropped the phone and let out a long, frail groan, then turned, slid slowly to the floor and sat with her back against the wall, knees pushed outwards, trying in vain to find relief.

She was thirty-three years old, London-Nigerian by heritage, petite by nature, with messy hair and a small, perfectly oval face. Her nose was sprinkled with pale freckles. As she sat there she could feel her babies moving inside her, a single disjointed form she imagined like the parts of a small seal, muscle, head and flippers, writhing against her pelvic floor. The antenatal class had preached the benefits of traditional breathing techniques, which, however, gave her no relief at all. Only ginger lollipops would do.

She had no one but Ray. She thought what a weird idea that was; she'd never wanted anyone *but* Ray. But now there was only Ray she felt alone. Her family had moved back to Nigeria the year before. Her sister was about to get married to a petroleum executive in Lagos and her mother was preoccupied with the preparations; she had no time for Diane. One daughter's power-move wedding trumped another daughter's morning sickness.

She let out another frail moan. She felt sad and also angry. It was the pregnancy hormones, she knew, but she did not believe it. She felt the world against her. She used to be lead commercial analyst for one of the largest groups of fashion magazines, now she was a misshapen woman in pain.

Her thoughts drifted. She thought of Ray's appearance on the television the night before, how glamorous he'd seemed in his uniform, no longer the dazzling boy she met ten years earlier but entering into a newly handsome phase, his face strengthened somehow by the marks of experience in it, the set of the eyes, the underpinning of the jaw. She watched his mouth as he talked, the shapes his lips made. And later she went online and saw the photographs and read on Twitter comments from women who seemed not to be able to contain themselves. *He can investigate*

36

me anytime. Form an orderly queue, ladies. She tried hard to be pleased for him. This was what he had always wanted, to lead an investigation of national importance. It was natural that he should love it, natural that under the studio's lights he should appear so star-like. In her gut she felt the nausea rise hotly like threads of steam, and tried hard not to feel that it was jealousy.

SIX

It was nearly five in the afternoon before Ray got back to the station from the Jericho flat with news confirmed by Forensics that the items of pirate costume found there had been worn by Poppy. They had been lying in the master bedroom as if discarded hastily, jacket by the door, sash under the window, eye-patch on the bed. There were other signs of haste too: wardrobe doors left open, a half-drunk glass of milk on the kitchen counter, things from the bathroom cabinet dumped in the basin. They had been unable to find the father's passport.

The manhunt was underway already, and Ray had spent the rest of the afternoon working with his team and co-ordinating the relevant agencies across the UK and Europe. He was tired but keeping it together, running on adrenaline, on his way now to brief the Super before going out with a major press announcement later in the evening. He'd missed two further calls from Diane. Going at pace up the stairs, the first person he saw in the corridor was Ryan.

That stopped him. Ryan's bony face, ridiculously lit.

'Big man!'

'What are you doing here?'

'Me? Just hanging out. Catching up, shooting the breeze.'

Ray looked disconcerted.

'Fucking with you. Got pulled in, see the Super.'

'What for?'

'Reinstatement.'

Ray looked at him. 'Joking again, right?'

'Straight up. Still getting my head round it. Early days, only got the call lunchtime. Still, who knows? Discharge a travesty in the first place, right?'

Ray looked dubious.

'How about you, though? Big on TV. Got that whole top man thing going. Smooth. Thing you do with your eyes.'

'I don't know what you're talking about.'

'Tough but soulful. People might even stop calling you The Other Wilkins.'

'No one calls me The—'

'Anyway, may be back soon enough to give you a hand. Like old times.'

Ray made an impatient noise, ignored by Ryan, who went on. 'Actually, come in a bit early to catch you about something.' He explained about Mick Dick.

Ray shook his head. 'Can't do that, Ryan. Basic confidentiality.'

'Come on, Ray, throw me a bone.'

Ray regarded him with a critical eye. 'You're really here about reinstatement? So there'll be a process to go through, am I right? Reports, submissions, testimonials? If it comes out you've been

39

poking around, interfering in ongoing police investigations, how do you think that's going to play?'

'Okay, thanks, Mum. So what, shall I pop round see Nadim?'

Ray grimaced. 'Just don't say I sent you.'

'Course not. Wouldn't dream of getting you in trouble. Head boy.'

Something passed between them then, some shared pulse, a moment of fellowship or mutual irritation, or something else, unnameable but sharp, then they were gone in different directions.

Ryan found Nadim in the COMINT suite, sitting in front of three screens, watching a news feed on a fourth and listening to something else on her headphones.

'Ray sent me,' he said.

She was surprised to see him – and behaved for the first few minutes as if she thought he'd broken into the building – but pleased. Her tolerance levels were higher than her colleagues'; besides, Ryan reminded her of her younger brother Khalid, currently keeping a low profile after getting into some bother with the local imam. And if Ray had given the nod, she was happy to pull out record details for him.

Michael Dick, deceased. Incident called in at 9.05 a.m. by a PC alerted by a family living on North Hinksey Lane who had found the body a little earlier, at the side of the road, after walking their dog on the adjacent meadows. Fatal injuries sustained by the victim consistent with being struck by a car: traumatic damage to head, thorax and locomotor system, massive internal haemorrhaging, blood loss and shock.

Ryan was shaking his head. 'Odd. Nothing on that lane most of the time 'cept kids on bikes. Completely deserted at night. Don't suppose there's any CCTV? Outside the school?'

'No.'

'Witnesses? People in the houses along the lane? Heard something, saw something?'

'Everyone asleep.'

'Time of death?'

'Pathologist puts it at around two thirty a.m.'

He thought he'd misheard at first. 'Say it again.'

'Two thirty.'

He sat there, breathing. Two thirty. Just quarter of an hour after he'd seen Mick Dick. He was probably the last person to have seen him alive. He saw him again in the compound, the way he stood, the way he looked at him, terror in his bloodshot eyes, his hand trembling when he took it away from his face. He heard him speak. *This is fucked up. It's a mistake.* Like a man in shock.

'You all right, Ryan?'

He swallowed. 'Yeah. Yeah, fine. Got visuals?'

Images appeared on one of the screens. Man tumbled in a ditch, one shoeless foot upraised, face hidden under an arm, sad comedy of a pratfall. A twisted leg, hand grasping nothing, wet patch of midriff. Mortal remains. Then shots of things, possessions, brightly lit in a studio: a wallet, bunch of keys, black hooded top, grey trackie bottoms, underwear, pair of cheap battered running shoes.

'Can you zoom in there?' He peered at the muddy shoes, frowned, sat there thinking while Nadim watched him.

'No phone?'

41

Nadim called up the inventory. 'No phone found, apparently,' she said.

'Really?'

Nadim read the transcript. 'They searched the area, as per. No phone found.'

Ryan remembered then that in fact a phone wasn't one of the things Mick Dick had shown him at the compound when he'd turned out his pockets, and for the first time it struck him as odd that he didn't have one with him. He murmured to himself for a while.

'What's going on, Ryan?'

'I knew him. Not close. Just at school. He was famous for sports when I was famous for doing fuck all. Forensics finished yet?'

'Not quite.'

'Give us a ding if other stuff comes in?'

'Sure.'

'By the way, got to tell you. Maybe coming back.'

She looked shocked. 'Really?'

'Stuff to be sorted out. But yeah, maybe. Going to see the Super now.'

'Good luck.'

There was a tone in her voice and he squinted at her. 'What's he like?'

She shrugged. 'Different from the old Super.'

'Good way, bad way?'

'They're calling him Barko. Likes to give orders. He's got his fans.'

'Bet Ray's not one of them. He likes all the nice and polite stuff, yeah?'

Saying nothing, she gave him a look.

'Don't worry about me,' he said. 'I can get on with anyone.'

He waited twenty minutes at an empty desk at the edge of the open-plan, attracting glances, which he ignored. No one spoke to him. He thought about Mick Dick, dead in a ditch just quarter of an hour after he'd seen him. Thought about those muddy shoes: Mick Dick must have run straight across the water meadows in the dark instead of the long way round on the lighted path. Why was that? Thought about what he'd said, how he'd behaved. Something had frightened him, not just the thought of going back inside. Something worse. Not just fear either. Panic, the panic of a man who's got himself into trouble. *A mistake.* That's what Mick Dick had said. Ryan knew about mistakes, their fatal attraction, their horrible persistence; he knew about the way they sucked you in, twisted you inside out, the way they grew legs and teeth, hunted you down. A mistake could strike instantly or lie in wait for years, chase you across your childhood, through all your fondest hopes and spoiled dreams, in and out of marriage, fatherhood, prison, all the way to a compound of hire vans on a rainy night in July, the last place ever to go, where there's nothing left to do but turn to the last person you'll ever see and say, 'This is fucked up, man. I made a mistake.'

But what mistake? What had Mick Dick done?

A door opened, he looked up.

'The Superintendent will see you now.'

Detective Superintendent Wallace leaned back in his chair, a short, wide length of old muscle done up in tight white shirt and

43

crisp dark uniform, and gave Ryan a long, expressionless look; and Ryan looked back, standing there in his trackie bottoms and old Loop jacket, noticing details. A clean, round head fuzzed with stiff grey hair. Colourless eyes, squashed nose, narrow mouth sharpened at both ends. Shovel hands with thick, short fingers. DSU Barko with everything under control, nothing superfluous on display, watching Ryan carefully from a hidden place behind his eyes, like a poker player. Like all poker players, he must want something. Which was interesting. After a moment he rocked forward in his chair and put one of his meaty hands on a couple of folders. He'd turned them over as soon as Ryan entered, though not before Ryan had read their labels. *Diversity, Equality and Inclusion Strategy. Thames Valley Police vs DI Ryan Wilkins.*

'You've made mistakes, son,' Wallace said in a confidential tone.

Ryan acknowledged it.

'I know your type. I've read your file, I know what you're like.'

'Yes, sir.'

'Had a problem with the Bishop of Salisbury, did you? Had a problem with the provost of Barnabas Hall, Oxford? You're the problem. I don't like problems. I like solutions.'

'Got it.'

Another long, silent stare without expression. But by now it was obvious what he wanted.

'I see the deal,' Ryan said.

Wallace's eyes narrowed. 'Deal?'

Ryan nodded towards the folders. 'You seen my record, my results. I'm not stupid. Bad discipline let me down, lack of control. Straightforward then. I show the suits discipline, you get the poor white trash boy into your stats. Diversity bollocks, right?'

44

For the first time the Super showed a flicker of emotion, a tightening of the mouth; it could have passed for the beginning of a smile, immediately suppressed. 'All right then, smart boy, let's cut to the chase. Big question. How do I know you can deliver?'

'Easy. I want it. You know it's true. Bet you could hear it in my voice when you called.' He held his eyes. 'You want me to jump through hoops, I can jump through hoops. I can jump through hoops all day. Not only that, I'll believe in the hoops, I'll make the hoops mine. I'll fucking autograph those hoops. Sir. Give me a chance, I'll prove it.'

The Super watched him closely. If he was encouraged by what Ryan said, he didn't show it. He said, in a low voice, 'Try it on with me and I'll put my fucking boot through you.'

'Fair enough.'

Wallace made a show of deliberation, which Ryan politely tolerated.

'This is how it works then,' he said at last. 'A process, like I said. Interviews, panels, evaluations. Anger management course. I told you on the blower, three things to keep in mind. Answers to the questions they're going to ask you about the bishop and the provost and all the crap you threw around in the past. I can help with that. Attitude, that's your responsibility. Live or die by it. And your record since discharge. It'd better be clean. I don't just mean legal. Employment record, everything. If there's a hint of anything, anything at all, makes them think you're still a delinquent who shits wherever he likes, they'll dump your reinstatement application on its arse before you can say, "Look at my records, I'm really quite smart." I want your eyes on the ground, nose clean, underwear spotless. Am I understood?'

'Got it.'

'Finally, remember this. I'm supervising the whole thing. Me. It's personal. Keep that front and central.'

'Sir.'

He gave Ryan a final long, hard look. When he spoke it was a growl. 'As of now, I give you no better than fifty-fifty. So you better prove me wrong.'

It was the sort of growl that sounded well rehearsed to Ryan, who'd heard a few, but he swallowed a snort and went out grinning.

He went past the Super's PA and gave her a wink. 'Nice old boy,' he said, and went across the open-plan whistling.

He'd stopped whistling by the time he got to work at the end of the day. Another dreary night on the Osney industrial estate: inky cloud-splot on a much-used blotting-paper sky. To his surprise, his manager's car was on the forecourt and there was a light on in his office.

His manager, Carl Crapper, was a middle-aged man with an unfortunate name and a crumpled, disappointed look. It seemed to Ryan that at some point, many years earlier, he'd attempted to grow a moustache and had forgotten to shave off the failure that resulted. He had a scowl so ingrained he must have been born with it. He didn't like Ryan.

He was bent over the desk when Ryan went in. He looked up. 'You're late. I been waiting nearly ten minutes.'

'Oh yeah? Any major break-ins?'

He gave Ryan a look. 'I was just leaving you a note.'

'Okay. Need a hand with it?'

Carl's scowl deepened. 'Cost came through today from

46

Thames Valley Police. Call-out charge for last night. Couple of hundred quid.'

'Yeah?'

'Recorded as *No Action Required*. In other words, a false alarm.'

'Deer got in the compound.'

'You called in the police 'cause a deer got in the compound?'

'No.'

A silence followed. 'Why then?' Carl said at last.

'I called them in 'cause it's procedure to call them in. Any suspicion, *any suspicion*, do not hesitate. I'm quoting from the handbook. Might be crap procedure but I didn't write it. That'd be you.'

Carl's face went through various contortions suggesting psychological trauma but in the end he left the desk and went past Ryan to the door. There he stopped and turned.

'Far as I'm concerned, you owe this company two hundred pounds.'

'Far as I'm concerned, you're pissing in the wind and your front's all wet.'

'I'll be taking this to Derek.' Derek was the owner.

Ryan called after him, 'Don't forget to change your trousers.'

Sitting in the silence afterwards, he felt a small but unmistakable twinge of unease. He remembered what Wallace had said about an impeccable employment record. He knew he had a faulty control button. Usually it didn't bother him. But it was different now.

As so often when he gave himself a talking-to about his behaviour, he found himself thinking about little Ryan. That shining, serious face. That high-pitched, truthful voice. He began to smile. What were children for if not to make us better than we were without them?

47

SEVEN

The next afternoon Ray returned to Garford Road with Livvy. Detective Sergeant Livvy Holmes, thirty-seven years old, mother of three, had been in the force exactly twice as long as Ray and had risen half as high. She was highly competent. When they talked she had a habit of saying little but keeping her eyes on him. Her eyes were beautiful, softly creased at the edges, but they did not express any sort of appreciation – rather, he thought, a contained scepticism – and he wondered if she judged him.

It was another sunny day, and the quiet, comfortable street with its mature trees, old red-brick walls and carefully trimmed hedges regarded them with a look of complete innocence, as if to deny that anything in any way distasteful could ever happen there. They went together to the nursery, which occupied a listed plain stone building once a carriage house halfway along. Inside, it had been turned into a children's paintbox: blue walls hung with silver netting filled with pink balls, green tables, purple toy boxes and an area of red and orange chequered playmats, where they sat on small yellow chairs with nursery manager Natalie

48

Bunting, who was trying to add to her previous statement, her pale face blurred with distress. On the table was some of Poppy's artwork, boldly drawn pictures of houses, trees and people in colourful greasy crayon. In one she had written 'Daddy' next to an enormous figure in a boat. Every picture featured a smiling sun with long eyelashes, red lips and a handbag.

'She's such a bright girl, so cheerful, so lively. She makes friends with everyone, children, adults, everybody. Everybody loves her.'

Natalie gave Livvy a list of the nursery's staff going back two years, two dozen names of teachers, contractors involved with maintenance and gardening, and occasional helpers and work experience students, and told them a little about the staff on duty that day: Mrs Bronwen Davies, team leader; Ms Deborah Collins, nursery assistant; and Ms Harriet Spivey, work experience student. She identified them on the nursery website. Mrs Davies was a heavy-set, motherly-looking lady of forty-five, who had been with the nursery nearly fifteen years. She worked mornings only and on the day of Poppy's disappearance had left the building at lunchtime. Debbie Collins was twenty-seven, a newly qualified assistant, keen and competent. Just after lunch, however, she had fallen awkwardly while playing in the garden and had gone to A&E with a suspected sprained ankle. Which had left young Harriet to help Natalie for the rest of the afternoon.

'She's only just taken over from our last work experience person, a trustee's son. Luckily, she's a sweetie.'

She was, in fact, Natalie's niece. Most of the work experience students were relatives of the staff or trustees; it helped give the place its family air.

'We'll just need a quick word with them, nothing major. If

you let Detective Sergeant Holmes have their contacts later, we'll organise that.' Ray cleared his throat. 'But I'd like to ask you about Dr Clarke.'

A flutter seemed to go through the young woman; she settled herself in an unnaturally natural pose, and a flush spread across her cheeks.

'Did you see him at all that day?'

'It wasn't his turn to pick her up.'

He held her eyes in silence, waiting.

'No,' she said at last.

'Contact you?'

She shook her head.

A longer silence.

'What's your opinion of Dr Clarke, Natalie?'

She began four different sentences, flushing more intensely still until her face and throat were mottled with burgundy patches. Ray flicked his eyes towards Livvy who was regarding her intently.

Ray said, 'Have you had any social contact with Dr Clarke, Natalie? Outside work.'

She bit her lip; nodded. 'Rachel was always my friend, though. Is my friend. I'd never do anything to . . .' Her voice guttered and went out.

'I understand. We're not interested in your social life. What I want to know is your view of Dr Clarke as a father.'

She nodded, collected herself.

'He's a good father. Devoted. He loves Poppy very much.'

'It must have been hard for him not seeing her so often. Especially since the court order. Perhaps he confided in you.'

A tiny nod.

'What did he say?'

He'd said plenty. Slowly, cautiously, Natalie elaborated. Dr Clarke was a sensitive, wonderful, talented, charismatic man. Also, it was clear, angry and vengeful. He suffered the restrictions placed on his contact with his daughter as a monstrous injustice, and his instinct was to defy them in whatever way he could.

'Are you aware of him breaking the terms of the order?'

Another tiny nod. 'Sometimes he picks her up when he's not meant to. He can't help it. He has to see her, he says.'

'Did he ever talk to you about wanting to take Poppy away altogether? Any place they might go to?'

Now she rallied. 'Never. No.'

Ray watched her as he spoke. 'This morning we got some pictures from Wychwood School's CCTV camera on Bardwell Road. They show Dr Clarke's silver Mercedes passing at four fifteen p.m., travelling in this direction.'

Natalie's mouth opened, closed again.

'But you didn't see him.'

'I didn't see him. I promise.'

After a pause Livvy took over. 'Can you tell us again everything that happened at home time? I know you've given a statement before but it often happens that people remember new details if they think again.'

Natalie repeated what she had said earlier. Rachel had been slightly late; the other children had all been picked up already. She popped in to talk to Natalie for a moment while Poppy slipped outside to play on her own in the afternoon sunshine. After only a few minutes they went out and found the driveway empty. Hunting distractedly in the nursery garden – across the lawn, among the bushes, behind the Wendy house – hearing Rachel shouting frantically in the street, Natalie had known straightaway that something had gone wrong. She felt – she struggled to describe it – a horrifying ill-fitting absence in the usual shape of things, and she ran inside to call the police.

At no point, however, had she seen anything unusual in the street.

'Nothing at all?'

'Nothing.'

'No one hanging around?'

'No one. It was a quiet day, hardly anyone about.'

'And you heard nothing?'

'Nothing.'

Waiting until her crying subsided, Ray thanked her at last and they rose with difficulty out of the tiny chairs.

'Except . . .'

'Except what?'

While she was talking to Rachel, Natalie had heard Poppy outside laughing. Of course, there was no reason for her not to laugh; Poppy was an imaginative child, she could amuse herself for hours, playing on her own with dancing games, skipping games. It was just that the sound of her laughter had stuck so heartbreakingly in Natalie's memory.

Ray and Livvy stood together in the street outside.

Livvy was blunt and decided. 'She's telling the truth.'

Ray agreed. 'Poppy laughing. That's interesting.'

'Because her father had arrived to take her away?'

'If not him, who?'

52

They stood there a moment longer, then Livvy went back to the station and Ray lingered, looking round the nursery garden, trying to feel his way into scenarios. It was hard. Everything lulled him, the sunshine, the hush, the smooth combinations of beech and magnolia. He walked down the empty driveway to the pavement, thinking about Poppy's laughter. It was four thirty. At just this time, on just such a quiet, sunny day, she had stood where he stood now, laughing. And then she had disappeared.

He felt his tiredness. It filled him like water. Scrolling through a news feed on his phone, he read the headlines – POLICE HUNT FATHER, FATHER ON THE RUN, DOES THIS MAN KNOW WHERE SHE IS? – all accompanied by headshots of Dr Clarke, an unsmiling man in the sort of blue scrubs associated in the public imagination with medical mass murderers like Harold Shipman. Ray winced. At the lunchtime press conference, in the hubbub of excited questions after the announcement of the police search for Dr Clarke, he had made the mistake of not correcting the impression that Poppy's father was a 'suspect', not merely a 'person of interest', and by the time the Superintendent had intervened, the breaking news was half written. He thought now of the Super's terse comment afterwards: 'There are a hundred ways, Ray, to politely tell a journo to fuck off. Use them.'

He thought again of Poppy laughing in the street. Was it because Dr Clarke had appeared?

The sun blazed. He put on his Ray-Bans and looked about. Garford Road was short: four large houses down one side, glimpses of brown brick and gables behind tall hedges, and, on the other, the old stone building of the nursery sitting placidly on its long green lawn. At the cul-de-sac end, half hidden by hedges,

53

trees and creepers, were three more houses and their gardens. A leafy street, seeming narrower than it was because of the builders' pickups and transits parked down one side. A street of scents, birdsong, butterflies. Quiet. The sort of street Ray himself had grown up in. Standing there, he closed his eyes for a moment and listened to the faint noises in the streets around: well-behaved schoolkids walking home after chess practice or violin lessons at the private girls' high to the north or from the even more private Dragon to the south; workmen calling to each other from houses along Charlbury Road, keeping their voices low, their language clean; a dog-walker crisply issuing instructions to her red setter or pair of French bulldogs. Familiar, comforting sounds. Ray himself had been one of those private schoolkids, had taken those violin lessons, walked those dogs through such safe, leafy streets.

He opened his eyes again and looked towards the end of the road. As Poppy's mother had said, Dr Clarke wouldn't have attempted to pull into Garford Road, he would have parked round the corner in Charlbury Road, thirty yards away. It would take less than a minute to walk there with a small girl. Once in his car, he could take one of the side roads back to the Banbury Road, the main route north out of the city, quickly connecting with major roads east towards the London airports or south to the ports with their fast, frequent ferries to northern France. Since the appeal for information as to Dr Clarke's whereabouts, they had received several sightings, including one by a woman who claimed to have seen a man answering Dr Clarke's description and a small girl eating in a McDonald's on the M27 just east of Poole, where the ferries leave for Cherbourg.

But as Ray stood there, a different thought came to him, and he turned back the other way, into bright sunlight, and looked towards the dead end of Garford Road. Unseen on the other side of those houses, he knew, were the Cherwell River, meadows and fields, very close, and country lanes leading out into the nearby countryside, patches of woodland at Elsfield, Water Eaton and Beckley. Close and largely deserted. Before he could pursue this thought his phone rang. He took a breath and closed his eyes.

'How are you feeling?'

He could hear her breathing quietly with effort.

'Diane?'

'Where are you?' she said in a whisper.

'Garford Road.'

'Her nursery? Any news?'

He was wary of answering. Diane's interest in Poppy Clarke seemed unhealthy to him; in her emotionally fragile state, she became anxious so quickly.

'I can't talk now.'

There was an awkward pause. 'The antenatal class tonight,' she said at last. 'That's what I was calling about. You won't forget?' In her tone he heard a note of accusation.

'Are you well enough to go? You sound bad.'

'I just need you there.'

'I'll be there.'

'I know you're busy. You have to find that little girl, I know that.'

A green light was pulsing on his phone. 'Babe, a call's coming in from the office. I'll see you this evening.'

If she said anything else, he didn't hear it. Livvy's voice said, 'Boss? Can you come in? The father's here and he's kicking off.'

EIGHT

In North Hinksey Lane Ryan stood looking at the remains of Police Incident tape littering the scrub above the ditch where Mick Dick's body had been found. There were no other signs to mark the spot; the caravan had moved on. He looked about him. On one side of the road: water meadows spiky with sedge, a feathery line of distant willows and, beyond them, Osney industrial estate, where the van rental place was. Everything shimmering in the sun. On the other side of the road, set above a bank of untidy grass: a row of large semis. Ryan listened for a moment to the monotonous rumble of traffic on the ring road behind them. Like lots of country villages, North Hinksey was no longer in the countryside.

He knew it pretty well. He used to come down here from New Hinksey, meet the Botley lads, go into town or up to Cumnor for parties. Michelle was with him then. Before that, he came on his own to fish in the stream. Twelve, thirteen years old, in and out of trouble. Never caught anything but that wasn't the point. The point was to keep out of his father's way. He remembered sitting in one of the fields behind the pub, hidden in the bushes so no one would see him and alert the Oxford and District Angling Association. He remembered bird sounds, tree sounds. Water moving through sunlight green and yellow, darkening in cloud shadow, breeze stippling the surface. He didn't even see a fish. Stayed there seven, eight hours, until he got hungry and went home at last to a beating.

He stood next to the ditch, thinking. Mick Dick had left Osney at around quarter past two and headed straight here, in such a rush he'd run in a straight line across the pitch-dark meadows. Why? Why did he take off towards North Hinksey so fast? Ryan thought again about his terror in the compound. Was he trying to get away from someone?

He looked along the lane, imagining the car coming round the corner, picking up speed. Mick Dick panting, hauling himself through the scrub, blundering oblivious and distracted into the road, then the thump and lurch, scream of engine, the heavy body flung sideways like a bag of builder's sand, dumped in the ditch, the car swerving on, noise fading to silence. Ten seconds was all it would take.

He looked at the road, at the houses twenty yards away on the other side. No skid marks on the asphalt. No one woken by the commotion. Turning, he walked fifty yards along the lane until he came to a path rising between the houses and went up it, and found himself two minutes later standing at the side of the ring road, lorries thundering past, whipping up the air. Was this where Mick Dick was coming, to be picked up and taken somewhere else? Or was he going on, through the pedestrian underpass? Ryan looked across the roaring dual carriageway. To the north it was all Cumnor house roofs up to Dean Court at the top of the hill, to the south all countryside, green pastures rising to Chilswell, the darker shape of Youlbury Woods, the lowering hump of Boars Hill, the wide blue sky. Where was he was trying to get to? Ryan stood there for several minutes, lost in thought, letting the gritty traffic-wind scour his face, then turned away, went back down the path to the lane and got into his car. He looked at the address he'd written on his hand, put the car in gear and moved away. In the bushes the police tape waved goodbye.

In Weldon Road he found the house and pulled up outside. It was a small semi, like most of the houses in New Marston, with a pebbledash front, oblong windows and paved forecourt. Quiet, solid working people lived here. Outside the houses were vans, taxis, small economical cars. Weldon Road was a side street, its quiet broken only by the siren of an ambulance on its way to the nearby John Radcliffe up the hill.

She answered the door still dressed in her nurse's uniform and stood there suspiciously as he explained, before letting him in and taking him through to a small back room with a bright pine-veneer floor and plain walls, where they sat at the kitchen table. Narrow French windows gave onto a patio set out with green plastic garden furniture.

'Nice place.'

'I rent it with a girl from work. I've had enough of men for a bit.'

She had short blonde hair, a snub nose and pale lips, and she looked at him with that half-shy toughness he'd seen in other young mothers. Her name was Charlene.

'This is Ashleigh, by the way,' she said.

The little girl sat at the table with a dish of Smarties, staring at him. She had coffee-coloured skin and floppy black hair done up in bunches with red and black ribbons, and depthless dark eyes, unblinking. Mick Dick's daughter. Without taking her eyes off Ryan, she solemnly brought a Smartie up from the dish and put it in her mouth and forgot to close it. Ryan gave her a wink which did nothing to deter her utter absorption in him.

'But if we're going to talk about Mick, I'm going to put her in the other room for a minute, let her watch some TV.'

When she came back she started. 'So, you saw him that night, where you work. What do you want to ask me about? I already talked to the police.'

It was more than he'd done himself, he was aware. His own interest, he mentioned delicately, was running parallel to the police line of enquiry. And what he mainly wanted to know was what Mick Dick had been doing in North Hinksey.

'Probably didn't know himself. Thing about Mick was, he just did stuff. You know? Without thinking. Or someone else give him the idea. That was his other thing, always doing stuff for other people. Wore me down in the end. You reach a point when you say enough's enough.'

She'd split from Mick while he was still inside. No point in waiting till he came out, she knew already that Mick wasn't going to change; in fact, he needed a fresh start as much as she did. Besides, she had her daughter to think about. After his release he'd moved in with them for a few weeks until he got his own place.

'He had a place?'

That was interesting.

'Out at Horspath. Mobile home. You know those things?'

Oh yes. He knew everything about a trailer, the wind-sensitive instability of it, the dim interior lighting, kitchen of clip-together cabinets, living room with its carpet tiles and matching armchair where his father would sit with his brew every evening staring at the television, tiny bedroom where he and Jade slept side by side on mattresses no wider than their bodies. He remembered the smell of it, brew, gravy and Calor Gas, the way the thing moved at night and the noises it made, mad twitterings of plastic and metal. Nothing wrong with it really except its size. Some cars were bigger.

'I took Ash there,' she said. 'It was all right. Till he got back on his feet.'

She gave him the address and he put it into his phone as she talked about Mick Dick's last weeks. He was searching for work, something in construction (he'd done a bricklaying course in Grendon), though once employers knew he'd been inside they tended to lose interest. Twice a week he came to take Ashleigh out, never missed. He was always good with his daughter. She'd seen him only a couple of days before his death.

'And how was he that last time?'

She shrugged. 'Same as usual.'

'Not upset about anything?'

'No.'

'Anything on his mind?'

'Mick's problem was not having stuff on his mind.'

He asked her if Mick had a phone.

'Why?'

He told her that there had been no sign of it at the compound or at the scene of the accident.

'No mystery there. Typical Mick. He'll have lost it. He could never keep hold of his phones. Another thing used to drive me mad.'

'Okay then.'

He asked about the people Mick hung out with. She didn't think he'd taken up with his old friends. He'd always been happy on his own, in fact. He visited his mother in Littlemore every week.

'Anyone else?'

She thought. There was a guy the prison service had fixed him up with as part of the release package, to help him find work, a 'mentor'. Mick had liked him, but she didn't know anything about him. And she couldn't think of anyone else Mick was in regular contact with. His life had shrunk.

They stood at the door.

'Wait a minute. There was a guy rang here once wanting Mick. Don't know if he caught up with him. Something about money.'

'Interesting.'

'What was interesting was that he wanted to *give* Mick money.'

'Get a name?'

She frowned. 'Crabb? Croft?' She gave up. 'Sorry.' She'd told Mick about him but Mick hadn't reacted so she'd left it at that.

It was time for Ashleigh's tea. Ryan thanked her and stepped out onto the driveway.

She was looking at him.

'You think there's something not right about Mick's death?'

'Don't know yet.'

'Wouldn't waste your time. He didn't make enemies, for one thing. People liked him. And an accident like this is just typical Mick. God,' she said, 'that man.'

Ryan thought she was going to get angry but she began to cry instead. 'I did love him,' she said, 'but I had to move on. For Ash.'

Ryan nodded. There was no more to be said and he walked to his car, and sat in it a moment, thinking. So Mick Dick had a place of his own. That was interesting. Why then was he sleeping in hire vans? He couldn't answer that question so he put the car in gear and drove away.

NINE

Dr Sebastian Clarke was waiting in C3, a dim windowless room used for voluntary interviews. A swarthy man with an outdoorsy air, he was wearing tailored pale blue chinos and a navy blue shirt with the sleeves rolled up. A photogenic slick of long black hair fell slantwise across his forehead. His mouth was large and dominating. Ray went in and sat opposite him, put his folder on the table between them, and switched on the recorder.

DR CLARKE: I can't believe this bullshit.

DI WILKINS: Thanks for coming in. It's a voluntary interview. You're free to end it at any point. But we always do them under caution and record them. No need to be alarmed.

DR CLARKE: You're the guy in the press conference, aren't you? The one dropping the hint I'd kidnapped my own daughter. *Police Hunt Father. Father On the Run.* Did you see those headlines?

DI WILKINS: So you saw the conference.

DR CLARKE: [silence]

DI WILKINS: Why didn't you get in touch?

DR CLARKE: Sorry, what's your name again?

DI WILKINS: DI Wilkins.

DR CLARKE: Well, DI Wilkins, let me tell you. I got in touch the instant I saw you wanted to talk to me, which was the same instant I found out that my daughter had gone missing. Which is when I went into a newsagent's in Brockenhurst this lunchtime after two nights camping in the New Forest. So I'll ask you, DI Wilkins, not to jump to conclusions and make these insinuations, because it won't do you any good and it will only make me angrier than I am already.

DI WILKINS: When was the last time you saw Poppy, Dr Clarke?

DR CLARKE: Christ. You're really not getting it, are you? I've come here to ask *you* questions.

DI WILKINS: There are a few things we need to get clear first.

DR CLARKE: Fuck that. I want to know what her mother was doing when she should have been keeping our daughter safe. Have you asked her why she was always late picking her up? Why she used to leave her on the pavement outside while she was gossiping with her friend indoors. Have you?

DI WILKINS: [silence]

DR CLARKE: I want to know if you've spoken to her brother yet. The junkie uncle. Who took her away with him for a weekend in London without telling anyone when she was two. Have you?

DI WILKINS: [silence] When was the last time you saw your daughter, Dr Clarke?

DR CLARKE: Jesus, this is pathetic. All right then. I saw her a week ago, Wednesday.

DI WILKINS: Where?

DR CLARKE: At her nursery.

DI WILKINS: [silence]

DR CLARKE: Is there a problem? Do I need to justify seeing my own daughter at her nursery?

DI WILKINS: Do you recognise this? For the tape, I'm showing the interviewee a copy of a ruling issued by the family court in Oxford.

DR CLARKE: [unintelligible]

DI WILKINS: Please speak clearly for the record.

DR CLARKE: You really are unbelievable. Yes, for the benefit of the record, I recognise it.

DI WILKINS: You see the date?

DR CLARKE: What a farce. Yes, I see the date.

DI WILKINS: You understand that if you went to Poppy's nursery on Wednesday last week, you were breaking the terms of this court order?

DR CLARKE: Yes, again. Yes. I broke the terms of the court order for ten minutes outside her nursery last Wednesday and I was gone before her mother came to pick her up, late as usual.

DI WILKINS: And did you also go to Poppy's nursery on the day of her disappearance?

DR CLARKE: No, I did not.

DI WILKINS: No?

DR CLARKE: Do I also need to say things twice for the record?

DI WILKINS: Is this your car? I'm showing the interviewee a photograph taken by the camera outside Wychwood School on Bardwell Road.

DR CLARKE: You know it is.

DI WILKINS: So if you didn't go to Poppy's nursery, what were you doing in Bardwell Road?

DR CLARKE: [unintelligible]

DI WILKINS: Please speak clearly for the—

DR CLARKE: I changed my mind.

DI WILKINS: You changed your mind?

DR CLARKE: I was going to see her, but her mother had made such a fuss about Wednesday I changed my mind at the last minute. How do you think I feel about that now? If I'd have been there, I could have kept her safe.

DI WILKINS: So you didn't see her. So what did you do?

DR CLARKE: I drove to the New Forest. As I said. Listen, all this is pointless. I want to know what you're doing to find my daughter.

DI WILKINS: Was anyone with you on your trip?

DR CLARKE: Agony. Absolute agony. No. The point was to get away on my own.

DI WILKINS: Did you see anyone while you were there?

DR CLARKE: No, I kept to myself. Oh God, haven't you finished yet?

DI WILKINS: Do you recognise these items of clothing? For the record, I'm showing the interviewee photographs of a child's pirate costume.

DR CLARKE: [silence]

DI WILKINS: These articles of clothing were found at your apartment yesterday.

DR CLARKE: [unintelligible]

DI WILKINS: Please speak up for the record.

DR CLARKE: [noises of weeping, distress]

DI WILKINS: Dr Clarke?

DR CLARKE: You fuck. You fucking fuck. You have absolutely no idea, do you?

DI WILKINS: [long silence]

DR CLARKE: Do you have children, DI Wilkins?

DI WILKINS: Not yet.

DR CLARKE: You'll learn things you didn't even realise you didn't know. That costume was the last thing I bought her. She wore it the last time she was allowed to come to my flat. And I left it on the floor because I wanted to pretend she lived there with me and left her stuff lying around like that all the time. But I don't expect you to understand that. [More weeping]

DI WILKINS: [silence] Terminating interview.

Ray got up and left the room. Outside he met Livvy, who had been monitoring the interview. She looked away as he approached. Was she judging him? When she looked back, she just raised her eyebrows, a gesture he couldn't interpret.

'Obviously he didn't take her,' he said quietly.

In fact, Livvy had been told that CCTV footage had just been located of Clarke's car entering the Summertown parade of shops, driving away from the nursery, at 4.20 p.m. – ten minutes before Poppy went to play outside. They looked together through the two-way at Dr Clarke sitting in C3. A change had come over him. All his handsomeness had come off. His hair fell awkwardly across his face, his mouth had shrunk and buckled, and he sat with it open, looking vacantly at the wall, a father terrified about his missing daughter.

'Talk him through procedures. Give him my number. Tell him we've spoken to the brother already.'

'Sir.'

He forced his mind elsewhere, to darker things.

He said what they didn't want to say. 'We're looking for a snatcher.'

She breathed out. Nodded. Held his eyes.

They began to organise accelerated interviews of the men identified in the SOR review.

'Another thing. The meadows behind Garford Road. Do you know where I mean? By Wolfson College.'

'Along the Cherwell.'

'We need to search them. The river too. And further out, Elsfield way. The woods there. Anyone could drive there in ten minutes.'

'I'll get on it.' Livvy hesitated. 'By the way, your wife called. Just to remind you, she said, about an antenatal class this evening.'

'Did she say what time?'

'No.'

He looked at his watch, thinking ahead to his calls with the liaison teams in Europe, his briefing with the Super, the evening press conference. 'Doesn't matter. Let me know when the search can start, will you?'

'Sir.'

She went into C3 to talk to Poppy's father, and Ray stood there a moment, absorbing the new information, summoning his strength. Up to this point they had been looking at a parental. Now, almost certainly, they were looking for a paedophile. He remembered what Maisie had told him: the window for finding Poppy was shrinking fast.

TEN

'Fucking men,' Jade said, 'The useless sex. What do they do? Piss off and leave us to do everything or hang around and fuck things up. Don't know which is worse.'

Neither did Ryan. He hardly ever interfered with Jade's rants. The capacity of her mind impressed him; she had the magical gift of blending wide-ranging philosophical arguments about human behaviour – men suffered from something she called Dick Brain – with detailed descriptions of her ex Darren's personal lack of hygiene in the toilet or his habit of using chapatis as a Kleenex when eating curries hot enough to make his nose run.

'Talking of useless men, don't you think it's time you visited Dad?'

Here Ryan protested. 'He's not useless. He's evil.'

'When I said "useless", I didn't mean him, Ryan.'

Their father, convicted of the attempted abduction of little Ryan, was in custody. He was a chronic alcoholic. At first he had been in category C Huntercombe Prison but during the first few months of his sentence, while drying out, he'd been involved in a violent incident with an inmate and two prison officers, and was now on temporary transfer at Grendon, where he complained frequently about being housed with the murderers and sex offenders.

Ryan stated that he would rather go blind than see his father again. Even as he said it, he had an uncomfortable feeling that Jade would somehow find a way to persuade him. He understood the arguments for making the visit. Deprived of alcohol, his father might well be a different person, more reasonable, less vindictive, not quite so bitter and twisted. She – and others – had repeatedly told Ryan that it would be good for him personally to meet his father, to resolve the issues between them. He didn't believe that bullshit, however. And he noted that Jade had not visited Grendon herself.

'Daddy?'

'Yeah?'

'Mylee can wear my costume if I let her, can't she?'

Little Ryan and his cousin huddled in the doorway, their faces wholly intent on the question, a picture of seriousness to be captioned *World Leaders Address Key Issue of Our Time*.

Then bath time. Bath time was always seven p.m., sometimes with Mylee, sometimes without. Tonight little Ryan was on his own. He sat in the white enamel bath with a plastic crocodile in his mouth and a thoughtful expression on his face.

He made a conversational noise and his father took the crocodile out of his mouth.

'What's that?'

'Crock diles are strange, aren't they, Daddy?'

70

'They are, yeah. Big teeth and stuff. Bad breath. You wouldn't want to kiss one.'

Little Ryan thought about that for a while. 'Is Auntie Jade strange?'

'Not the same way, to be fair. She can be a bit shouty.'

Little Ryan contemplated this, chewing on the crocodile again. 'Is Mylee?'

'Nope.'

'Mylee is my cousin.'

'Correct.'

'And my friend, Daddy.'

'Yeah, she is.'

There was a silence in which the crocodile briefly returned to the mouth. 'Am I strange?' he asked at last.

'You? No, never. Most normal person I know.'

'I like conversations.'

'There you go. Crocodiles don't. Crocodiles don't know what conversations are. Anyway, they've got nothing to say for themselves. It's just chomp chomp, gobble gobble all day long with them.'

Little Ryan heaved a sigh. 'The thing about stranger danger, Daddy, is you shouldn't say yes.'

He hesitated. 'What?'

'When they ask you to get in the car.'

Ryan, sitting on the toilet seat, gave his son a long look.

'Learn that at nursery, did you?'

His son nodded. 'And, Daddy, you shouldn't say yes when they say do you want a sweet.'

'Fair enough. When did they tell you this?'

71

'Now.' Little Ryan corrected himself. 'Today.'

Ryan could imagine it. In nursery schools up and down the country smiling young teachers telling children how not to be snatched like little Poppy Clarke. Word had gone out that the father was not a suspect any more. He could imagine their calm voices explaining patiently what can be explained and avoiding what can't, the great horror that lies behind the stranger in the car with his packet of sweets and his cheeky smile.

'Not Smarties, Daddy.'

'What do you mean?'

'You can't say yes to a Smartie.'

'Okay.'

Little Ryan began to list all the sweets you couldn't say yes to. His knowledge of sweets was extensive and it took him a long time. After a while Ryan found himself thinking about Mick Dick again, turning questions over in his mind. What had he been doing at the compound? He hadn't stolen anything. What was he scared of? Since speaking to Charlene, Ryan had talked to a couple of guys from school who'd stayed in touch with Mick Dick. Neither could understand why anyone would want to harass him, let alone kill him. Like Charlene had said, he'd never made enemies. He'd been a friendly sort of guy, for a violent criminal. When he went down there was a plea deal on offer if he spilled the beans but he never did. There were people grateful to Mick Dick, not angry with him. Perhaps, Ryan thought, he had mental health issues. Quite likely, in fact. Chronic low self-esteem. Good old-fashioned paranoia. But, then, he'd never thought Mick Dick took himself seriously enough to go wrong in the head.

Little Ryan said, 'But Daddy, I don't *know* any stranger dangers. Auntie Jade's not a stranger danger. Mrs Welbeck's not a stranger danger.'

And Ryan reluctantly began to explain the concept of a stranger who might be a danger.

When Jade came back from her shift at the Co-op, little Ryan was in bed, satisfied with his conversation, and Ryan was on his way out when Jade asked to have another word with him.

'It's not about Dad again, is it? You just done that one.'

It was a different one: the one where people had been calling the house to talk about this fellow who'd been killed, Michael Dick. Jade was suspicious. She wanted to check (narrowed eyes, beady mouth) that Ryan wasn't taking an inappropriately close interest in his death, or, putting it another way (irritated now by Ryan's reluctance to deny it), of sticking his big nose in where it wasn't wanted, interfering, in other words, in an official police investigation, which, unless she was mistaken, had been explicitly discouraged, or even formally ruled off limits, by Superintendent Wallace, who happened to be the same guy supervising Ryan's reinstatement procedure ('Seriously, you couldn't make it up, the actual same fucking fellow, Ryan!'), leading her to observe (eyes suddenly prominent and threatening) that if Ryan continued to behave like a complete knobhead, his reinstatement process was likely to end up in the waste-paper basket.

Ryan made little contribution to this conversation, in fact exiting the house without speaking, though, as usual, he was struck by his sister's forcefulness of expression and tenacious grip on the situation.

ELEVEN

Grove Street lies just north of the Summertown shops, a high-value narrow strip of late Victorian terraced cottages, built originally for the workers in local factories (buttons, toffee, caps), occupied now by the upper-middle classes, doctors, academics and business executives, who have refurbished their miniature properties with knock-through sitting rooms of cool whitewashed walls and exposed chimney breasts, ultra-modern kitchens with bespoke cherrywood cabinets and Modena granite surfaces, light-filled attic bedrooms with stripped pine floors extending the full depth of the house, and tiny back gardens ingeniously remodelled with timber work-rooms, brick rotundas and water features. They are the Fabergé eggs of housing. And, in the knock-through of one of them, sitting cross-legged on a rug, attempting to perfect her antenatal breathing technique, Diane was anxiously trying to find comfort. It was nine thirty. She was angry with Ray, and she felt this anger moving in her, a dark flow, a sluggish current washing through her like nausea.

She heard the key turn in the lock and breathed lighter, stronger, but to no avail.

Ray was into the room and already in view when he realised he'd forgotten the antenatal class. His face hesitated between several different expressions before settling on exasperation. He held up his hands. 'You wouldn't believe. I was just leaving to get to it, quarter to eight, and I was called out to Elsfield; we've started a search in the woods out there. False alarm as it turned out but I've only just got away. Babe,' he said, 'I'm so sorry.'

She turned a sweat-shiny face towards him. 'The class started at seven,' she said in a voice both dull and edgy.

A moment passed. His eyes slid away and she began to tremble. 'A search in the woods?'

He nodded, grim.

'I thought you were looking for the father.'

He shook his head.

'You think she was snatched? A paedophile?'

'I'm afraid it's a possibility.'

She looked at him a long moment without speaking again, an expression on her face he couldn't decipher. Something of disappointment in it, and of exhaustion, but something else too, something stronger, fear perhaps. Or was it disgust? He was just formulating a comment of general positivity when she opened her mouth and something slid out, a stream of lemon-coloured liquid. Once started, she couldn't stop it, moaning as she clutched her distended stomach as if to squeeze all the poison out of her, and Ray ran past her to get kitchen roll.

★

Later, he sat in their spare room with his laptop, gazing at it blankly, trying to muster the will to turn it on. He was tired. On the keyboard was a scribbled post-it note put there by Diane earlier in the day: *Call your father*. It didn't make him feel any better. He stood and stretched, trying to ease his aching back. There wasn't much space in the room. Over the previous few months it had filled up with baby stuff: packages of clothing, tiny outfits of denim dungarees and branded T-shirts, sleepwear in calming pastel colours, romper suits decorated with rainbows. His father had sent matching coats in the colours of the Nigerian flag. There were also – he noticed now with discomfort – two pirate costumes with eye-patches and cutlasses, as if Diane was going to give birth to three-year-olds. Taking up the space where he used to keep wine was a two-seater pushchair, their major purchase so far, a sleek, compact, computerised model from Baby Dynamic, more robot than pushchair, the season's must-have piece of baby infrastructure. Contemplating it all, he felt disquiet. For nearly four years he and Diane had been trying to have a baby, but now he felt less ready to be a parent than ever. He'd watched Diane's joy turn to misery as her punishing pregnancy took its toll. From the beginning she'd suffered: sleeplessness, back pain, vomiting. Hallucinations at one point. She could find no relief, she was never at ease – and now, to make things worse, she was upsetting herself about Poppy Clarke. They'd begun to argue – about the birth (Diane wanted it at home), pain relief (she was keen to avoid all unnecessary drugs), their children's diet, discipline, education, future lives. They argued about childcare, their careers, where they should live. He had found himself saying things he didn't even know he believed, and heard Diane's views

76

with shock, like those of a stranger. That was it, he thought: they had become strangers. She couldn't bear for him to touch her.

He felt worn, slack. Briefly, he remembered the energy of his youth when he was still single, still properly handsome, when he could see it in the girls' eyes, hear it in their voices. 'Hey, Ray, want to hang out Friday?' But those days were gone.

He turned his thoughts to his father. He did not want to call him. The retired businessman had become more outspoken as he'd got older, harsher, more macho. 'I don't want to hear these excuses, Ray. I didn't raise you to complain. Be a man.' He was proud of his son's position, his prominence in the Poppy Clarke investigation. Over the last three days he'd called several times, wanting to talk about it, censorious, incredulous.

'The mother,' he'd say. 'I've seen pictures. Pink hair, I ask you. What was she thinking? Her child, Ray! Does she think the world is safe? These people in their expensive English houses, I know them, thoughtless, careless. They can thrive here, in their comfortable little corner. Anywhere else in the world, I promise you, they go under. Think of them in Lagos, Ray! Think of them in Accra, Dakar. Five minutes, under they go, their houses, their possessions, their children. I'm not kidding.'

Ray thought about Poppy's father, he remembered the way he had wept in the station. What was he doing now? He imagined him back in his nice, empty canalside flat, sitting alone, lost in his nightmare, praying as he had never in his life prayed before, for Poppy to be alive.

We're all thoughtless about what is most precious to us until it's too late. Perhaps fathers more than most.

He glanced again at his laptop, remembering the briefing

Maisie Ndiaye had given to his team that afternoon. Though as yet they knew nothing about the perp, Maisie had outlined some likely features. Almost certainly male, most likely white. Given the success of the abduction (most attempted abductions fail), he could be a slightly older, experienced guy, thirty-five to forty. Not a first-timer, not an opportunist. Probably without drug or alcohol addictions. Possibly in full employment, perhaps as a professional, but socially inhibited with low self-esteem and, almost certainly, mental health issues. They had, in fact, already begun to interview known paedophiles in the area, trawling through records of their past activities. Even at this early stage there were images and descriptive accounts Ray could not get out of his head. Looking around the room at the miniature clothes, the toys, all the child-friendly items, he felt suddenly scared.

At midnight he was too exhausted to work any more. Too exhausted to fall asleep either. For a long time after he got into bed he lay in a sort of swoon, at the mercy of his imagination, crowded by images which came and went without his involve-ment: a tree-lined avenue, a sunlit driveway, a little girl laughing and the shadow of someone stood nearby; and the voice of Natalie saying, over and over, 'A quiet day, such a quiet after-noon, hardly anyone about.'

TWELVE

He was waiting for her when she arrived at seven thirty. Nervous, flushing, she dropped her keys twice at the door, flicked timid glances at him as they went inside. Once inside, she began to speak.

'Last night, on the news . . . They said he was no longer a—'

'This isn't about Dr Clarke, Natalie.'

They sat again on the tiny yellow chairs. It didn't look as if she'd slept; her eyes were small and watery, a sort of strained astonishment in them, as if, as the hours passed, she believed less in what had happened.

Ray said, 'You told us it was quiet. Deserted. Out there, in Garford Road, where Poppy was playing.'

'It's true. It was.'

'All right. But here, in the nursery, there must have been people coming and going all day.'

'Well, yes.'

'I want to know who was here, throughout the day, the whole day. Not just staff. Everyone you remember. Parents, delivery men, everyone. People you were with, people you saw, people you only glimpsed, people you just overheard. Take your time. But try to remember everyone, no matter who they were or how briefly they were here.'

After a hesitant start, she became methodical, organised. It was a side of her Ray hadn't seen earlier. Beginning with the arrival of the postman, she went through the day in chronological order, listing the staff who arrived shortly after she did, the children and their parents, their carers, their siblings, the woman who delivered the milk, the woman who brought the lunches, a neighbour returning three balls kicked into her garden, a boy from the newsagent's who dumped some flyers on the doormat, then the different parents and carers who arrived in the afternoon to collect their children, ending with Rachel, the last parent to arrive. It was an impressively detailed list and there was no one on it who could be plausibly described as suspicious.

'Is that everyone? No one else? Did you hear anyone talking to someone else? Did you hear anyone talking outside, even if you didn't see them?'

No.

'See anyone outside through a window?'

No.

And then: 'Actually, I saw Sam.'

'Who's Sam?'

'One of the kids who helps out sometimes. Three o'clock, Harriet had just made our tea.'

'Get a good sight of him?'

'Just brief. Going past that window there.'

'What was he doing here? Working?'

'No. The day before he'd been with the kids and he'd left some of his frisbees in our store, and he told me he'd come back to pick them up. So I assumed that's what he was doing.'

'Work experience kid?'

'That's right.'

'Related?'

She flushed. 'We don't just take *my* relatives. Earlier this year we had the son of one of the trustees, and before that Bronwen's daughter, and—'

'I understand.'

The first children had begun to arrive and he said his good-byes.

'I didn't ask. I don't suppose there's any news?'

'No.'

She swallowed, blinked and turned to face the children.

Outside, he wandered. The lawn was set out with tricycles and wheelbarrows, scooters and playmats. Under the wall of a neighbour's house a wooden climbing frame was set into a sandpit. The whole garden seemed to have been designed like a child's painting. Walking beyond, round a shrubbery, he came across the outside store. The door was open and he went inside, into green shadows and vague smells of damp, and stood there inhaling until his eyes adjusted and he could make out the objects around him, garden umbrellas, tins of paint, a lawnmower, bales of purple netting, boxes of balls, ribbed plastic panels of a Wendy house. And, by the door, a pile of frisbees.

He bent to pick one up, turned it over. On the underside was written thickly in waterproof ink *Sam Baloch*. For a moment he stood there thinking. Then he put the frisbee down and went back to the nursery to get Sam's address from Natalie.

As soon as the door was answered he knew the outcome of his visit. Samama Baloch stood there, seventeen years old, polite, quizzical, floppy-haired. He was going to study to be a doctor, Natalie had told him, but was taking a year out in order to spend time with his younger sister, Alaya, who had MS.

Ray sat with Sam and his parents in their front room. After being offered tea, coffee, homemade scones and a variety of herbal drinks, he asked his question.

'Did you go to Magpies nursery the day before yesterday?'

'No.'

'You were going to pick up your frisbees.'

'I forgot.'

'So you weren't walking in the garden there?'

'No.'

Ray thanked them all and left.

Ray and Livvy talked in his office.

'She assumed it was Sam passing the window. But that's all it was, an assumption. She remembered Sam was coming back and her brain told her that's who she was seeing. She didn't get a proper look at him at all.'

'Okay, not Sam. Young, though?'

'She couldn't say.'

'But Asian?'

'She's not even sure about that. Hooded is all she remembers for definite. And a sense it was a man.'

'A man. Indeterminate age, unknown ethnicity.'

'In the nursery grounds two hours before Poppy was taken.'

'Something? Nothing?'

'It's all something until proved otherwise.'

They looked at each other. Livvy went to get coffees.

THIRTEEN

Cuddesdon Park was off the main road on the eastern side of Horspath, a neat plot of well-kept trailers separated from surrounding farmland by a white picket fence. Tubs of flowers bordered the driveways and sculptured woodland animals struck cute poses by front doors. It was a warm, scented evening, the wide sky veiled in twilight, Oxford glowing faintly in the distance like a child's night-light in a shuttered room, and quiet, no one about, as if the park was occupied entirely by old age pensioners, all now tucked up in bed and soundlessly asleep.

Ryan left his car at the end of the lane and sauntered between trailers until he came to Mick Dick's, the last in a row, close up against the wooden fence bordering a field of rapeseed. Lights off. No answer, of course, when he knocked on the door. No movement in any of the other caravans either, no curtains twitching, no lights coming on. It might have been midnight, not nine thirty. He walked round the trailer until he came to the bedroom window, and found it smashed. Someone had put a brick through it – he could see it lying on the carpet inside. He went back to the front door and tried it. It opened.

The trailer was even smaller than the one he'd grown up in but newer, two-tone, cream and beige. Neat little place. He could imagine it nice to live in, compact and tidy. But not now. Chairs had been overturned, furnishings slashed, mirrors cracked. The kitchen was awash with the debris of ransacked cupboards, spilled cereal, pasta, broken biscuits, packets of soup. In the bedroom, drawers had been emptied, clothes scattered across the floor. He picked his way through the mess, stopping occasionally to examine something, a torn manilla envelope (in which he found a bunch of papers setting out the terms of Mick Dick's release from Grendon), child's mittens, a wallet (with nothing in it) and correspondence (mainly flyers, a few official notices from the council, nothing personal). In the bathroom, still sellotaped to the mirror, was a creased photograph of Mick Dick and Ashleigh at a funfair, Mick Dick looking awkward as if afraid to drop her, Ashleigh concentrating on not dropping her candy floss.

He left everything where it was. After ten minutes he was ready to go. But on his way out he noticed a homemade business card stuck in the frame of the door. It had a name and address on it. SHANE COBB, FACILITATOR.

That was interesting.

He put it in his pocket, closed the door carefully behind him, and walked back down the deserted driveway to his car, where he sat for a few moments, gazing across the twilit fields.

One possibility was simply that local teenage morons had sussed the place was empty and gone on a spree. Another was that Mick Dick had enemies after all. Is that why he was sleeping in hire vans? Did that explain his terror, his rush across the muddy fields, his broken body in the ditch?

He gave Charlene a call.

'That guy who wanted to give Mick Dick money?'

'Yeah. Crabb or something.'

'Was it Cobb? Shane Cobb?'

'That's it.'

Ryan sat there a few moments longer. Interesting.

Who was this Cobb and why had he been trying to give Mick Dick money?

Also: what the fuck was a 'facilitator'?

Something had frightened Mick Dick, someone had smashed up his place. The more Ryan thought about it, the more it pissed him off, and he sat there among the peaceful Cuddesdon fields feeling angry and helpless until he realised he was once again late for work.

Carl Crapper was waiting for him in his office, his scowl so pronounced it completely obscured his eyes and gave an unfortunate prominence to his moustache.

'Name Mick Dick mean anything to you?' Ryan said before he could speak.

Taken by surprise, the manager struggled to begin whatever he had been waiting to say and was easily interrupted.

'Michael Dick, if it helps to have his name in full.'

Carl began again.

'Big lad,' Ryan said. 'Black. You'd notice him.'

The manager said, 'What I'm trying to say to you—'

'Got a little girl, Ashleigh. Four, five.'

'What I'm trying—'

'Dead,' Ryan said. 'Dead in a ditch in Hinksey two nights ago.'

Carl stopped speaking.

'Puts it in perspective, though, don't it?'

By this time Ryan had put on his security uniform and was sitting at his desk, firing up the monitors. 'Are you staying long?' Ryan asked. 'Want me to put the kettle on?'

Carl, flushed and sweating, was not to be deterred. He regrouped and said his piece addressing Ryan's poor time-keeping, bad attitude and careless decision-making, topics very familiar to Ryan, all of which, in fact, he was prepared not to dispute. But then Carl brought Mick Dick into it. He'd read about him, in fact. And he knew his type. Big black fucking lazy criminal.

Ryan felt himself lose a little bit of self-control. 'What was that you said?'

There was a dangerous edge to his voice, which Carl ignored.

'Listen. Just because some vagrant—'

'Vagrant? Vagrant, Carl? I said he died in a ditch, I didn't say he lived in a fucking ditch. Can we have a little respect?'

Carl's body language and general expressions indicated that no respect would be forthcoming, in fact, and Ryan lost his self-control entirely.

'I'll tell you why, Carl. 'Cause he wasn't lazy, that's why. 'Cause he tried his best. 'Cause he had a little girl he visited twice a week and never missed spite of all the bollocks. 'Cause he made mistakes and paid for them, not like some fuckers, Carl. 'Cause when he died, his ex broke down and wept.'

Carl made a contemptuous gesture, enraging Ryan further.

'Who's going to weep for you, Carl? Your cat? Your *AutoTrader* subscription? Look at yourself, Carl. Think you're Lord of Van Hire, don't you, King of Punch the Fucking Clock? Well, take a giant look in the mirror, have a look at your pre-stained shirts and trousers two sizes too small. Think you're a cut above? You drive a nineties Vauxhall Vectra spray-painted with go-faster stripes, and you live on your own, and you have no friends and you have no lovers, Carl, and no relatives except a sister in Hove you haven't visited in fourteen years, and no hobbies except annoying people, and no kindness, Carl, and less intelligence, and no idea that you look exactly like what you are, Carl, which is why, Carl, I'm not going to sit here and listen to you give me a lecture about the value of human life, because the truth is, Carl, you think you're top brand but you're nothing but a special offer multi-pack of piss!'

By the time he'd finished shouting, Carl had retreated to his Vauxhall Vectra and driven off, and Ryan was left standing in the doorway of his shed, still shaking with the mantra of his words, panting and righteous in the marvellous heat of his anger, as Carl's tail lights disappeared, and the noise of his engine faded to silence, and Ryan's heat began to cool, and, along with the evening's summer chill, he felt the first faint inkling of having, once again, gone too far, and heard, somewhere in his memory, the voice of Superintendent Wallace telling him that it was absolutely necessary for him to have an impeccable record of conduct at work.

FOURTEEN

'Any recent experiences of anger, Ryan?'

Dr J. Tompkins, BSc, PhD, QOP, his anger management counsellor, sat opposite him on a comfortable chair in the small meeting room on the first floor of St Aldates station. It was their first session. Her eyebrows made politely questioning arches.

He mimed searching his memory.

'You haven't behaved in a way you've regretted later, said anything you wished you hadn't said?'

'Well,' he said at last, 'not with anyone what didn't deserve it.'

'That's interesting.'

She kept her eyes constantly on his. It was a technique she had. She used a soft, inviting voice and left silences.

'Just a joke.'

'That's why it's interesting.'

'I've got to do this course for the rehab,' he added after another lengthy silence.

She ignored this. She kept her eyes on his until he looked away. She'd been trained to do that, he knew. Trained also to radiate

89

calm and assurance, to invite confidences. She was good at it. She'd already promised to never judge him, and though he could probably make her break her promise, he didn't want to. He liked her. He liked her teacher glasses, her long, straight brown hair, her neat mouth poised to speak but only at the right moment, her hands that made such quiet gestures in the space above her lap. He liked the way she introduced herself informally as Jill, though he'd seen already, upside down on her folder, her official name and letters of qualification. But he didn't like her silences.

Dr Tompkins moved her mouth into a smiling position. 'Why don't you begin by telling me a little bit about yourself?'

He stirred, shifted about a bit. 'It'll all be in the file.'

'What's in the file has been written by other people. I'm interested in what you might say yourself. Tell me what's important to you.'

He blew out a big breath, fidgeted. 'Got a kid.'

'Lovely.'

'Yeah. He is and all. Nearly three. Not like me.'

'In what way?'

'Well, he don't lose his temper for a start.'

'Which you don't do any more.' She smiled again, without showing her teeth. She never showed her teeth, he'd noticed. 'What's his name?'

'Ryan.'

'Must be a family tradition. It's your father's name too, I think.'

She held his eyes until he looked away. 'In the file,' he said.

'I've read it. Written by someone else.'

'Yeah. That's a tradition as well.'

Neither of them showed their teeth.

'What about friends?'

The question took him by surprise.

'Never mind,' she said at last. 'Let's talk a little bit about anger. Just in case, Ryan, you ever experience it in the future.'

So, anger. An emotion, like lust, pulling us towards its source. A seductive emotion, narrowing things down, simplifying them. Blocking out everything else, what we're doing, what we're saying, any thought of the consequences. Damaging others, those we love, damaging ourselves.

'Yeah. Or standing up for ourselves. Bringing down the bad guy. Getting justice done.'

Her calm remained unruffled. 'Absolutely, Ryan. At the right time.' She made the smiling expression. 'At the wrong time, unfortunately, it wrecks our relationships, ruins our careers. Causes us to make terrible mistakes, mistakes from which we sometimes never recover.'

He sat there while she talked, thinking of Mick Dick and his mistake: something from which he had never recovered. Maybe, he thought suddenly, that expression on Mick Dick's face had been anger. Could it have been rage that drove him across those water meadows? Something to think about. He thought too of the card he had found at Mick Dick's trailer for Shane Cobb. He surreptitiously glanced at his watch; there would just about be time to pay him a visit before work.

'Any of this sound familiar?' she asked.

He made an ambiguous gesture.

She let another silence grow between them. She had the gift of releasing these silences into the room, like bubbles, fragile and breakable. They made Ryan scared to breathe in case he burst them.

'Listen,' he said at last. 'Not being funny, but I'm not, like, a big talker about feelings. This counselling's all about outcomes, right? I can learn. That's my thing. Techniques, whatever. I can do all that. Get it down, tick the boxes, everyone wins.'

She relented. Perhaps, Ryan thought, she felt sorry for him. In any case, she spent the next twenty minutes teaching him breathing techniques, the means to break emotional momentum, to lift the red mist, to give him time to deal with the thoughts causing the anger. And he was soothed. Something about the exercises' dull regularity and quiet repetition reminded him of primary school, the hush of it, no raised voices, walking quietly in single file, sitting cross-legged in rows on the dusty, waxy floor of the hall, gazing at sunbeams, hearing, like distant traffic noise, the pleasant drone of the teacher's voice. He breathed slowly, remembering. And for a moment he thought that the anger management course was going to be helpful. Then Dr Tompkins asked him to try an exercise.

'Think of an instance when you were angry. Remember it. Just briefly. Ten seconds.'

He wasn't prepared, wasn't ready; he saw it too vividly, the scene at Hinksey Point six months earlier. Suddenly he was in it. The trailer door hanging lopsidedly on its hinges where he and Ray had smashed it in. Little Ryan clinging to him, his terrified sobbing in his ears. Then his father, in cuffs, coming through the broken door, the man who had just abducted his son, coming out of his lair in his alcoholic's stained vest and badly fastened trousers, with his scrawny tattooed arms and dangerous, lumpy hands, turning his grey face towards Ryan and sneering at him. The man who had just been terrifying his son, sneering now with a sneer he remembered from his own childhood, the sneer that had taunted him as he cowered in the corner of the caravan, as he writhed on the lino trying to evade his father's boot, the sneer that told him he could do what he wanted, because he, Ryan, was too weak, too pathetic to stop him.

So he saw it and felt it all again. And felt himself running towards his father again, screaming, a half-brick in his hand, and hitting him with it, swinging it, pounding his head, trying hard to kill him, concentrating on it, doing his best to make every blow split open the skull, though continually mistiming it, seeing to his horror and fury how his father continued to sneer, even as the blood ran down his face into his mouth, as he heard himself screaming in a childish voice he hardly recognised, *Die, you fuck, you cunt, you fucking cunt, you fucking*—

'Ryan?'

He untangled himself on the chair, unwrapped his arms from around his head. For a moment he seemed to hear the faint after-noise of a feral keening, like a child imitating an animal; then the room was quiet again.

'Ryan?' She used her most tactful voice.

'I'm all right now.'

She was looking at him with a mild professional concern, but time was up and she let him go without further questions, and he went gratefully out of the room and made his way in a daze down the corridor as far as the vending machines, where he could stop, get his breath back. He was cross with himself. He had to be stronger than that; only his strength, that gristly toughness acquired in childhood, kept him safe. He got a bottle of water from the machine. Gradually he calmed down; at least he was always able to do that, he had the knack of moving on fast. Policemen and women came past him up and down the corridor, carrying things or chatting to each other. Normality resumed. He looked at his watch: he could still get to Cobb's. But a voice came down the corridor as a well-packed uniform appeared out of a small group of admin staff and turned into Superintendent Wallace.

They stood together in the little cafe area under a wall-mounted television. Without looking, Ryan sensed how other officers moved away slightly, as if to give Wallace his due space. Wallace did not need space, however; he pinned Ryan in the corner and brought his broad face up close.

'Word says you're dipping into one of our cases ongoing. Comment?'

He had no comment. Wallace's face remained close to his.

'Michael Dick. Hit and run.'

'Oh yeah. I know what it looks like but the thing is—'

'Driver of the car turned himself in last night.'

He was taken by surprise. 'Really?'

Wallace's eyes widened.

'I mean, is it solid?'

'Fibres from Michael Dick's clothing stuck in the smashed front driver-side headlight of his Vauxhall Astra. Yes, it's solid.'

'Who is he?'

'No one of interest to you. Sales assistant, twenty-two years old living in Botley. No priors. No connection to Michael Dick.'

'What happened?'

'He was driving home after hanging out in a car park of a sports club at the end of that lane. According to his statement, Michael Dick suddenly ran into the road out of the bushes. It was dark. Didn't see him till it was too late. Had no chance of stopping.'

'Left it late to come forward.'

'Why do you think that is, bright boy?'

Ryan didn't have to think. 'Off his face when it happened, I suppose. Popping pills or whatever in that car park with his mates. Waited till he was clean again.'

'There you go.' Wallace remained uncomfortably close. 'Something else. Two teenage boys from Horspath picked up vandalising a newsagent's in Cowley admitted to trashing a mobile home in Cuddesdon belonging to one Michael Dick.' He spoke now in a lower tone. 'I've no interest in this Michael Dick. Neither do you now. Your job is to prove to me that you're no longer the sort of guy goes rogue. So prove it. Am I making myself understood here?'

Something in Ryan's expression must have failed to reassure him because he pushed his face even closer and lowered his voice to a more dangerous growl. 'Listen, son. It's not hard. You want reinstatement, you toe the line. Otherwise I'll dump you in a second.'

'Got it.'

There was a moment in which Wallace seemed to be demonstrating how long he could go without blinking; then he silently withdrew. Ryan wiped the condensation of his glare off his face and turned to go, but his attention was caught by the television screen, where there was a news announcement about the missing girl, Poppy Clarke. DI Ray Wilkins appeared on screen, handsome and plausible in crisp uniform, and next to him a young woman with pink-tinted hair, tearful and trembling, trying to say something, trying to address someone, pleading.

FIFTEEN

The television 'newsroom' was a small stage set positioned in the corner of the studio, a construct of fake walls and furniture as temptingly artificial as a children's play area. Under fierce lights Ray sat behind a partial desk trailing cables, between the news anchor on his left and Rachel Clarke on his right, avoiding looking at the activity going on out of camera shot, the cameramen moving at the edge of the set, the director making gestures, the make-up lady murmuring to the producer, assorted gofers with clipboards and bottles of water. Making an effort to zone it all out, he concentrated on what Rachel was trying to say, willing her to get through the script. She hadn't managed it in rehearsals.

Now that they had ruled out Dr Clarke as a suspect, and were working on the assumption that Poppy had been taken by a person or persons unknown, a new strategy followed. It was now over ninety hours since Poppy had disappeared, and they had decided to make a direct appeal live on lunchtime news to Poppy's abductor. It was probably their last chance.

Ray watched Rachel as she struggled to speak.

The script had been carefully put together by specialists from the Missing Child Team in the National Crime Agency, every word weighed and judged, words to describe Poppy, her joy in life, her future, words to describe her mother's love for her, words to make her agony irresistible under those exposing lights. But they were not words written by Rachel, nor even for Rachel. They were for Poppy's abductor, all of them, each one carefully chosen to speak directly, intimately, to him, to make it possible, even now, for him to spare her. For Rachel there were no words possible, just the unbearable thought of Poppy herself, as only she knew her and as only she imagined her now, which she couldn't endure. So the words choked her.

The director gestured, the cameras cut to the anchor, Ray helped Rachel off the set.

'It's okay,' he said. 'It doesn't matter. It has more impact like this. Much more.'

He did not believe it.

They sat together in the green room afterwards. Rachel said, 'She's already dead.'

Ray began to protest.

'I don't really believe it,' she said, watching him. 'I just say it to see if I can survive if it becomes true.'

'We can get your statement out in other ways. We'll release it now to the media. We can quote from it in the posters and leaflets.'

She didn't seem to be listening. He wondered if she was on medication. Her leg was twittering, as always.

'We called her the trouble monkey,' she said. 'Always making mischief. We used to laugh about it. But the truth is, Sebastian was jealous of her. He hated the time I spent with her. We fought about it. We fought over her. There were times . . .' She paused, eyes closed, trying to control her breathing. '. . . there were times I blamed her.'

They sat in silence.

She wiped her face, became brisk. 'You don't have anything to go on, do you? No leads. When you talked, you didn't mention anything. Or is there something you want to keep out of the press? Something you're hiding?'

He thought briefly of the man in the garden. They couldn't even confirm his existence yet: no one else at the nursery that day had seen him. 'We need a sighting,' he said. 'It will come. It always comes.' He didn't need to say that it might come too late.

They sat in silence again. She began to cry. 'I'm stuck in it. That moment. Coming out of the nursery, seeing the empty driveway. I dream it. I see it when I'm awake. It's so vivid I could be sick. Blue sky, birds singing, sunshine on the lawn, everything screaming at me that Poppy isn't there. I've always loved the smell of cut grass; now it'll be the smell of when I lost her. Right then. Middle of the afternoon. Broad daylight. An ordinary day. Oxford. *Oxford*,' she repeated harshly. 'Not Mogadishu.' She was shaking her head; her voice had begun to come apart. 'And no one saw anything. *No one!*'

She began to sob.

'That afternoon,' she said, 'everything broke.'

Ray said after a moment, 'I promise you this, we will continue to do everything we can, we won't give up, and in the end we will find her.'

She held his eyes. 'I know what that means,' she said. 'I know what you'll find.' And then, with a bitter laugh: 'Do you think I blame *you*?'

She got up and walked away, leaving Ray behind. For a while he stayed there, staring at the wall. Then he called Magpies and got Natalie on the phone.

'Did someone come to the nursery to cut the grass that day?'

She went to check and came back.

'It looks like they did. The agency send someone every week. I wasn't aware of anyone being here so he must have just arrived and got on with the job.'

'Could he be the man you saw through the window?'

There was a long pause. He could almost hear her trying to remember.

'I don't know,' she said at last. 'I think I would have recognised him.'

He called Livvy and asked her to check it out, and sat there, thinking. The COMINT team was reviewing the camera footage on all the main routes out of Oxford, at all the service stations, fast-food outlets, cafes. He longed for a sighting here, a glimpse of a girl in a pirate costume walking across a forecourt to the toilet, a small face in the back of a car. It would at least give them a chance. At the same time they were also searching the woods near Elsfield. Here, he dreaded a sighting. He knew what it would be: clothing, something under a heap of leaves, signs of digging.

On his phone he read an email update about Rachel's brother, David, the 'junkie uncle'. Dr Clarke had repeated his feelings about him to several papers, which had printed them alongside

100

pictures, with the result that David had been attacked in a Bristol shopping centre and was now in a local hospital recovering from a ruptured spleen.

He had some texts from Diane too. One read *ANTENATAL!* She followed it up with *Any news?* She was still fixated on the missing child. Reflecting, he realised that, though he hid it from himself, he now no longer believed that Poppy would be found alive. Pulling himself out of his chair, he walked up and down, fighting his nausea. He was his father's son: others might go under, he would not. Deliberately, he forced himself to check his shoes, his trousers, his jacket; he brushed a speck of lint off his thigh. Then his phone rang.

Livvy said, 'Boss? The guy cutting the grass. Tariq Sayyed. The agency confirms he was there that afternoon. Cover. The regular Magpies gardener was sick.'

'Okay. We want to talk to him. Run him through the systems, get a line on him, and give me a call soon as. No delay. I've got some baby stuff to do now but my phone's on so call me soon as you can.'

'Got it.'

He sent a text to Diane. *See you there.* And made his way out of the building.

SIXTEEN

Seven o'clock. Ryan sat in his car on Pinnocks Way up at Dean Court, a long street of boxy semis with vans, motorbikes and kiddies' bicycles left haphazardly on kerbs and bald grass verges as if abandoned in a hurry. He shouldn't be here. It had been explained to him. Mick had simply been the victim of dangerous driving. But what explanation was there for the look on Mick's face in the compound, or his flight across the meadow? What was the 'mistake' Mick had made?

He looked impatiently at his watch. He'd been waiting two hours already, parked across the road from a house with a dog-eared flat-roof porch and a post-civilisation front garden stocked only with the sort of plants ugly enough to outface the coming eco-disaster. But now, at last, a man came slowly down the street and turned in at the gate, a small man with an overlarge head, taking quiet, careful steps, glancing from side to side. When a light came on in the front room Ryan got out of his car and went across the street.

Shane Cobb looked at him puzzled when Ryan asked if he could come in and ask a few questions.

'What about?' He had a soft voice.

'Facilitating.'

He let Ryan in.

They sat in a front room obviously used as a dumping ground for things in need of repair, cracked games consoles, legless ironing boards, buckled hard drives, parts of vacuum cleaners, a bicycle without handlebars.

'This what you facilitate? Handlebars on a bike sort of thing?'

Cobb said mildly, 'I can do a bit of anything. Repairs. Deliveries. Removals. Gardens, I've done a lot of those. Build a wall, I can do that now. Walk a dog.' His voice was childlike, sing-song with modest pride. 'Anything people need doing. Things they keep putting off. I know software too. Often I go into a place and help them out for a week or so, sit in the office, clear up a mess, get things straight.' He smiled. 'I can juggle,' he said unexpectedly. 'I've done street entertainment.'

'Oh yeah? Coco the Clown?'

'Children's parties. These days, though, I mainly do repairs and gardens.'

Ryan took all this in. 'Bit of an odd job man.'

'I prefer Facilitator.'

Ryan wondered if he was all there. With his large head and placid manner, he was like a child himself, a little disconnected.

'So,' he said pleasantly, 'what would you like me to facilitate for you?'

'Answers to some questions about a guy you know. Mick Dick.'

Now Cobb went pale. Swallowed hard. 'Are you police?' His voice was a whisper.

'Why do you ask that?'

'No reason.'

'Heard about Mick?'

Cobb managed to nod his head, but only just. He seemed
to be having problems holding himself physically together. 'On
the radio.'

'Hit and run,' Ryan said.

Cobb's eyelids fluttered as he nodded. As Ryan watched, his
pale face slowly darkened, his eyes bulged and he began to make
short, croaking noises. Struggling in his pocket, he brought out
a packet of prescription pills and swallowed three of them dry.

'I got issues,' he whispered at last. 'Health. Things upset me.'
A crinkly grey vein stood proud of the side of his ungainly head.
'Be all right now,' he said after a while. It did not look a certainty.

'See Mick much recently?'

He shook his head.

'But you been calling him. Wanting to give him money.'

Cobb looked at him warily.

'Owe him, did you?'

A cautious nod.

'How did you know him?'

Cobb's eyes darted this way and that.

'Doing a bricklaying course, maybe?'

Nodded at last.

'How long you been out?'

'Six months.' A whisper.

'What were you in for?'

'Supply of class A, three to five. I made a mistake,' he said,
'in my choice of associates.'

Ryan nodded. Making mistakes was becoming a bit of a theme. 'How's the facilitating thing going?'

Cobb shook his head sadly. 'No one wants to know when they find out you done time. Same for Michael.'

'What's the story with the money then?'

Cobb's eyes went all round the room. 'I needed it.' He'd shrunk into himself as if trying to hide from the memory of it. 'Needed it bad. Sometimes, inside, things happen if you can't pay. Michael lent me. No one else would. Only Michael. Got me out of a jam. I wanted to pay him back.' He was pale again with remembering it. 'He was a good friend to me inside. Sort to do you a favour. We were good friends.'

Ryan watched him. If Mick had been scared of somebody, it wasn't this guy. Cobb was fragile. Prison hadn't been kind to him. He looked shattered by the experience. Ryan could imagine Mick Dick taking poor Cobb under his wing.

'How about enemies? Mick make any enemies inside?'

'No. Everyone liked Michael.'

'What about the screws?'

'No.'

'Outside then?'

Cobb shook his head. 'Never heard it.'

'You don't know why anyone would want to kill him?'

Cobb's eyes widened and his mouth fell open, revealing some shadowy dental work. He shook his head soundlessly, fumbling for his packet of tablets.

Ryan tried another tack. 'He was looking for work. Know anything about that?'

Cobb relaxed slightly. 'Yes. He used to talk about it. He did

105

the bricklaying in Grendon, same as me. Other things too. But it's hard once you get out. The way people look at you. It can mess up your mind.'

'Grendon set him up with someone to help him, a mentor.'

Cobb brightened a little more. 'That's Thomas Fothergill. Yes. Michael liked him a lot. Admired him.'

'Who is he?'

'You don't know? Very successful local businessman. Has his own company, Baby Dynamic, out on Garsington Road. Rich, he's very rich. But a *lovely* man.' At the thought of it, he suddenly relaxed. He smiled and a confiding twinkle came into his eyes. Ryan almost felt warm towards him, and for a moment they both sat there, as if recognising a small but genuine consolation. 'You should talk to him,' Cobb said. 'I think Michael was spending more time with him than anyone else.'

'Okay. One more thing. When was the last time you spoke to Mick?'

'Last week.'

'And how did he sound? Worried about anything? Frightened?'

'Oh no. He was very happy.'

'Really?'

'Talking about things he was going to buy his daughter when he got work. Never heard him happier. His luck had turned, he said. Tom was going to help him get a job.' Reflecting on that, Cobb's face fell again. 'And now he's dead,' he murmured to himself.

He sat there in silence, holding his chest, hunched into himself, looking lonely, like a child abandoned on a railway station bench. Poor, fragile Cobb, one more victim of his own mistakes.

Ryan waited a moment but Cobb said no more, so he got up. 'All right, thanks. Mick Dick's ex could probably use the money, by the way. Bringing up Mick's daughter and that.'

Outside, he sat in his car. Cobb had given him very little, perhaps because he had very little to give. His questions remained unanswered. What had Mick Dick been scared of at the compound? Why had he run across the meadows in the pitch dark to get to North Hinksey? But if he couldn't see Mick Dick's death any clearer, a different picture was coming dimly into view, men thrown together, helping each other in hard times, comradeship of sorts: youth boxing champion Mick Dick looking out for little Cobb in Grendon; Fothergill, millionaire mentor, offering out-of-work Mick Dick a helping hand outside. That was sort of interesting.

He sat there in his car. He remembered what the Superintendent had said to him; he should probably let it all go now. Definitely he should let it go. What was Mick Dick to him anyway? Childhood friend? To be honest, he'd hardly known the guy. Just a big man in a compound gone quivery with fear, saying, 'Ryan, Ryan, man, *you* know, I can tell. You know what it's like to be out of luck.'

So he went to work.

SEVENTEEN

Meanwhile, in the front room of an old stone house in North Hinksey, only two hundred yards from the spot where Mick Dick had been killed, Diane and Ray sat cross-legged on a rug holding hands with five other pregnant couples. Ray was distracted, she could tell just from the way he was holding her hand.

The house was grand but shabby with a posh, hippyish vibe. In the wood-panelled hallway, leaflets advertising baby products (including Baby Dynamic's smart pushchair, which Diane and Ray had already bought) were mixed with ones for massage, reiki and past lives therapy. Marianne, the antenatal and hypnobirthing teacher, was a bare-foot middle-aged woman with a grey bun wearing a long, lumpy knitted cardigan; she had spent twenty years as an NHS community midwife followed by ten more as a psychic medium and energy healer. Her naked feet with their long, elegant, somehow thoughtful toes would be the abiding memory for many of her expecting mothers and fathers. Sessions began with hugs and smiles, both of which, Diane noticed, Ray struggled to perform. Then a few words for reflection. Men and women. How different are they?

'Some of these differences we hide. Some of our similarities we hide too.'

Marianne invited people to make their own comments. Someone said the differences were social, someone else that you can't ignore biology. Someone said men earn more. Diane said nothing. Ray didn't even seem to notice what was going on; out of the corner of her eye, Diane could see him resisting the urge to check his phone for updates.

All the couples were middle class, their babies were all due at the end of October, and all the mothers except Diane were conspicuously healthy – glossy and placid, hair shining, skin fresh, looking as if they exuded country scents of new leaf and meadowsweet. In discomfort, they were cheerfully stoical, and their husbands were proud and bemused, making well-informed if off-the-point comments (about amniotic fluid, the pubic bone or pelvic floor) in smiling deference to their partners – except for Ray, who said nothing, did not smile, and behaved as if he wasn't actually with Diane or even at an antenatal class. She tried not to think about him. She tried not to feel the tiredness in her face, the prickling tremor in her mouth, the thin yellow crust around one of her eyes. But though she didn't look at Ray, the others did, the women especially. They'd seen him on TV, the handsome police guy stating his determination to bring back little Poppy, chaperoning the bereft young mother. Marianne asked each of them to say a few words about their own experience of pregnancy, dads as well as mums, and when it came to Ray's turn to speak Diane could feel the intensity of their interest in him, as if they wanted not only news of the investigation but some personal intimation. In fact, he had to be prompted by Marianne to say anything at all, and when he did speak it was only to say he'd been busy, a comment so disconnected that Diane had to look away.

While they practised their breathing exercises ('Imagine you are very softly blowing out a candle') she thought ahead to the birth and, once more, saw nothing but differences between Ray and herself, more arguments about childcare, diet, nannies. He'd accused her of behaving as if the twins were solely hers. She replied: 'There's no room in your mind for me at all, is there?' Such were her thoughts as she blew out imaginary candles; she didn't want to feel like this, she wanted to be nurtured, like the other women, confident, she wanted to feel, as they obviously did, all the excited anticipation of becoming a mother. She wanted to look good, she wanted not to feel sick. She wanted Ray back. And, in fact, suddenly, there was a moment, even as she was thinking these things, when, shifting position next to him, a pain went through her so sharp and unexpected that she instinctively turned to him in the old defenceless way, and his hand, as if it had moved of its own accord, was already squeezing hers, and they looked at each other as they used to.

Then his phone rang.

He got to his feet without saying anything, his mind already elsewhere, and went out into the hallway. The silence in the room was profound, as if they'd all stopped breathing in order to hear what was being said outside. Only a low mumble of conversation came through. Then a loud exclamation.

A moment later Ray came back into the room at speed. He

looked stricken. His eyes sought Diane's, but he said nothing except to make a hurried apology to Marianne; then he was gone, and they heard only the slam of the front door. Now everyone was looking at Diane, in their faces a mixture of anguish and awe, and she felt again a seasick wave of nausea.

Green Street is a narrow, ill-lit strip of mismatched terraced houses in the middle of east Oxford, that cramped maze of graffitied brickwork, bijou coffee shops and overflowing bins, a shabby-chic district of students, immigrants and hipsters. There are strange scents in the air, world music coming out of open windows and endless lines of parked cars choking the pavements. Ray and Livvy found a spot two blocks away and sat there a moment, talking about Tariq Sayyed, the man who had done the garden at Magpies on the day when Poppy disappeared.

Five years earlier he had served eighteen months for sexual assault against a child.

Ray repeated his disbelief.

'He was filling in at the last minute. A one-off. The agency wasn't aware.'

Ray still couldn't believe it.

They got out of the car and walked through streets loud with music to a house scabbed with mouldering pebbledash.

Sayyed answered, wearing green bib overalls, and after they told him who they were he led them inside to a small front room, where they were introduced to his mother, a woman of solemn dignity, who rose with difficulty from her armchair, spoke briefly to her son in a foreign language and left the room.

Sayyed was a spare, strong-looking man with a closed

111

expression and careful eyes. He closed the window and drew the curtains, and sat nervously while Livvy said they had some questions they wanted to ask him.

''Bout what?' He had a thick West Riding accent.

They explained.

'Yeah, I were there, mowing lawn.'

'On your own?'

'Yeah.'

'What time?'

'Got there 'bout quarter to four. I were at another job at St John's before that. Left Magpies 'bout quarter past, up to Binsey.'

'There are people who can verify that?'

'Yeah. College gardener at St John's. Another fella up at Binsey. Met him there 'bout five. Traffic were bad.'

'You weren't at Magpies at three?'

'No. Just said. I were still at St John's.'

He kept his eyes on Livvy. In the short silence they all heard Tariq's mother moving, slowly and heavily, in the next room.

'At Magpies you were filling in for the regular agency gardener.'

'That's right.'

'Been there before?'

'No.'

'What did you do there?'

'Just the lawn, like I say. Half an hour tops.'

'Talk to anyone while you were there?'

'No need. I were told where everything was.'

'See any of the children?'

112

His look narrowed. 'No. I could hear them from time to time but I were working round back.'

Silence resumed. From the next room came the creaking of a chair.

Ray said, 'You understand why we're asking you these questions, Tariq?'

'Yeah.' There was a pause, and he looked at Ray for the first time. 'You want to know what's happened to Poppy Clarke.'

'What has happened to her?'

'I don't know.'

Ray said, 'Five years ago you were convicted of a sexual offence against a minor and given a three-year custodial sentence, reduced, after assistance given to the prosecution, to eighteen months, which you served at HMP Stafford, near Stoke.'

Sayyed glanced towards the door. 'Do you mind keeping your voice down, please?'

'And you're currently registered on the national sex offenders' database as a danger to children.'

'Yeah, all right.' Now there was a growl of defiance in his tone.

'And there you were, at Magpies, *a nursery school*.'

'Didn't take her.'

'There's no eyes on you from the time you arrived at Magpies till the time you arrived at Binsey.'

Tariq leaned forward and hissed at them. 'Read my file. I were never involved with children that young. She's of no interest to me.'

Ray winced. He said, 'Have you received information from anyone about Poppy Clarke?'

'No.'

'Do you know anything about her whereabouts?'

'No.'

'Do you know anything at all about her?'

'I know she's in danger.'

'How do you know that?'

Tariq was animated now. ''Cause she's been taken by a man what has the same urges I have. Instead of having a go at me, why don't you listen for a minute? At Stafford I did the Core SOTP programme. Now I'm lead member of two local sex offender support groups. It'll all be in my file. I didn't just serve time, I took responsibility for what I did, and I paid my debt to society. The work I do now is about protecting children from people like me.'

'Then tell me what you think has happened to Poppy.'

'If she's lucky, she's been taken by someone who'll end it quickly.'

In the silence he looked at them both intently.

'Sorry if that offends you. I'm trying to help here. I know how he thinks, what he feels.'

Livvy made a noise and turned away.

Sayyed nodded bitterly. 'Yeah. I get it. You're disgusted. Listen. You can't afford to be disgusted. You should be listening to what I'm saying.'

Ray managed to speak. 'Go on then.'

'I'm talking about something you both know. The sexual urge. Gets stronger when it's forbidden, don't it? You want to fuck another man's wife, another woman's husband, you know it's wrong but you can't stop wanting it. You have to resist. But sometimes the urge's too strong. That's right, int'it? Sometimes it's uncontrollable. Well, the man who took Poppy . . . he'll have been out of control.'

Ray muttered something under his breath.

'You don't like it? I don't like it. Blokes I work with don't like it. Think we want to have these urges? I know men can't face people, run away, go to live alone on a houseboat out at Kidlington, whatever. Volunteer for chemical treatment. I know one bloke tried to castrate himself with a Stanley knife.'

Silence.

Sayyed said, 'Before you can do anything, you have to understand people like me.'

'She's four!' Ray shouted. 'She's not someone else's wife, she's a little child! Don't give me this bullshit about forbidden desire!'

He locked eyes with Sayyed, who said after a moment, 'I'm sorry I've upset you. But you have to understand. You're not looking for someone who thinks this is a little child. You're looking for someone who thinks she's the only person who can take away his desire.'

Outside in Green Street, darkness had fallen. They walked down the middle of the road.

Ray said, 'The girl he tried to anally rape was eleven. Eleven!'

In the car they talked, their voices low and downbeat. It wouldn't be hard to pinpoint the times of Sayyed's movements – and, if confirmed, it didn't seem that there was much of a window for him between four thirty, when Poppy disappeared, and five o'clock, when he arrived in Binsey. Assuming that the timing of Sayyed's earlier college job checked out, he also couldn't be the man Natalie glimpsed through the window at three.

'And there's another thing he's right about. No evidence of his interest in children so young. But I want someone on him twenty-four seven. He's connected. All those groups. And I don't buy his psychobabble about managing his urges or about the shame.'

'Sir.'

They exchanged a look.

'If he's right about Poppy's snatcher being out of control . . .'

He looked at his watch. It was late. Diane would probably be back at home, in bed by now.

'I'm heading back to the office. Drop you home?'

Meanwhile, in the house in Green Street, Tariq Sayyed helped his mother to bed. She wanted to know what the two strangers had come for.

'Nothing. It were a mistake.'

He kissed her goodnight and went downstairs to make a phone call.

'They're coming,' he said in a low, angry voice. 'Course they are, what did you fucking expect? No, I didn't. They didn't ask. Course they can find out if they look. I don't know. Don't call me again, all right? They'll be watching me now. No. I can't help that. You're on your own.'

And as the night hours went slowly by, in the blessed silence of one and two o'clock, long after DI Ray Wilkins had left the office and gone home, long after Tariq Sayyed was asleep, night security guard Ryan Wilkins sat in his plastic-roofed shed on the Osney industrial estate in the usual fug of coffee and diesel, listening to the tickle of distant traffic on the ring road at Hinksey and an occasional bird waking out of a dream, trying not to think about Mick Dick.

After being breathed on so heavily by the Super at the station earlier, he'd left a voicemail for Nadim warning her not to pass him any more information about the case. She'd responded by sending him thanks – and, as a parting gift, a copy of the driver statement.

It was what he would have expected, an exercise in self-justification. The guy said he'd spent the evening talking to mates in the car park of the tennis and rugby club at the end of North Hinksey Lane. No drink was taken, naturally, no substances, just cigarettes and conversation. Time had passed, unnoticed. Then, at two thirty, realising how late it was, he'd driven carefully and responsibly homeward down North Hinksey Lane. It was a dark night, drizzle hanging in the air like smoke. Quiet. As he proceeded with all due care and attention along the straight section of lane, where reckless drivers have been known to speed up, a man leaped suddenly out of the bushes in front of his car. There was no time to stop or even swerve out of the way, no time to do anything. He'd barely registered what had happened until he was further down the road, and then it seemed too late, too pointless, too frightening, to do anything; besides, he was in a state of shock, a fact corroborated by a doctor, whose statement was part of the submission.

Ryan wasn't interested in any of this. He focused on the driver's brief description of the man he had killed:

It happened so quick. The road was empty then suddenly he was there. He must have jumped out of the bushes. I didn't see his face.

One hand was flung out, the other was up at the side of his head. Then the car bucked and he disappeared.

Ryan thought about Mick Dick's fear in the compound, his urgent flight in the dark across the water meadows: a man trying to get somewhere, as fast as possible. He stared at the statement again. Something snagged. Why was one of Mick Dick's hands up at the side of his head? He thought of a detail that wasn't there, a non-existent phone, saw how it could fit into the picture, a man running somewhere, telling someone he was on his way, reporting what had happened in the compound, whatever that was, listening to someone, forgetting to think about the road.

But there was no phone. There was only Mick Dick, one hand up, one hand out, frozen in the instant before the car wiped him out.

Two o'clock turned into four o'clock. Ryan went out and did his rounds. The industrial estate lay about him flattened in the moonlight like a film set. Noises came to him: brief petulance of a motorbike on the ring road, plaintive hoot of a bird nearby. On the forecourt suddenly a muntjac deer appeared, fragile, almost insubstantial, an image of fear. Then gone.

Ryan went back inside. He told himself not to think about Mick Dick any more. Just out of interest, though, he googled Baby Dynamic Ltd. and looked at their website. They made cots, car seats, pushchairs, all very high-tech, chic and expensive. Their bestselling product was a computerised pushchair with all the programmable features of a high-end sports car. Their offices were in the business park; there was a photograph of a glass cube rising neatly from the gridlines of the car park like a three-dimensional mathematical model, sleek and chic and a million miles from the sand-and-gravel world of dumpsters and hard hats which was Mick Dick's natural habitat. There was a photograph of the owner, Tom Fothergill, on the website too, Regional Businessman of the Year four years running, a blandly handsome man in an open-necked shirt, his stylishly cut hair ruffled by the breeze. Personally, Ryan wasn't keen on million-aires; like bishops and the provosts of Oxford colleges, they got his back up. But Fothergill looked interesting. His face was open but his hands were clenched.

Still, Ryan knew that he shouldn't go anywhere near him. He knew he should drop the whole thing.

So he sat there, through four and five o'clock in the morning, telling himself that.

EIGHTEEN

Garford Road again. The pink brick walls still glowing in the morning sun, breeze-filled beech trees polishing the air, the gentle insistence that nothing bad could happen there. Ray knocked on the door of the impressively gabled villa, stylish but respectful in dark green muscle-fit denim jacket, white tee and sky-blue cropped trousers, listening to the well-behaved quietness of the street behind him, a child's voice, a workman's van, birdsong. He took off his sunglasses and stood waiting under the arched doorway.

Marjorie Willoughby was a stout, almost square lady of advanced middle age bearing a striking resemblance to Winston Churchill. She had spoken to a policewoman already but Ray told her he had an additional specific question and she led him to a spacious, light-filled room with a view of a walled garden of flowering creepers and raked gravel paths, and sat him on a chesterfield upholstered in dusky pink velvet.

Her voice, when she spoke, was at odds with her appearance, a small, sweet whisper. She confirmed that on the morning of

Poppy's disappearance she had visited the nursery briefly, in the middle of the morning, to return three balls found in her garden.

'It's something I do about once a week. I don't mind. I think children should hurl balls around as much as they like.'

Ray agreed. But he wasn't interested in the balls, he said, but in what she might by chance have seen later in the day. Her upstairs windows overlooked the nursery garden.

She blushed, as if found out. She lived alone and had no grandchildren; she liked to linger sometimes in her bedroom and watch the children play.

'Do you know Poppy by sight?'

Mrs Willoughby nodded.

'Did you see her that day in the nursery garden?'

'I don't remember seeing her at all that day. I told the police lady that.'

Ray nodded. 'Is there any chance you saw a man in the nursery garden in the middle of the afternoon?'

She seemed to drift off. Sighing, she turned to the garden, as if for consolation.

'I forget so much these days.'

'A young man. Walking past the building on this side. Perhaps wearing a hooded top.'

She looked up at him sharply. 'Good God. Yes. Yes, I did. You're quite right. It made me so cross.'

'Cross?'

'Well, they have their own facilities, don't they?'

'I don't understand.'

'At the properties where they're working.'

'You think the man had been . . . relieving himself in the garden?'

Now she stopped to consider. She was embarrassed. It seemed in retrospect a foolish thing to have thought. But something about the man had made her think that. Some furtiveness.

Ray asked for a description of him but it was clear she had no memory for details. A young man, perhaps. Youngish. Wearing a hooded top, certainly. But no, she didn't see what he looked like, and couldn't say what ethnicity he was, or how tall, or anything else.

'Sorry.'

'But you think he was a workman?'

'Oh, he was definitely a workman.'

'How do you know?'

'Over his hooded top he was wearing one of those hi-vis vests, and was carrying a helmet.'

Throughout the morning the temperature rose. Sunshine flooded the city, daubed its pale stone monuments in yellow light, buttered the tourists. In Kennington the midday heat woke Ryan earlier than usual, and he got up, fatigued, dressed in his trackies and sat in the kitchen with a mug of tea, feeling irritable. It wasn't just the heat, it was the itch in his mind, the nagging questions without answers. At home time he went to St Swithun's and picked up Ryan and Mylee from nursery and took them to the swing park, and watched them tottering to and fro, between roundabout and see-saw, swings and climbing frame, flushed and utterly absorbed in what they were doing. And at last he couldn't stand it any more and made the call.

A voice recited one long multi-part word, 'Baby-Dynamic-tomorrow's-baby-care-with-smart-solutions-for-your-baby's-needs-how-may-I-help-you?'

Ryan asked to speak to Tom Fothergill.

'Who may I say is calling?'

'Just tell him it's about a guy he knows, Michael Dick.'

'And your name, sir?'

'Well, that don't matter.'

There was a short silence. 'We have a policy at Baby Dynamic of always—'

He gave his name and there was another, longer, silence. The sun was in his eyes. He waved in the general direction of the children.

'Hello? I'm sorry, Mr Fothergill isn't available at the moment.'

'You told him it's about Mick Dick, right?'

'What we suggest is that you send an email to our enquiries address on our website and we'll be able to consider what you say.'

'Listen, not being funny, that's not going to work. I need to speak to him urgent. It's important, right?'

'I'm sorry, sir, there's nothing I can—'

'I'm not calling about some pushchair costing five hundred quid or whatever.'

'Our pushchair range starts at one thousand, three hundred—'

'I don't want a fucking pushchair, all right? Listen, is there someone else there I can talk to? Hello? *Hello?*'

He sat there bunched in fury. Little Ryan came over and he held up his hands.

'Sorry, won't say it again.'

'Mylee heard it too.'

He shouted across the playground, 'Sorry, Mylee!'

He knew very well what he should do now. The words of the Superintendent and, in fact, Jade were clear in his head. It was a natural point at which to give up.

'Hey, Ry! Mylee! Want to go for a drive?'

As soon as he got back from Garford Road, Ray went up to see the Super and, ten minutes later, they had pivoted the investigation towards the construction workers. Five guys from the Hub came in to help them with the new interviews; the Super instructed Forensics at Grove to redo their work on the vehicles; the techies in Nadim's team began to run every piece of information they had through new configurations, tracking all the workmen's movements in and out. Charlbury Road stood quiet and dust-free all day while men in hi-vis jackets and hard hats, their day's pay docked, waited surly and silent in the waiting areas alongside the interview rooms. Gradually Ray and Livvy built up a cross-referenced minute-by-minute timetable of every movement of every workman in the area that day.

The hours passed.

Nothing new came to light.

'We must be missing something,' Ray said. 'We need to go back over it all.'

Morning turned to afternoon.

One by one the men's stories checked out, synced. They couldn't find a discrepancy anywhere. No gaps, no anomalies. All the men working in the area had alibis.

Wallace came down to Ray's office. 'This lady, Ray. Her

eyesight okay? Do we really think a construction guy's going to take time out of his work day to kidnap a child?'

Ray said, 'There's a detail here, something we can pull on, I can feel it.' But he no longer sounded confident.

Wallace went away again.

Other issues nagged for attention. Responses to Rachel's television appeal were still coming in. The woods out at Elsfield were still being searched. Ray called Diane, warned her he was going to be late, cut the conversation short, knowing that staying in the office was a way of avoiding going home.

At the Baby Dynamic office Ryan sat in reception with little Ryan and Mylee, who were quickly – and justly – bored with the surroundings: black leather sofas on which they must not put their feet; glass-topped coffee tables which they must not lie on, nor lick; long, skiddy floor across which they must not slide, laughing as they fell. There were windows two storeys high full of car park and clouds, Baby Dynamic signage tasteful as artwork and brightly polished steel-panelled receptionist's desk with brightly polished steely receptionist behind it talking on the telephone, telling someone that the package for Tom hadn't been collected yet and someone else that Sanjeev Gupta was on the phone with a query about the launch in Delhi, while all the time avoiding making eye contact with Ryan until he got off the sofa and came over to talk to her again, looking like he might not be physically able to contain his irritation. She was saved by the appearance of another lady who emerged briskly out of the lift to intercept him. Unlike the receptionist, she knew a little about Fothergill's involvement in the mentoring scheme, but seemed to think that

Ryan was part of the programme, repeatedly telling him that it would be far better if he made his request via the channels set up by prison services for that purpose.

Bitterly reflecting how much easier it is when you can just flash a badge, he became impatient. More loudly than he intended, he mentioned a dead man in a ditch, a subject offensively out of place in the surroundings. The brisk lady became abrupt and hushed. There was nothing she could do. Sorry. She turned decisively to go. Putting a hand on her arm, perhaps more firmly than he had meant to, and raising his voice, perhaps a little louder than he had intended, Ryan elaborated on the terror and violent death of an ex-convict, who wanted only to get work and watch his little girl grow up.

She offered to call Security.

Now visibly agitated, he followed her to the lift, pointing out more loudly still that a quick conversation was all he was asking for, a couple of minutes at most, what was so difficult about that, what was her fucking problem?

At the lift, she turned. 'Just because he has a charitable foundation doesn't mean he gives handouts to *everyone*,' she hissed.

Silence had fallen in Baby Dynamic. The receptionist was looking at him. A DHL guy at reception was looking at him. Mylee and Ryan, frozen in the middle of a game, were looking at him. There was something concerned in their expressions, and though he felt the urge, in front of them all, to verbally smash up everything around him which deserved smashing, he fought it, looking for another way out, one that might not involve meekly giving in to these fucking, *fucking* . . . And then, glancing round, he saw one.

★

In the end Ray left the office and went out to Elsfield for an hour or two to supervise the search in the woods. Police and volunteers moved slowly in long wavering lines through the trees, heads bowed, picking at the ground with their sticks as if in some obscure rural rite, half agricultural, half religious. Members of the white-clad Forensics team moved behind them, another sect. Occasional shouts marked the irrelevant discoveries of out-of-place objects: a woman's left-hand glove, a pair of football shorts. His mind still ran on workmen and towards the end of the afternoon he went back to St Aldates to read the new forensics report. It was identical to the old forensics report: nothing of any interest in any of the workmen's vehicles parked in Garford Road that day.

Livvy left to go to a meeting at the Hub. It was now over a hundred hours since Poppy had disappeared. He was very tired. Diane called him and he found it impossible to concentrate on what she was saying, something about her blood pressure, something else about her feelings of dread, something about men, their uselessness. In the end she became angry and rang off without asking what time he would be home.

He called Mrs Willoughby and spoke to her again, and she repeated what she had told him before.

'And you're sure he was one of the workmen?'

'Well, why would he have a *helmet*?'

He sat at his desk without an obvious task in hand. His tiredness filled him again and his mind began to drift. He thought about Livvy. He knew nothing about her except for the fact that she had three children and had brought them up on her own, a fact he found intimidating. He thought about his father. There

127

was another message from him on his phone, which he was ignoring. He knew he ought to go home but he did not want another argument with Diane, and the thought of the spare room with its piles of baby clothing and boxes of toys filled him with dread. He leaned back in his seat to rest. Just for a few minutes. He told himself that he wouldn't go to sleep. Just rest. Just for a few minutes.

And now Ryan drew up at the side of the lane at Bedwells Heath and turned off the engine. Below them was Fothergill's house. It was very big, a geometric arrangement of glass, weathered steel and zinc, granite panels and timber, poking out of the woods like the corner of a futuristic city, strikingly at odds with the green meadows falling in a long swinging dip towards the distant spires of Oxford, obligingly offering themselves below as a lesser attraction. Ryan had followed the DHL courier as he left the Baby Dynamic office with his 'package for Tom', out of the city and up to Boars Hill, his Peugeot making banging noises as they trailed the bike past the gorgeous villas along Foxcombe Road and the gardens of the even more gorgeous mansions hidden from view in their acreages of private woodland, all the way to Fothergill. He was police: he knew how to find people.

It was now late afternoon. Little Ryan said, 'Daddy? Are we going to have our tea now, Daddy?'

Ryan said not just yet, and his son subsided into soft disgruntlement, abetted by Mylee.

Ryan looked out of the car window. Despite having once lived only half a mile away in Bayworth at the bottom of the hill, he'd never been up here before. Bayworth was for the agricultural poor, Boars Hill for the nouveau riche, the cryptocurrency entrepreneurs and big tech executives, who had bought up the old Victorian villas in order to knock them down and build mansions after their own fancies – half-timbered Elizabethan hunting lodges, turreted Scots baronial castles, eco-ranches in cantilevered glass and steel – all discreetly hidden among the beech and oaks. It was not Ryan's world. It brought out the worst in him.

'What d'you think?' he asked the children. 'Shall we go and say hello? Nice and friendly like.'

After he had leaned on the intercom buzzer on the wall beside the gate for the third time, a voice responded.

'Come to see Tom,' Ryan said. He gave an explanation, smiled and made door-opening gestures for the benefit of the security camera. The children looked about to see who he was gesturing at.

There was silence. The gates did not open. Peering through them, Ryan could see at the end of a long curving drive a length of low pale wall, a long stretch of glass and a display of glazed Scandinavian timberwork surrounding a shiny black oblong entrance. As he watched, two people came down the steps and emerged into the light. One was a teenage boy dressed in Goth black wearing headphones and a backpack, who didn't lift his eyes from the ground as he shambled along the front of the house, followed by a slim woman stepping out elegantly in green country-wear and riding boots. Ryan gave a two-fingered whistle and she turned her head just long enough for him to catch a glimpse of clean-cut chin, celebrity-chic sunglasses and weighty swish of ash-blonde hair; then she was gone.

He whistled again.

'Daddy?'

'What?'

'Auntie Jade says, always remember not to lose your rag.'

'Thanks, I'll be fine. I can always do that breathing thing I told you about.'

Little Ryan looked doubtful.

At last a voice spoke out of the intercom. 'Mr Fothergill isn't available at the moment.'

'Thing is, I know he's here. And he'll definitely want to talk to me, I know he will.'

'Please make contact with the chief executive's PA at his business premises.'

'Not about business.'

'Mr Fothergill arranges all his mentoring sessions at the office.'

'Not after a mentoring session either.'

'His PA will deal with other unsolicited private matters too.'

'Tried it already, worked about as well as this is working.' He breathed in and out in a deliberate fashion, without benefit. 'Listen, not being a dick but can't you just put someone on who knows what they're doing?'

He tested the gates.

'Please move away from the entrance.'

He shook them again in exasperation.

'Move away from the gates before we call the police.'

He stood there unresolved on the edge of anger.

'Daddy?'

The little voice distracted him. 'What?'

'Are you breathing?'

He could hear himself breathing in fact, a noise like fat in a hot pan, and after a moment, with effort, he turned away.

Back in the car, he gradually calmed down.

'Thanks,' he said, when he could.

'You're welcome.'

His son's face was serious, shining and unreadable.

'Know what?' Ryan said. 'You're the politest person I know. Never got the hang of it myself somehow. But you give me an idea.'

Ray jerked awake in his chair and grovelled for his phone which he had knocked onto the floor. Panicking, he snatched it up, saw the caller and made a despairing face.

'Ryan.'

'Ray, mate. Didn't wake you, did I? Listen.'

Ryan explained what he wanted.

'Easy peasy. One posh boy to another.'

Ray said, 'Are you insane?'

'What you mean?'

'I'm not doing that.'

'Just a chat. In and out. Ten minutes tops.'

'I'm not even working the case.'

'All you have to say is, DI Wilkins, just want to ask you a few quick questions, Tom. Simple as.'

'You know what's going on at the moment.'

'Yeah, you're napping in your chair 'cause you've done all you can and you're waiting for the next move. I know what it's like, mate. Staring at your phone won't make it happen any sooner.'

'Don't push it, Ryan.'

'What time's Diane expecting you back?'

He didn't answer.

'You can pop in on your way home. Thing is, Ray, you're polite, you know how to talk to people like him.'

'Forget it.'

'There's this stunning babe there too, did I mention?'

'Oh please.'

'And if you ever need a van, I can get you a great deal down at our place.'

'I don't even know why you're interested in this Michael Dick.'

There was a brief silence.

'You know what? That's a fair point.'

'Well?'

'I guess, maybe, it's a friendship thing.' He left a pause. 'Remember friendship, Ray?'

'I can't believe I'm hearing this.'

'And a getting to the bottom of it thing. And a seeing justice done sort of thing.'

'I can't believe I'm listening to it.'

'And did I say? Mick's got this little daughter'll grow up without her dad now.'

Ryan counted off the seconds, grinning.

Ray said, 'Oh, for Christ's sake, Ryan. Where does he live?'

'Cheers, mate. What friends are for, eh?'

NINETEEN

Tom Fothergill sat at his dining table reading spreadsheets. The twenty-seater table had a walnut top mounted on weathered zinc legs, and it stood in the centre of the polished concrete floor of the sharp-edged room, sleek but antique, like something from Noah's ark, if Noah had been a Bauhaus-trained Italian designer. One of the dining-room walls was taken up with a circular artwork of children's handprints created from Rhône Delta mud; behind another – cutaway – wall were the great plate-glass windows overlooking Hinksey Valley.

Fothergill was forty-eight years old, fit and trim in jeans and heavy-duty cotton shirt, sleeves rolled to his elbows. He had a regular face – firm jaw, straight nose, wide mouth. His sandy hair, which had started to recede, was cut short, giving his face an open, almost naked look. When he smiled he showed regular teeth, unusual in an Englishman. Otherwise, in a well-bred sort of way, he was very English, frank and confident, though his tendency to talk about intimate things often confused people who couldn't tell whether it was careless or deliberate. In general, he was brisk and focused, as multi-millionaires often are.

When Ray went in, he rose at once to greet him. 'I've seen you on television. You must be under enormous pressure. Are you bearing up? Can I get you something? Juice? We have some fig cordial from a dealer I know in Anatolia.'

Ray said, 'Thank you, no. I don't have much time. Just one or two questions to ask you.' As he spoke, he checked his phone; he'd asked Livvy to call, whatever the time, as soon as there was a sighting or a lead from the television appeal.

'Of course. I just hope you're making progress.' Ray made a non-committal noise. He looked at his phone again; he wanted to finish here as quickly as possible.

'You can't speak about it, I understand. But what could be more terrible?' Fothergill shook his head. 'Do you have kids, Ray?'

Ray admitted that his wife was expecting twins.

'I've got just the one,' Fothergill said. 'Grown-up, or nearly – though it never ends, the love, the anxiety. Never.' He smiled. 'You'll find that.'

Ignoring this, Ray reminded Fothergill of the purpose of his visit.

'Let's go into the living room. We'll be more comfortable there.'

They stood in front of the vast expanse of glass, looking out into the evening darkness, where silhouetted patches of woodland below had shrunk into themselves, blots of shadow blemishing the grey fields that flowed down, smoothly indistinct, towards the embers of Oxford flickering faintly in the distance below.

Fothergill was still talking about children. 'Parents would do anything to keep their kids safe, I know I would. Of course, sometimes, we have to rely on others. People like you, Ray. In a sense, in situations like this, you take on a parental role. You'll feel it, the pressure, bound to.'

He looked enquiringly at Ray, who made another non-committal noise.

'But I'm holding you up,' Fothergill said. 'What questions do you want to ask?'

'It's about one of the men from Grendon you've been mentoring. Michael Dick.'

'He's not in trouble, is he?'

'I'm afraid he's been involved in an accident.'

Now Fothergill's conversational ease failed him. His face went slack. 'What happened? Where is he? Can I visit him?'

'The accident was fatal.'

Fothergill's reaction was extreme. He began to speak, could not. He sat down in a chair.

Ray watched him. 'I'm sorry to give you this shock.'

Fothergill sat trembling. He said weakly, 'I can't believe it. With all my guys from Grendon, I worry, you know, that they'll get involved in something they shouldn't. But this! And to Mick! I can't believe it. A sweet, sweet man.'

He wanted to know details, many of which Ray didn't know himself. It was several minutes before Ray could begin to ask Fothergill the questions Ryan had given him.

Fothergill confirmed that he'd been mentoring Michael for a few months. They'd hit it off straight away. Yes, he'd also been paying rent on Mick's mobile home at Cuddesdon. 'Via

135

my charitable foundation.' It was construction work Michael wanted, and Fothergill, who had plenty of contacts through various local business associations, had fixed up trials for him; he'd felt that it was only a matter of time before someone took him on. 'That's what I kept saying to him. Don't despair. It's going to happen.'

'Was he despairing?'

'I don't think so. He was a naturally upbeat sort of person.'

'His prison record will have played against him.'

'Yes. But when people met him, saw what he could give them, you could see them changing their minds. He was such an open man. Big and strong too, a powerful man; it makes a difference in that world. It's funny, isn't it?' he said. 'I know what he did, the violence, but whenever I met him I was struck by how placid he was. I was much more worried that someone would take advantage of him.' He bit his lip, as if to stop himself from being upset again, and looked for a moment out of the window. He began to talk about the mentoring scheme which he had set up and his confidence came back. Ray watched him. He was reminded of other millionaires Ray had met: he saw things as clearly defined, asked direct questions, sought practical solutions. He was brisk and on-point. A tiring man to be with, perhaps. As he continued to talk, a youth slouched into the room, dressed in a grey hooded top featuring the slogan *Jesus is My Homeboy* and skinny black jeans.

'This is Jack,' Fothergill said. 'Jack, Detective Inspector Wilkins.'

Jack gave Ray a blank teenager stare, turned and slouched out again.

Then a young woman passed through the room, equally obviously the babe Ryan had mentioned, slim and leggy in jeans and loose sweatshirt; she turned her head just long enough for Ray to glimpse a narrow Botticelli face and delicate features, lips parted slightly, dark eyes drifting incuriously across him, before going on, leaving behind only the disturbance of her perfume.

'My wife,' Fothergill said, 'Ros Kerr, the artist.'

She looked about twenty years younger than him.

Ray said, 'Just a few more questions.'

It was clear immediately, however, that Fothergill had little information to give him about Mick Dick's private life. Mick had never talked about his experiences at Grendon and only occasionally about his ex-wife. The one person he did mention was his daughter, clearly the most important person to him.

'What about friends, associates?'

Fothergill shook his head.

'And when was the last time you had contact with him?'

'I'm not sure when we last talked.' He looked at Ray enquiringly. 'You'd be able to find out from his phone records.'

'We haven't located his phone. It's possible he'd mislaid it.'

Fothergill smiled wryly. 'He couldn't seem to hang on to phones, it's true. Well, let's see. I think, perhaps, we last talked a couple of weeks ago.'

'And did he sound upset? Worried about anything?'

'Not at all.'

'Frightened?'

'Frightened? No. Why do you ask that?'

'Do you know any reason why he might have had enemies?'

Fothergill actually laughed. 'I can't imagine Michael having enemies. Just not the type. No. That was one reason I was so confident about him getting a job.' He began to talk again about the way his mentoring scheme got people into work, and Ray waited for an opportunity to make his excuses and leave, only half listening. Fothergill's wife reappeared in the dining area, visible through the cutaway gap in the partition wall. Ray noticed that she had changed into a thin summer skirt and silk blouse. She stood at the table leafing through an art book with a bright lamp behind her and in its light her body was clearly visible inside her skirt, the long curve of her thigh, slender hips, faint line of flimsy underwear. As Ray watched her, she glanced up and met his gaze with the same incurious look as before, and held it a moment, then went on reading. She did not alter her position.

It was time to go. Ray stood and Fothergill began to apologise.

'I've kept you too long, Ray, I'm sorry.'

He showed him out. As they went down the hall, Ray looked back but Fothergill's wife had gone.

'Look here,' Fothergill said. 'If there's anything else I can do, will you let me know?'

'About Mick Dick?'

'Of course. But I was also thinking about the little girl who's gone missing. I have resources. What's the point of money if not to put it to good use? That's what people miss, Ray – the charities, the science and medical funding, educational programmes set up by people like me, fortunate people who have made a bit of money and who want to make a difference. All my initiatives have been local. If your investigation needs more resources, think of me. I mean it. Let's keep in touch.'

He insisted on giving Ray his private phone number, and they stood together for a moment at the bottom of the entrance steps, at the beginning of a runway of sunken lights leading off into the evening darkness. Peppery smells of grass and trees hung in the night air around them. His handshake was predictably firm.

And then Ray's phone went. He took the call straight away, immediately tense. There was a short silence, then Livvy told him that there had been a discovery in the Elsfield woods. The body of a small girl.

For a moment he couldn't speak. He closed his eyes. 'I'll be there in ten.'

He hung up.

'What is it?' Fothergill cried, but Ray didn't answer. He went fast towards his car, trying to breathe normally, feeling a numbness in his hands. He didn't look back as he accelerated up the drive and out of the opening electronic gates, watched by Fothergill still standing at the foot of the steps.

TWENTY

Poppy Clarke's naked body had been lying for four days in a shallow grave in a dry gulley in the Elsfield woods. Parts of her pirate costume were discovered nearby, jacket, sash and bootees, along with her socks. The eye-patch and ribbons were missing, probably taken as trophies. She had been killed within two or three hours of her abduction, asphyxiated, her underpants pushed down her throat. Held in one of her fists, still closed, was a Love Hearts sweet.

Ray went straight from the crime scene to the house in Park Town to tell Rachel. It was midnight by then. He would never, as long as he lived, forget the way she opened her mouth, the dislocating bend of her face, the noise she made. Then he accompanied her to the mortuary at Grove, where they were met by Dr Clarke, who had been informed by Livvy, and stood together on either side of the gurney far too big for the little body on it. As they walked out of the cold chamber Dr Clarke attacked Ray with big ineffectual blows and Ray held him until he went limp and began to cry. Back at Park Town, Rachel was given tranquillizers by a police doctor and put to bed. Her elderly parents had arrived to look after her. They sat silently in the living room, looking at Ray as if for instruction.

The mother spoke. 'When was she . . . when did she . . . ?'

'We think probably within an hour or so of going missing.' He hesitated a moment. 'We're sure she died quickly.'

The mother wept into her hands. The father looked at Ray with disgust.

'Who could have done it?' he said. 'Who can have done such a thing?'

Ray had no answer.

Outside the house, Park Town was thickly dark, shadow clotting the little gated gardens, but the sky was already pale at the horizon, and somewhere a wakeful bird was muttering to itself. It was now four o'clock. He went straight to the station to prepare for the media storm that would ensue, though there could be no adequate preparation for the chaos of the next twenty-four hours, the vicious spike of emotion, the howling across networks, public and private grief, disintegrating press conferences, abusive phone-ins, all the demented ventriloquism of social media trolls, violent blame for the mother with her pink hair and moneyed bohemianism, outrage at the negligence of the expensive nursery, condemnation of the slow and stupid police, unbearable knowledge that we are creatures who do these things to our children.

At some point Ray talked to Diane. The news had reduced her to a whisper. She asked questions requiring answers she could not endure, what she said was often incoherent, and her silences seemed fraught with pain. Sometimes she talked about the murder, sometimes about her pain and loneliness, as if they were connected, and perhaps to her they were. There was a note of accusation in her tone.

'Please, Ray,' she said. He did not know what she meant.

He hadn't slept for twenty-four hours; his tiredness swamped him, he was submerged in it. Diane's voice came to him over a surf-like purr in his ears, and shrank to nothing, to a dial tone. Had she ended the call, or had he? A text came from his father asking for news but he could not think of news, he thought of Rachel lobotomised in Park Town, Dr Clarke writhing in his canalside apartment, and, beyond that, only the immediate urgent things to do. At St Aldates there was the hush of frustration and anger so like the hush of disgrace. He tried to keep calm; he remembered his police training which had drilled into him that anger solves nothing. But he could feel his rage burning steadily under everything else. He addressed his team, spoke several times to Forensics, video-conferenced with Maisie Ndiaye and her team at the Hub, moving numbly from one task to the next. As he walked to the Super's office for another briefing he received a text from Tom Fothergill. It read: *I realise now what your call was about last night. My thoughts are with you and, of course, with the little girl's family. Remember what I said. Do get in touch if there's anything I can do. Regards, Tom.* For some reason Ray was disconcerted, as if a stranger had shared with him an intimate secret. Briefly he remembered Fothergill's wife looking at him through the cutaway wall, the expression on her face, the way she was standing; then he knocked on the Super's door and was called in.

While Ray talked, the Super stood against the window, a solid, dark shape in his uniform, details of his face indistinct, lost in the late afternoon sunshine, as if he had become a monolith, a totem of authority to be placated, unreadable, unmoved by the constant torment of geese on the river behind him.

Ray brought him up to date with the latest from Forensics. There wasn't much. Microfibres on her pirate costume were consistent with the interior upholstery of a vehicle – a common sort used in many different vehicles.

'Tyre tracks?'

'He didn't need to go off-road, there's an asphalt lane leading right to the edge of the woods.'

'Luck? Local knowledge?'

'It's possible he knows the area. The nursery too. How deserted it would be, what time to turn up.'

The Super spent a long time just looking at Ray. 'This is our biggest case for years.' He left a long silence. 'And we've got nothing,' he said at last, 'except the body of a little girl.'

His tone was emphatic. The silence he left was emphatic too.

'I want everything thrown at this, everything. I don't want what's possible, Ray. I want what happened. I want the bastard who did this. I'm backing you, so take the resources you need. But now you have to deliver.' He moved away from the window and sat at the desk. 'Right, plan of action. Take me through it.'

Ray went through key areas. Interview and re-interview all relevant men on the national sex offenders' register, shake them down, widen and intensify the questions; even if none of them was the perp, someone somewhere knew something. Interview and re-interview the nursery staff and related people who regularly came into contact with Poppy. Trawl CCTV on all likely routes towards Elsfield. Expand Forensics' examination of the

143

crime scene, the body and clothing. Examine vehicles identified in the Garford Road area at the time and not yet analysed by Forensics. Re-sweep the woods, interview people living or working near Elsfield.

Even as he listed these things he realised how many of them had been done before.

'What about the guy in the nursery garden? That anything?'

'Nothing's come of it yet.'

'*Come on*, Ray. We've got no new lines of enquiry. No angle. Nothing to pull on. Where are we, what are we doing? Give me your gut.'

Ray hesitated. 'I keep coming back to the sound of Poppy laughing.'

The Super looked interested. 'Meaning?'

'I think she knew whoever took her. Someone she trusted. Someone she was friendly with. Going back to the SOR will give us the sex offenders we know about already. But what about someone we don't know about? A friend of the family. Someone connected to the nursery. Someone she saw regularly.'

Wallace nodded at last. 'Get to it, then. No shilly-shally, let's find this bastard now.'

TWENTY-ONE

Ryan drove to Van Central for the beginning of his shift, slightly late. He was still thinking about Mick Dick. He'd decided to call it quits, finally. There was no more he could do. Nothing reported by Ray from his conversation with Fothergill led anywhere; besides, the Super's discouragement weighed in his mind more and more heavily. Since their conversation at the station, Ryan had attended an interview by a panel of independent 'arbiters' and a second anger management session, both under the Super's watchful eye. He could feel his reinstatement application hanging in the balance. Having taken the decision, he felt relief as he pulled onto the forecourt at Van Central, which disappeared when he found Carl Crapper waiting for him.

He was posed in the doorway of the office, unusually purposeful.

Ryan went the route of affability. 'Carl! Don't worry about it, mate. It's okay. Can't say I wasn't distressed, course I was – who wouldn't be, after the death of a friend? But you know me, Carl, I don't bear grudges. Let's move on, eh?'

Carl didn't move at all, except to hold up a piece of paper, a letter with a familiar crest in its letterhead.

'Derek's had a letter.'

'Okay. I won't tell him you've taken it.'

'Which he's passed to me to facilitate.'

'Everyone's at it, Carl. Facilitate away, mate.'

'From the office of Detective Chief Inspector David Wallace of the Thames Valley Constabulary. To the effect that we are invited –' Carl paused, corrected himself – 'that *I* am invited to submit a report to him concerning your performance at Van Central, to include, and I'm quoting, aspects of discipline and manner.'

Ryan's heart sank. But he made his face smile. 'Glad for you, Carl. Obviously they wouldn't trust just anyone with this sort of responsibility. And you deserve it. When you're ready for a chat just let me know and I'd be happy to go through it with you.'

Carl did not appear eager to accept that offer. 'You're on notice,' he said loudly.

'Got it.' Ryan had been on notice most of his life, he was generally unbothered by the fuss made by the people who put him there, but he recognised the danger of the current situation.

Carl wanted to be frank with Ryan, he said. It was his nature to be frank. He'd not been happy with Ryan, he said frankly. *For some time*, he added for emphasis. Ryan had often pushed him too far. Him, a reasonable man, a commercially minded man, a man of integrity, a man charged with the responsibility of making Van Central Oxford's *premier van hire choice*, a task which . . . et cetera, et cetera. For a moment he lost the thread of what he was saying. But Ryan had pushed him too far, he said, finding it

146

again. He mentioned the expensive false alarm which had needlessly brought the police out to the compound; he mentioned Ryan's failure to lock the van left on the forecourt that evening, as reported to him by a female member of staff, who had also reported persistent refusal by Ryan to clean up after his night shift; he mentioned various instances of insubordination and repeated failures to turn up to work on time; he mentioned . . . The list went on. The only way for Ryan to cope with it was, in fact, to stop listening and try out the breathing techniques which he'd learned from Dr Tompkins.

Twenty minutes or so went by.

At length Ryan became aware that Carl had come to an end. He was peering fiercely at Ryan, had been perhaps for some time. Ryan made his face smile again. 'Nice one, Carl. Totally makes sense. Yeah. And I just want to say how glad I am to have the opportunity to prove to you what a valuable member of the team I can be.'

After Carl had gone, Ryan sat in his plastic shed, reflecting. He needed to knuckle down, to forget about Mick Dick. But he brooded. He didn't want to, he couldn't help it. It was something Carl had said. Forget it, he told himself. What did it matter? He began to distract himself with more urgent, personal things, things he needed to do to head off Carl's report, strategies to placate Superintendent Wallace. But the thought of what Carl had said kept coming back. He began to brood again.

Ten o'clock gave way to eleven.

At last he could stand it no longer and went out onto the forecourt with a flashlight. Everything was quiet and still, the night air scented with petrol vapour, drains and the sour-mash soil smell of the water meadows. Unlocking the compound gates, he went inside and walked up and down the aisles among the sleeping vans until he found the one he'd parked that night, a silver Ford Transit with a black driver-side wing mirror; it loomed out of the shadows with a blandness very like innocence.

Carl had said he'd left it unlocked. Ryan knew he hadn't.

Shining his light on the driver-side door, he saw nothing at first; but, as he played the light up and down the panel, faint scratches appeared, like hairline cracks, in the glass of the side windscreen above the door handle. For a while he stood there thinking, then he turned away and went back down the aisles to the corner of the compound where he'd put the van that night and shone his light around on the ground and through the fence into the darkness on the other side, lighting up lumpy wasteland beyond, scrub of alder bushes and goose grass and a black ditch running away towards Hogacre. Again he stood there for a moment; then he went out of the compound and round the edge of the waste ground and spent ten minutes in the ditch searching up and down. And at last he found what he was looking for and carried it back to his shed.

It lay on his desk, a narrow thin blade of metal, commonly called a 'slim jim', ancient tool of car thieves, one of Mick Dick's signature accessories. He must have thrown it into the ditch when he'd heard Ryan come out. He remembered Mick Dick saying that he'd found all the vans locked. True enough. But now Ryan knew that he'd actually broken into one of them. Why? To spend the night in it, like he'd said? Then why didn't he just tell

Ryan what he'd done? At least then Ryan could have locked it up again and avoided getting into trouble later.

It was a puzzle. He sat there with the slim jim in front of him, thinking. Eleven o'clock gave way to twelve, twelve gave way to three and four, and he sat there brooding.

TWENTY-TWO

'Don't look for a monster, Ray. He will appear as ordinary as you.'

Maisie Ndiaye spoke slowly and precisely, weighing her words. She rarely smiled. Sometimes she lifted her elegant hands from her lap and made a gesture of affirmation or doubt. She did not make the mistake of being definite but was always precise.

A paedophile, she said, may function most of the time in a completely normal way with colleagues, even friends, who never for a second suspect him of any sexual interest in children. He could be a sociable person, friendly, someone naturally able to engage a child in smiles or talk or even a game.

Ray thought once again of Poppy's laughter.

A man, Maisie went on, who feels childlike himself, who has extreme difficulty being adult. He may have learned to a high degree how to function as an adult but that's not how he feels. Inside, he's confused and angry. Though he feels connected to children, that connection is sexualised and violent. A forbidden connection, all the harder to resist. All the time he remains outwardly normal, friendly, an ordinary man.

'Someone Poppy knew?'

'It could be.'

'Someone she knew well?'

Maisie raised her eyebrows.

He wondered out loud about Poppy's laughter, as if she were playing a game with someone she felt comfortable with, about the complete lack of commotion when she went off with him, about the timing of the abduction, as if the perp knew Poppy's routines and the habits of her mother. 'Someone she had a relationship with already,' he said.

'Do you have anyone in mind?'

He didn't.

They moved on. Ray asked if the perp might act again.

'Very likely. His desire is mixed up with his confusion and anger. It will be intense. Irresistible.'

'Could it be soon?'

'Depends on his self-control. As I said, it's very probable he's learned to function normally most of the time. Given the media coverage of Poppy's case, I'd expect him to lie low now for a while, at least until the media loses interest.'

She thought further. 'Your theory about Poppy knowing him well.'

'Yes?'

'She was holding a sweet in her hand, wasn't she?'

'A Love Heart.'

'You could ask her mother what Poppy's favourite sweets were. If they were Love Hearts, it might be more than a coincidence.'

★

The rest of the morning went by, rolled over him, left him dazed. He interviewed three men with previous convictions for crimes against children, trying not to think of them as monsters, was interviewed on national radio, addressed his exhausted team. The forensics work on private vehicles parked in and around Garford Road was almost complete; it had given them nothing. All the possible suspects on the SOR had been interviewed at least once, without result; they seemed genuinely not to know who might have killed Poppy Clarke. Working through the personnel at the nursery with Livvy, they had a minor surprise: one of the trustees was Thomas Fothergill of Baby Dynamic. He remembered now Fothergill telling him about his educational initiatives. It explained Fothergill's interest in the case. When Livvy called Natalie, she confirmed Fothergill's involvement. He was the main investor in the nursery as well as a trustee. He had always taken a keen interest in its running, she said, often visiting them. His son had done work experience with them; Ros Kerr, Fothergill's wife, had created artworks for their displays. After the abduction he had called Natalie several times to find out if there was any news.

At lunchtime Ray's father called him at the office, which he never did unless he wanted to make a point. The point was that Ray mustn't get down, mustn't lose hope, it wasn't the Wilkins way. He'd seen him on television looking tired; not tired, *defeated*. But he knew his son was equal to anything, anything at all. It was kindly meant, sternly delivered. Ray was monosyllabic, unable to cut the call short, unwilling to prolong the conversation.

'And what about this monster, Ray? I know you can't tell me how close you are to catching him; just tell me that you will.'

'I will, *Baba*. You know I will.' But the words felt scratchy in his mouth.

In the evening he went to Park Town to see Rachel. On the living-room floor she sat in her dressing gown, her face unfocused. The backs of her hands were crusted with scabs. From the sofa her parents watched her anxiously, as they might a child. She had been prescribed sedatives, they said, to help her sleep, though she did not sleep but existed all the time in a somnambulist state.

'I wanted to ask her a question.'

'You can try.'

He asked, and she turned to him and looked at him a long time, frowning, as if he'd asked a question with no meaning she could think of. She hadn't been informed about the sweet in Poppy's hand nor about the eye-patch and ribbons taken as trophies; the police therapist had advised against it. Nor had there been any public announcements about them either.

'Her favourite sweet?' Her voice was slowed down, out of sync with her mouth.

'Yes.'

'Of course.'

He waited.

'Love Hearts,' she said.

TWENTY-THREE

The day of the funerals was still and warm. At eleven o'clock, at the tiny, perfectly formed church of St Martin's in Bladon, where the Churchills have their family graves, there was a private service for Poppy attended only by Rachel, Dr Clarke and their respective parents, though floral tributes from members of the public were so numerous they had to be piled outside the door, where they partly blocked the path, and journalists and cameramen loitered like perverts outside the lychgate on Church Street and along the lane behind the graveyard. Shortly afterwards, at twelve o'clock, at the brownish-brick crematorium in Oxford, a service was held for Michael Dick, also attended only by family – his mother, his ex-wife and his daughter. There were no issues with excessive bouquets or loitering media. The sun poured down on both alike, on church roof and crematorium arcade, on gnarled yew surrounded by tilting gravestones and on cypresses casting full-blown shadows on lawns that lay around them still and smooth as pools of green water.

*

Four hours later, there was a knock at the door of a house in Littlemore, and Mrs Dick got up with difficulty to answer it. She was short and hunched, all elbows and knees, with an inquisitive expression on her crumpled face, and, cursing softly, she unhooked herself from her oxygen machine and made her way down the hall to let Ryan in.

They sat together in the parlour, decorated by the deceased Mr Dick in floral patterns faded now by years of dusty sunlight but still crowding the small room with insistent foliage, to which Ryan added his bunch of condolences. Mrs Dick's voice might be worn almost to crow-bark by emphysema but her memory was still sharp and for ten minutes she quizzed Ryan with raspy questions about his mother and father and Jade, and whatever the little one's called.

'Ryan.'

'Ryan, yes.' She looked sceptical. 'Got your nose?'

'Not yet.'

'Pray to the Lord he never does.' She let out a long trickle of almost silent laughter.

She talked about Mick Dick then, his childhood, his sporting achievements, his missed opportunities. Her memories were vivid. Occasionally, with great effort, she clambered to her feet and got something to show him, a photograph of Mick holding a regional youth boxing trophy or crouching on a football field, the fingertips of one hand resting on the turf. In one photograph, dressed in a suit too small for him, he was accepting a certificate from a frail old man in an elegant cape.

'His Duke of Edinburgh,' she said with pride.

Mick Dick's childhood had been a golden age of promise and

innocence and she remembered it in detail. Occasionally she had to pause to recover her breath, pressing her small face into the mask attached to the machine at the side of her chair. It was clear that she spent most of her days here in the tiny room, the things she needed within reach, radio, glasses, packets of medication on the table beside her, the lamp behind her chair, where she sat surveying her past, the framed photographs on the little sideboard, the commemorative knick-knacks – ashtray from Porthcawl, tea tray from Penzance – and the foliating decor done by her husband in the year her son Michael had been born.

She held a small unframed photograph of a grinning five-year-old whose smile seemed too big for his face. He'd been a lovely child, affectionate, polite. A happy boy, always laughing. It was a shame he'd had to grow up, turn into a man, start getting into trouble, making mistakes. She looked pointedly at Ryan. '*You* know,' she said.

She talked herself into silence. 'But he was good to me,' she said at last.

On the carpet by her armchair was a familiar police-issue transparent plastic bag, and Ryan drew her attention to it. He couldn't help himself.

'See you got his effects back.'

'Lassie in uniform brought them round, young enough to be my granddaughter nearly.'

'Can I take a look?'

Her gesture of permission seemed to also express the triviality of such things in a time of grief.

In the bag there was nothing unexpected. Ryan remembered

the hooded top and trackie bottoms from the compound, the muddy trainers from the police photos. The keys and wallet too. In the wallet there was nothing but a five-pound note and a business card for Thomas Fothergill, CEO of Baby Dynamic.

'Thought the world of him, Mick did.'

'And there was nothing else? Just these?'

She shook her head.

His visit was at an end. He got up to go.

'Only the ribbons,' she said.

'Ribbons?'

'For Ashleigh.'

Mick Dick was always buying little gifts for his daughter, sweets, cheap toys, a hat, a pair of socks; he liked to have something to give her whenever he went round. There had been hair ribbons in the pocket of his trackie bottoms which he must have bought for Ashleigh. That was her assumption anyway. They hadn't been in a packet but sometimes Mick acquired things, as he put it, 'wholesale'. Anyway, she'd taken them round to Ashleigh the next evening.

Ryan thought back to his visit to Charlene, the little girl in her high chair staring at him, her big eyes, her coffee-coloured skin, her floppy black hair – done up in bunches with ribbons. He remembered the colour of them.

'Red and black?'

Mrs Dick nodded. 'Nice. Mick was good at picking out nice things.'

At last he said goodbye and left her and went out and sat in his car for twenty minutes. He remembered Mick Dick turning out his pockets in the compound. 'That's it, that's everything.'

But it hadn't been. He'd kept the ribbons hidden. Red and black.

Why would he do that?

Again he saw that look of terror on Mick Dick's face. Or was it horror?

In Grove Street Ray lay sleeping in the spare room. He'd come home at ten after completing late interviews with two people connected with Magpies, a caterer and a maintenance man, neither with any meaningful memory of Poppy, both with alibis. Diane was already asleep. In the spare room he read transcripts of old interviews with local sex offenders until midnight, when he finally crashed on the sofa, then lay there for ages unable to sleep, staring vacantly at the kiddie equipment surrounding him, transformed into sinister shapes by the deranging moonlight that came in through the uncurtained window. Now it was two o'clock and he had been asleep for ten minutes.

When his phone rang he snatched it up and staggered to his feet, shouting into it incoherently.

Ryan's voice said, 'Did you find the girl's ribbons? From the costume.'

Silenced, Ray looked about him, as if for the source of his confusion, and Ryan repeated his question, which he finally understood.

'No. No ribbons. The perp took them. Ryan? *Ryan?*'

But Ryan had rung off and did not pick up when Ray called back. Diane called out fearfully from the bedroom and he called back to reassure her, more aggressively than he intended, and continued to stand there in the disturbed silence, among the spare-room clutter, not knowing what to do.

Half an hour passed. Still not knowing what to do, he began to get dressed.

By the time Ryan rang again Ray was fully clothed, standing as before in the centre of the room, phone pressed to his mouth, and he spoke immediately: 'How do you know about the ribbons? *Do not hang up.*'

'What sweets did he give her?'

Ray's stomach lurched. 'How do you know he gave her sweets?'

'What they all do, mate. Stranger danger. Was it Love Hearts?'

There was a panting pause. 'For God's sake, Ryan, can't you just . . .'

Ryan explained. About Mick Dick breaking into the van at the compound. About Ryan collaring him. About the red and black ribbons that Mick had kept hidden in his pockets.

'Are you telling me that your friend's the—'

'Mick Dick? Nah. No way.'

'So how did he end up with the ribbons?'

Ryan took a breath, told Ray he'd taken a look inside the van. He had an idea, he said.

'Perp hires the van, right? Snatches the little girl. Leaves her body in the woods. Takes the van back to the compound. Walks away. Nice and neat, right?'

'Okay.'

'But say the perp gets home and suddenly remembers. Fuck! He's left the ribbons behind.'

'In the van?'

'In the fucking van. What'll the cleaners think when they find them next day? With all those photos of the little girl everywhere, everyone knows what she was wearing when she was snatched.'

'So he's got to get the ribbons back.'

'Yeah, but now the van's all locked up in the compound. He's no break-and-entry guy. What's he going to do?'

Ray answered quickly. 'Find a guy who is.'

'Turns out he knows someone. Someone who has an unfortunate habit of doing favours for the wrong people.'

'Your friend.'

'Yeah, my friend. I doubt Mick was told exactly what he'd be retrieving. But he realised when he found them in the van. He was shaking like a fucking leaf, Ray. At the time I thought he was frightened. More like horror, I reckon.'

'And the sweets?'

'Yeah. Like I say, I give the van the onceover just now, see if there was anything else to find. Turns out there was. Wedged under the seat. Cleaners must've missed them. Tube of Love Hearts, one sweet missing.' He paused. 'All looking a bit suggestive. Don't you think?'

Ray took a breath.

'The perp, Ryan. Who's your mate's friend? Who hired the van?'

'You won't have heard of him.'

'Who, Ryan?'

'Name's Shane Cobb. Ex-con up at Dean Court, Cumnor way.'

TWENTY-FOUR

Pinnocks Way lay quiet in the summer darkness, a little rough around the edges, untidy, sleeping it off, dead to the world. Cobb's house was dark, curtains drawn. They watched it from the opposite side of the street.

'Think he's there? I think he's there.'

No answer.

'Calls himself the Facilitator.'

'What?'

'What he calls himself. Got a little card and everything. Strange little guy. Health issues. Now I think about it, creepy. Ended up in Grendon and Mick took him under his wing. Course, he didn't know he was a nonce. Supply of class As what he was in for. But he told me one of the things he did was children's parties. I bet he fucking did.'

Ray hesitated. 'You said I wouldn't have heard of Cobb. But his name rang a bell.'

'Oh yeah?'

'I'd read it in one of the files. He does gardening.'

'Yeah, that's one of his things. So?'

'The agency he works for does the gardens at Magpies, the nursery. The reason we didn't pursue it was, he was off work that day; another guy filled in for him. But he's been going there every week for the last six months. Poppy would have known him. Got used to him.'

'You think it's him then?'

Ray looked at him. Nodded.

They were quiet for a moment.

'He was on his way here, you know,' Ryan said.

'Who?'

'Mick Dick. After he found the ribbons. Straight up here. Didn't understand at first. What's he doing running across the meadows in the pitch dark? I thought. Heading for that under-pass. It's the fastest way up here, to Dean Court. Fuck knows what he'd have done to Cobb when he got here. That hopped-up knobhead in a Vauxhall Astra probably saved Cobb's life.'

'Mick could have gone to the police,' Ray said primly.

Ryan looked at him.

'An ex-con?'

Ray looked away.

They looked again towards the house, which remained dark and blank.

'Think he's there? Know what? I think the fucker's gone.'

Ray made no answer. He got out of the car and Ryan followed him across the road, through weeds and down a side passage to the back corner of the house, where they stopped and looked round. In a back upstairs window there was a weak fringe of light round the edge of the curtains.

'Knew he'd be here. What's he doing up this late?'

'We'll wait for back-up.'

They waited a moment, their eyes getting used to the darkness of the garden, a region of unclaimed nature, listening.

'Can you hear something?'

Ray shushed him again. Together they waited. Quiet voices, two of them, both male, came down from the room above.

'He's got someone with him.'

'Jesus Christ.'

'That's it. We have to go in.'

Ray crept to the back door and tried it. Locked. The downstairs windows were all shut. Ryan crept forward with his shirt wrapped round his hand and, before Ray could stop him, punch-shoved the glass panel of the door with his palm, and it fell in with a soft crumpling noise thinning quickly to splinter-tinkle and silence.

Eyes furiously wide, Ray gesticulated. Ryan shrugged. The voices above continued as before.

'If you're not expecting it, you hardly ever hear it. Basic. What you looking at now?'

Ray gestured. 'I can't believe you kept it after your discharge.'

'Told you before, not police issue.'

'You mean not legal.'

'Legal, Ray? Legal? *You're* not fucking legal.'

'What are you talking about?'

'Pick up a warrant on the way here, did you?'

'Overriding need for speed.'

'You can override the fucking Glock then.'

They glared at each other.

163

'I'd forgotten how annoying you are.'

Inside, they reached the foot of the stairs, bumping together as they each tried to go up first, hissing and signalling furiously at each other not to hiss. At the top of the stairs they crept along the narrow landing. The voices in the room were clearer now, one older, quiet but menacing, one younger, distressed, both low and murmuring. They heard the older voice say, 'Not the way.' The younger one said, 'I didn't.' The older one said, 'Not the way I want it.'

They moved faster, positioning themselves on either side of the door. Ray counted down with his fingers and, taking a breath, kicked the door open and Ryan surged into the room, Glock out, shouting '*Armed Police!*', spinning round looking for Cobb and his companion until he realised there was no one else in the room, just the bed piled with clothes, wardrobe with its door hanging open, dresser with its drawers all out, and, on the windowsill, a radio playing quietly, some middle-class drama.

'Knew he'd've gone,' Ryan said. 'Didn't I say?'

Ray turned off the radio.

There was nothing to see beyond the mess. It was an ordinary little room, cheaply furnished. Full-length mirror on the wall by the door.

'Looks like he left in a hurry.'

Ryan peered here and there. 'Could be he left something behind.'

'Would he be so stupid?'

'Wouldn't trust him to do anything normal. He's a nut-job.'

'Someone's tipped him off. We've let him get away.'

Outside, back-up and Forensics were arriving, the usual circus of lights and noise, neighbours appearing at their windows to watch them, and, behind the vans and wagons, a familiar black Range Rover drawing up to the kerb, out of which Superintendent Wallace emerged, impassive as ever.

And half a mile away, walking down a deserted road in the stillness and quietness of the Oxford night, he turned suddenly in fear. But it was only one of those miniature deer that creep into the city at night. He was safe. Like the deer, he had the gift of disappearance. Adjusting his backpack, he continued along the street, quiet once more except for distant sirens bringing angry men to empty houses.

TWENTY-FIVE

The Super sat at his desk, barely contained in his uniform, jaw bulging, reading Cobb's file, and Ray stood silently in front of him. Ryan had been told to wait outside.

Shane Cobb, no middle name, born in Carterton, near Oxford, was thirty-five years old. He had been given up for adoption as a baby and had grown up in care, moving from one institution to another every few years. After finishing his education at local schools, he began a Plumbing Foundation Diploma at Oxford Energy Academy in Witney, abandoning it for lack of funds after six months. For two years he was caretaker at a primary school in Aylesbury, released after a complaint from a parent about a drawing he'd encouraged her daughter to produce. A few years later he was questioned as a material witness in connection with soliciting a child prostitute, but released without charges. Finally arrested on suspicion of dealing class A drugs, he was convicted and sentenced to five years, served at Grendon, category B facility in Buckinghamshire, released after three years, partly for good behaviour. Since then he had been registered as self-employed ('facilitator'), with a few regular freelance contracts, one of which was with Garden Solutions, the agency employed by Magpies.

There were only two personal contacts listed in the file, an aunt, estranged, living in Leighton Buzzard, and a childhood friend, Ronnie Pigford, once Cobb's roommate at a boys' home, though he had long since disappeared, last heard of living in Portugal; there were no signs of contact between the two on any of the devices recovered from Cobb's house in Cumnor. Cobb was a loner.

The Super threw the file onto the desk and fixed his unyielding eyes on Ray's. A minute passed without him blinking. His gaze was hard to read but in its depths Ray sensed a barely constrained dissatisfaction. When he spoke his mouth did not appear to open and his voice was low and compressed.

'This the bastard?'

'Yes.'

Ray went through the forensics with him. There was no doubt Poppy had been abducted in the van: her prints were on the inside of the passenger door; fibres from the upholstery matched those found on her clothing. The ribbons had been hers: DNA match confirmed that she'd been wearing them. Cobb had hired the van; it had been in his possession all day; his prints were all over it. CCTV cameras belonging to the Wychwood and Dragon schools had caught it going into the area at 4.05 p.m. – they'd assumed it belonged to the workmen in Charlbury Road. Half an hour later, the Banbury Road camera showed it heading north past the Summertown shops. A few minutes after that, the camera at the Marston junction showed it turning off the A40 towards the Elsfield woods. Finally, the camera at Van Central had recorded it drawing up on the forecourt at 7.30 p.m., and

Cobb – there was no doubt it was him – getting out and walking away hurriedly down the road. As a side note, a number of relevant items had been recovered from Cobb's house, including items of children's clothing and a laptop containing pornographic images of children downloaded from various sites and homemade video footage of children playing, apparently taken at Magpies nursery – and, significantly, a hi-vis jacket and workman's helmet of the sort Marjorie Willoughby had seen being carried by the man in the nursery garden.

'He was taking pictures of the children?'

'Yes. He'd been to Magpies several times, attending to the garden. On one occasion Natalie, the nursery manager, saw him playing games with them.'

'He was playing with them too? Christ almighty.'

'Including Poppy. He got close to her.'

A final detail. One of the workmen remembered seeing the van (black wing mirror) parked in Garford Road opposite the nursery at about four o'clock. It had taken the spot where he usually parked his own van, opposite Magpies. Of course, like the police, he'd assumed it belonged to one of the other workmen on site: just a van among all the vans.

'It fitted in. No one thought anything of it.'

All Cobb had needed to do was to get Poppy to cross the quiet road.

The Super simmered in his uniform. Without losing eye contact, he moved his head from side to side and Ray heard the vertebrae in his neck pop.

'He's the bastard killed our little girl. And now, you tell me, he's disappeared.'

Twenty-four hours earlier, at a Lloyds branch in town Cobb had emptied his bank account, taking out two thousand pounds in cash. Camera footage from Cornmarket showed him walking away from the cashpoint wearing a grey hooded top and jeans, carrying a backpack. Around the same time he'd switched off his phone.

'He's dropping off the grid.'

'Someone tipped him off. This Sayyed fellow?'

'I think it's likely. Cobb introduced Sayyed to the agency.'

'You talked to him earlier.'

'I did.'

'Ask him about Cobb?'

Ray breathed. 'I wasn't aware of the connection then. There's virtually nothing in Cobb's file to suggest he's a paedophile. It was hidden. Even in prison he was known as a drug mule, not a nonce. He's never been charged with a sexual crime, let alone convicted.'

A pause.

'What does Sayyed say now?'

Ray felt himself flush. 'We haven't located Sayyed yet. He hasn't been home. He's gone . . . somewhere.'

Another pause, longer and more dangerous.

'You realise, Ray, what the media's going to do with all this?'

Ray acknowledged it but did not back down. 'We can use it to our advantage. We've got APWs out for both men. CRA up and running. Multiple public appeals. Full coverage. Cobb's face everywhere.'

The Super considered this. 'Where will he go now?'

'I think he'll try to get out of the city as soon as he can.

Oxford's not safe for him any more. Too small. He has no vehicle. We've got twenty-four seven coverage up and running of all the local transport hubs.'

'He needs help. Anyone he can turn to? This Sayyed?'

'Perhaps they're together but I doubt it. Cobb's a loner. His aunt in Leighton Buzzard hasn't seen him in fifteen years, never wants to see him again, she says. We've got someone watching. We're digging for other contacts he may have.'

'Paedophile contacts?'

'Exactly.' They were shaking down the men on the SOR again. 'We're also interviewing staff at the foster homes where he grew up, all his work contacts, past and present.' He hesitated. 'He seems to have done gardening and basic clerical work recently for other schools and nurseries.'

'Jesus Christ. The papers are going to love that.'

'We'll get him. We'll get him soon.'

The Super looked at him without expression. '*You'll* get him, Ray. I already have your word on that.'

Outside the Super's office Ryan sat in a spare seat at the edge of the open-plan. He'd sat outside offices all his life waiting to be called in, usually to be shouted at, by headmasters, wardens, social workers and, later in life, police superintendents; he was used to having things explained to him by men (and women) putting on scary voices. It was only noise. So he sat there thinking about something else, Mick Dick, trying to imagine those last minutes of his life, the terror that wasn't terror, or only partly terror. Partly horror, partly fury. He could imagine Mick finding the ribbons in the van, his puzzlement to begin with, then his

170

first troubled thought of that girl who'd gone missing, whose picture was everywhere, Poppy Clarke in her pirate costume with her jacket and cutlass and red and black ribbons, four years old, just Ashleigh's age; then an inkling, the creeping suspicion of what Cobb was, a growing conviction of what he'd done; then the horror at the mistake he'd made himself in helping him; finally the rage that sent him running across the water meadows towards Cumnor but, as it happened, only as far as Hinksey and a night-time driver off his head. Ashleigh in his thoughts as he ran into the road.

The door to the Super's office opened and Ray came out. For a moment he hesitated and their eyes met, then he walked on without saying anything. The Super, standing in the doorway, made a brief gesture and turned back to his desk, and Ryan followed him inside.

Ryan said, 'Like old times, eh? Me and Ray.'

The Super ignored him.

'I can just duck out, if you want,' Ryan said. 'Ray's probably filled you in.'

The Super said nothing.

'Or, if you like, I can uncork the Mick Dick end of things for you.'

He waited. The Super was bent to his laptop, radiating tension. Ryan watched his face. You could tell a lot about someone from the number of times they looked at you. He hadn't looked at Ryan yet. He was still deciding what to do with him. A good sign.

He shuffled about, hands in his trackie pockets. 'So anyway,' he began pre-emptively, 'just glad I could help, really. Bit weird, obviously, the way it fell out, and I wouldn't even have followed it up, definitely wouldn't have interfered, if it hadn't been for that look on Mick Dick's face, and it was really only—'

'Shut up.'

Another few minutes went by. Finally the Super closed his laptop and gave Ryan the benefit of his small, inhuman eyes.

'You think you've impressed me, son?'

He hesitated. 'I'm going to guess no.'

'You lied to Nadim Khan in order to extract confidential information from police records.' A flat voice for a bald fact, but compressed, suggesting pent-up emotion liable to burst out at any moment.

'Well, yeah, but—'

'You persuaded . . . the other Wilkins to break professional codes of conduct by interviewing Thomas Fothergill about a case he wasn't even working on.'

'Yeah, that's true. But—'

'You removed an item from an official crime scene at Cuddesdon residential park.'

'Yeah, but like I was saying—'

'You searched a vehicle at the Van Central compound in Osney, removing items from it, contaminating another crime scene and very possibly invalidating evidence which we would want to rely on in a court of law. Jesus Christ, you're in the middle of a reinstatement process. I don't even know how you've got time to do all this shit.'

Ryan said nothing to that. Winced a little. The Super removed a file from his desk drawer and took out two letters, held one of them up.

'Report of one Crapper at Van Central. Says you're – and I quote – negligent, obstructive, offensive and, by the way, a smart-arse.' He held up the other. 'Report of Dr Tompkins, anger management counsellor. Says you're disengaged, says progress is disappointing, can't confirm that you're dealing with your problems.'

Ryan winced, fidgeted.

'Yeah. Just to say, how I got involved in the first place, total accident. I—'

'Not interested. I warned you, didn't I? How many mistakes do you need to make?' As he stared at Ryan his features suddenly contracted in anger and he slapped the table. 'Stop twitching! Christ's sake, you're like a child!'

Ryan blew out his cheeks, put his hands in his trackie pockets, took them out again, scratched his belly, grimacing, all the time trying hard to stop doing these things.

The Super still hadn't decided what to do with him. Ryan watched him recover his composure, take a breath.

Some time passed.

'How old are you, son?'

'Twenty-seven.'

'Got any siblings?'

'Sister. Jade. She's all right.'

'You got a son too.'

'Yeah. Nearly three. Best thing ever.'

The Super nodded. This was a change of direction. Ryan paid attention. Wallace began to speak, slowly, leaving gaps between the words. 'I've got a brother. Neil, couple of years younger.'

He paused.

Ryan said, 'Nice.'

'He's an idiot. Wasted his life. Mistake after mistake after mistake.' He gave Ryan a hard look, then got up from his desk and went over to the window and stood there looking out with his hands in his pockets; and after a moment, as if addressing the river, went on. 'There was a railway near where we grew up, half a mile away, a mile. Goods yard. Made a tremendous fucking racket day and night, noises like you've never heard, metal twisting itself inside out. When we were boys we used to piss about there, flatten pennies on the track, break into the vehicles left overnight, that sort of thing.' He left a long pause. 'This one night, there was a few of us there as usual. Neil was arsing around, being stupid. Also as usual. We had a fight – not a real fight, he was only twelve, I was fourteen. But I'd had enough of the wee toerag, so I left him there, went home. An hour later, messing about on the tracks, he gets his foot stuck. Of course. Typical Neil. Hears a noise about quarter of a mile away: goods train coming through, one of those old flatbed things. Also typical. Classic movie scene, we've all watched it, we all know how it turns out. He wriggles and wriggles and gets free at the very last second as the train goes roaring past.' He left another long pause. 'So he wriggles and wriggles,' he said in a quieter voice. 'And the train comes on. But his foot's stuck fast. Just at the end the driver sees him there and slams on the brakes but by then it's too late.'

He turned round to face Ryan, totally expressionless.

Ryan began to say he was sorry.

'And at the last second he wriggles free,' Wallace said.

He held Ryan's eyes.

'So there he is, gibbering at the side of the track. The train, it goes screaming past, sparks flying, shaking from side to side, and he's just standing there, in a state of shock, can hardly believe his luck, and he's saying to himself I'll never be stupid again, I won't be a toerag any more, I won't keep making these mistakes, and a girder jolts free from the last truck, swings out wide and low and lazy and takes off both his legs just below the knees.'

The silence went on so long Ryan could almost count off the minutes.

'You see what I'm saying, son?'

'Don't be like Neil.'

The Super smiled a long, ugly smile. 'Oh, I'm not talking about my brother here. I'm talking about me. I'm talking about failing to take responsibility. About my mistake leaving him there, which is what I think about now every single fucking day. See, you're not free to waste the rest of your life at Van Central like the dipstick you are, because you've got a sister, you've got a kid. You need to wake up to that, son.'

He arranged himself at his desk.

'Except for your interviews and courses, I don't want to see you here again. Now get out.'

He drove home slowly, thinking. A cheesy performance, even by the standards of the many cheesy performances he'd endured over the years. Sentimental fuckery, self-serving bullshit. He couldn't stop thinking about it, though. The crappy Peugeot stalled at every red light.

His thoughts drifted away to little Ryan. He didn't realise his father was a dipstick yet. But later?

He knew these moments, these little signs, these flashes of lightning in which he briefly saw himself from the outside. He'd spent a lifetime ignoring them. And was it now, after everything he'd put up with, everything he'd ignored, was it now, because of this cheesy, lump-in-the-throat, hard-man sob-fest (probably not even true), that he was finally going to pay attention? He almost laughed.

There was hooting behind him and he realised the lights had changed. He drove out of town, up the long strip of speed bumps into Kennington, still thinking, and by the time he pulled up in front of the house, he realised that in spite of everything this time it *was* actually going to be true. He *was* going to turn things round. This last chance, the last of so many last chances. No more mistakes. A new start.

Having thought it, he sat there relishing it.

He could get through the last stages of the rehabilitation if he just got his head down. He could make it good at Van Central too, he just needed to finesse his attitude, make sure his final report was an improvement on the interim one. And then . . . Detective Inspector Ryan Wilkins of the Thames Valley. Back where he belonged.

His phone went. It was Carl Crapper, who had been reviewing security camera footage from the previous night and wanted to know what possible justification there could be for Ryan leaving the premises unattended between the hours of two and four, though he left no natural pause for Ryan's answer and it was evident, in fact, that he didn't expect or want one, this was just his way of dramatising the real purpose of his call, which was to inform Ryan that his employment at Van Central was terminated with immediate effect ('forthwith' was the word he used, more than once, relishing it as if it were usually forbidden him), with loss of pay commensurate with the level of his negligence, and, of course, complete lack of references for possible future employers, and no further communication whatsoever from Van Central, except a courtesy copy of the final report to be sent now to the Chief Superintendent of the Thames Valley Constabulary, informing him of Ryan's dismissal for what Carl called, inaccurately but with obvious satisfaction, Grossest Misconduct.

There may have been more but Ryan didn't stay tuned for it. In silence he went into the house.

TWENTY-SIX

Media frenzy: a 'killer at large' circus. Raw noise of fury and blame, mob-hoot of broken-hearted feeling, blarts of outrage and accusation, outpourings on social media of murderous intent; a toddler tantrum of words, rabbit punch of headlines, HUNT FOR PAEDOPHILE, POLICE ONE STEP BEHIND, NO PEACE FOR GRIEVING PARENTS, unpunctuated agonies and bewilderment; and pictures – the terrible, addictive pictures – luminous girl in jacket, sash and ribbons on the one hand, pavement-grey man with overlarge head and queasy smirk of a mouth on the other, both trailing their unbearable captions, OUR ANGEL, FACE OF A KILLER. One of the lowest circles of this hell of emotion was reserved for the nursery school, now closed and unlikely to reopen, which had regularly allowed a man with paedophile tendencies onto their site and had even enabled him to interact with the children. And another, even lower, circle for the hapless Thames Valley Police Force (ARE THEY NAPPING?!), whose Superintendent now delivered most of the press conferences, his SIO, DI Ray Wilkins, sitting silently at his side.

Nevertheless, it was Ray who ran the first team meeting in-house, so crowded it had to be held in the conference room on the first floor, with standing room only and overflow outside the door. Manpower had been increased by fifty per cent in order to bring Cobb into custody. There was a feeling in the room, a low-grade hum of emotion: hatred for the man who had killed Poppy Clarke.

He outlined the operation, one of the biggest manhunts in British policing history, involving the co-ordination of forces across the country and beyond, shakedowns on a huge scale, door-to-doors, extensive forensics and communications analysis, interviews and re-interviews of all known associates, paedophile contacts, work colleagues past and present, prison-mates, neighbours, past teachers, care-home staff and anyone else who might give an insight into where Cobb would go. He reiterated that Cobb was likely to try to run, to get out of Oxford, which is why surveillance of public transport was so important. Success, he said, was very close now, very close indeed, it all depended on how they performed in the next two days, which is why he was setting a deadline for Cobb's capture of forty-eight hours.

A little ripple of attention went round the group.

Team leaders reported on new developments.

Livvy had spoken to Linda Mackay, the retired headteacher of the Aylesbury school where Cobb had been a caretaker. In Mackay's view, Cobb had been a quietly predatory presence who played games with his victims, made friends with them, before inducing them to do things for him, to make indecent drawings or to undress. Unfortunately Mackay had not been able to prove all the allegations, which relied on the claims of a single child, but she had been sufficiently alarmed to persuade the governors to approve Cobb's dismissal, which, she thought significantly, he had chosen not to fight.

Mrs Mackay had been told that there were dozens of indecent drawings, which the girl claimed Cobb had shown her in his storeroom. They were never found, however.

Ray spoke up. 'This may be significant. If they exist, we think these pictures may hold special meaning for Cobb. We haven't found them at his house in Cumnor, so where are they? With someone else? A friend, an associate? Might he try to retrieve them now? Livvy?'

Livvy had spoken to Ahmed el-Baz, a taxi driver who had supported Cobb's statements when he was questioned about the child prostitute several years earlier. He denied being a friend of Cobb, however, and claimed to have no knowledge of any drawings, nor of Cobb's whereabouts. He was under surveillance nevertheless.

Finally Ray stood to speak. The third person of immediate interest was Tariq Sayyed, who had not yet been located, he explained. He briefed the teams; there was more information about Sayyed in their folders. If they found Sayyed, they had a good chance of finding Cobb.

Questions came in. Sayyed was from Bradford. Was there liaison with Yorkshire?

He had many contacts in the South Asian communities and sex offender circles throughout the West Riding, and indeed the

North in general, Ray said. Yorks were currently shaking them down; the difficulty, Ray admitted, would be in locating him in such extensive social networks.

What about Oxford?

The same was true here: Sayyed now had wide, deep connections in the city; there were many people to help him. Too many, someone said. Ray could see in their faces a lack of belief, not least in him.

Where should they focus their efforts? They wanted his guidance. He had to acknowledge that they currently had no promising line of enquiry. Sayyed's mother had said she had no idea where he was. For two days his phone had not been used, there had been no activity in his bank account; none of his closest associates had told them anything useful. It was a deflating note on which to end. Ray did his best to rouse them, but they left the room in near silence, some of them shaking their heads.

In the deserted room, he sat alone staring at the terrible carpet.

Livvy went over to give him encouragement and, as she approached, he looked up, gazed at her blankly and said, 'I think I know where Sayyed is.'

TWENTY-SEVEN

It was Ryan's lowest point. The problem was, Ryan didn't know how to be low. He moved restlessly from room to room, failing to settle, twitching and gurning to himself, unable to concentrate, drifting into daydreams and forgetting what had happened, then suddenly remembering and setting off through the house again in a storm of fidgets, veering from thought to thought, deciding to go round to Van Central and damage Carl Crapper, looking at his watch to see if it was little Ryan's bath time yet, thinking of telling the Super to shove the rehabilitation process, he'd never wanted it anyway, going upstairs to get his stuff ready for work, remembering again that he didn't have any work, getting up and moving out of the room again, scratching and blinking.

Then there was the problem of Jade. He'd rushed through his usual shit-happens, it's-all-for-the-best-really speech. Nights at the compound? Glad to get shot of them. Never see Carlo the Crapper again it'll be too soon. Move on to something better, that was always the plan. Back on track, really. And the police thing? Well, yeah, but it was only a long shot, he wasn't ever banking on it, to be honest didn't think it was going anywhere, was it even the right thing to be doing, all the fucking rules and regs, jump through this hoop, jump through that hoop, and that Scots boss-man Barko on his case twenty-four seven? Puts it in perspective, though, don't it?

To all this Jade said nothing. Looked at him.

He said in a quieter voice, 'Yeah, well, I'll get something soon. Promise.'

To which she replied after a moment, 'You can promise me that now you've got time on your hands you'll go and see Dad like I asked you. Or are you going to be useless at everything?'

He fled upstairs to give the children their baths.

He watched them, little Ryan crooning to himself as he moved his crocodile in and out of the water, Mylee chewing a penguin. His son's body was pink, his arms and legs rounded, elbows dimpled. A sheen of blond hair fell in a short straight curtain to his eyes. Scattered on the mat were his clothes, dungarees and T-shirt.

'Daddy?'

'Yeah?'

'What was the little girl called?'

He knew at once who he meant. 'That little girl what . . . went missing?'

'Yes.'

'Poppy.'

His son considered this for some time. 'There's a Poppy in our class,' he said at last. 'She's not missing,' he added.

The crocodile leaped out of the water and plunged back in.

'Daddy?'

'Yeah?'

'When the Poppy that you know went missing was it when she was wearing her pirate costume?'

'Yeah. Yeah it was.'

After a while little Ryan heaved a sigh, something he'd learned from his aunt, a noise like someone very sadly imitating a cow. The crocodile went in and out of the water. After a while he began to croon to himself again.

Ryan tried to imagine what a child's fear was like. It didn't show, not the way an adult's did; it lived below the surface, in the nerves and glands, like some deep-lying medical condition, symptoms unseen. Ryan thought about his own fear, that feeling when he thought he'd lost his son in the supermarket. That had been physical too, but it rose quickly from his stomach to his throat, like a sickness.

Now the children were laughing, wriggling about and frothing the water. The crocodile and penguin cavorted together, little Ryan rocked Mylee by her slippery shoulders and Mylee clambered into his lap.

'Daddy!' he cried, laughing. 'She's using me as a farting bucket!'

Gradually they calmed down.

'Mylee is my friend,' little Ryan said.

'And mine,' Mylee said.

'And Ben is my friend. And Jake is my friend. And Jasmine is my friend when she's good.'

Ryan sat there watching, listening to his son chatter. He'd stopped twitching. He'd made a mess of so much, made so many mistakes, was more of a dipstick than even the Super imagined, but he hadn't made a mess of being a father. He could say that at least.

TWENTY-EIGHT

LOCATION: C3: small, dim, bare, airless, ugly.
INTERVIEWER: DI Wilkins in charcoal Fred Perry polo shirt with tonal vertical stripes, Ralph Lauren dove-grey chinos and navy penny loafers.
INTERVIEWEE: Tariq Sayyed in brown work trousers and tan T-shirt, one sleeve slightly ripped.
SOLICITOR: Malcolm Bradbrook in limp blue suit, white shirt and loose yellow tie.

DI WILKINS: Tariq Sayyed, you've been arrested on suspicion of perverting the course of justice. You're being interviewed under caution in the presence of your solicitor, and anything you say may be used against you in court. Do you understand?

TARIQ SAYYED: Yes.

DI WILKINS: So. Why run, Tariq?

TARIQ SAYYED: I didn't.

DI WILKINS: Was it to avoid answering questions we might ask you about Shane Cobb?

TARIQ SAYYED: No.

DI WILKINS: Do you recognise this? For the tape, I'm showing Tariq a photograph.

TARIQ SAYYED: It's the houseboat where I'm staying.

DI WILKINS: It's a houseboat on a deserted stretch of canal north of Kidlington. A place you mentioned to me as the sort of bolthole a man might go to escape things. Two days ago you were at home in Cowley. Why did you suddenly leave and go out there?

TARIQ SAYYED: No reason. I felt like a break.

DI WILKINS: Okay, Tariq. Do you recognise this? For the tape, I'm showing Tariq a photograph of a laptop.

TARIQ SAYYED: [silence]

DI WILKINS: It's yours, Tariq, registered to you. Retrieved by Forensics from a locked underfloor storage area in the houseboat where you've been staying. What sort of activity are we going to find on it?

TARIQ SAYYED: [silence]

DI WILKINS: I'll remind you, Tariq, that if any evidence is found of anything relating to a sexual crime, you'll have broken the terms of your release from prison and you'll be returned to custody. As you can imagine, this time it won't be a short sentence.

TARIQ SAYYED: [silence]

DI WILKINS: The only way to minimise that, Tariq, is to help us now with our enquiries.

TARIQ SAYYED: [silence]

DI WILKINS: Okay, we'll leave it there. You'll be charged in due course.

186

TARIQ SAYYED: [silence]

DI WILKINS: Have you spoken to your mother, by the way, to tell her what's happened? We'll get on and do that for you, then, let her know exactly what it is we find on your laptop.

TARIQ SAYYED: Wait!

DI WILKINS: What? You don't want us to call your mother?

TARIQ SAYYED: [weeping noise]

DI WILKINS: Take your time, Tariq.

TARIQ SAYYED: All right, all right, I heard about Shane on the news and I panicked.

DI WILKINS: Where is he?

TARIQ SAYYED: I don't know. That's the truth.

DI WILKINS: Tell me what happened on the day of the murder of Poppy Clarke.

TARIQ SAYYED: I got a call from him to say would I cover his shift at Magpies. That's it.

DI WILKINS: Did he give a reason?

TARIQ SAYYED: Just said he had something to do. The agency had approved him missing a session as long as he could set up cover.

DI WILKINS: Did he mention Poppy Clarke?

TARIQ SAYYED: No.

DI WILKINS: What sort of relationship did he have with Poppy Clarke?

TARIQ SAYYED: I don't know.

DI WILKINS: Did he ever mention the children at Magpies?

TARIQ SAYYED: [silence]

DI WILKINS: Tariq?

TARIQ SAYYED: I told him they were too young.

DI WILKINS: You knew he was a paedophile then? You knew he had 'urges'?

TARIQ SAYYED: [silence]

DI WILKINS: Did Shane Cobb abduct and kill Poppy Clarke?

TARIQ SAYYED: [silence]

DI WILKINS: Tariq?

TARIQ SAYYED: I don't know.

DI WILKINS: Have you had any contact with him since the day of Poppy's murder?

TARIQ SAYYED: He called me once. He was upset. He said . . . something had happened.

DI WILKINS: Exact words?

TARIQ SAYYED: He said there'd been a mistake. I wasn't to know what had happened. I didn't want to know either.

DI WILKINS: Where will he go?

TARIQ SAYYED: He'll be scared. I reckon he'll try to get out of Oxford.

DI WILKINS: He doesn't have a car, doesn't have much money. He'll need help. Who will he turn to? Who are his friends?

TARIQ SAYYED: Don't know. Since he came out, he keeps himself to himself. I was only ever in touch with him about work.

DI WILKINS: Is he in contact with other paedophiles in Oxford, Tariq?

TARIQ SAYYED: [silence]

DI WILKINS: Is he? Tariq!

TARIQ SAYYED: [silence]

DI WILKINS: Don't blow it, Tariq. You withhold information from us now and we find out later – and we will, you know we will – you're going back to prison for a very long time.

TARIQ SAYYED: I don't know anything about it. People know not to tell me.

DI WILKINS: Tell you what?

TARIQ SAYYED: What I've heard is, there's people here who . . . share stuff. Only what I've heard.

DI WILKINS: Stuff?

TARIQ SAYYED: [silence]

DI WILKINS: *Jesus Christ.* Give me some names.

TARIQ SAYYED: I don't know any names. Are you fucking joking? I'm not that stupid.

DI WILKINS: So you're frightened of them. Why?

TARIQ SAYYED: Some of them . . .

DI WILKINS: What?

TARIQ SAYYED: Only what I've heard. Some of them are important people. People with a profile, you know. Money. A lot to lose. You don't mess with people like that.

DI WILKINS: But Cobb did.

TARIQ SAYYED: I don't know that. He would have just been a waiter.

DI WILKINS: Waiter?

TARIQ SAYYED: Serve them up.

DI WILKINS: Christ almighty.

TARIQ SAYYED: I want to stop now, please.

SOLICITOR: We'll leave it there then, Inspector.

DI WILKINS: Terminating interview.

He stood with Livvy.

'We've got nothing to charge him with.'

She looked at him.

'He's not going to tell us any more.'

She looked at him again. Those judgemental eyes. 'I'm not sure he knows where Cobb is anyway.'

He nodded. They were silent for a while.

'Serve them up,' he said, half to himself. 'A waiter!'

With difficulty he controlled his breathing. 'Get all the SOR guys in again. All of them. If this ring exists, one of them knows something about it. Cobb needs help from someone.'

'Boss.'

'What about surveillance on that cabbie?'

'Nothing suspicious so far. Just his usual routines.'

She left and he looked at his watch. He was late for his end-of-day briefing to the Super. His phone rang and he glanced at it to see that it was Diane, before killing it and heading for the second floor.

TWENTY-NINE

Two hours later they sat separately on the sofa with bowls of quinoa salad. Neither had eaten anything. Neither paid attention to the television which was quietly showing the news. Ray was looking at his phone. Diane was looking at Ray, her eyes dull and saggy.

'I called you today.'

He didn't hear.

'To tell you about what happened.'

Now he looked across.

'I rang the antenatal hotline and they called me in.'

'Why?'

She ignored his question though she carried on looking at him. 'Don't worry, I got myself to the hospital.'

The doctors had investigated a possible placental abruption, she said, but it turned out to be a false alarm. Minor incidental bleeding only, generalised pain. She said all this without expression. Ray almost began to ask why the hell she hadn't called him before remembering that she had.

'Babe—'

'I told you, Ray.'

'Told me what?'

'Told you I didn't think I could do it on my own.'

Feeling this as a provocation, he said nothing.

'But it looks like I have to,' she said. 'You're obviously too busy. Or you have different priorities.'

He began to argue, half-heartedly at first; gradually they backed themselves into a conversation of tight-lipped comments and silences, in the middle of which, surreally, another Ray appeared on the television screen to assure them, along with the rest of the population, that he was doing all he could, and they stopped talking, as if out of politeness, to listen to him until he had finished. Then Ray's phone rang and, not recognising the number, he went into the kitchen to answer it.

It was Tom Fothergill. His brisk, forthright voice was loud in Ray's ear.

'I've just seen the news. Shane Cobb. There's something you should know.'

'What?'

'The day the girl was taken, he was with me.'

For several minutes after they finished talking Ray stood there frowning at his phone. Then he went back into the knock-through to explain that he had to go out again. Diane looked at him strangely.

'This is what you were like when we met.'

'I don't know what you're talking about.'

He felt his tiredness like a form of anger.

192

'You went there before. To see this Fothergill.'

'So?'

'And when you came back you told me all about him, his business, his money, his house.'

'Yes?'

'But you didn't say anything about his wife.'

He didn't reply.

'I saw her picture in the paper. An artist.'

He shrugged.

'And before that, a model for Lancôme.'

'For God's sake, Diane.'

'I know you, Ray. It's happening again, isn't it?'

He could hear the bitterness in her voice. He looked at her a moment. He said quietly, 'I'm not that person any more.'

'I know what you're like when you've had a drink.'

There were things he could say. About pregnancy hormones. About round-the-clock pressure of his case. But he couldn't actually say them, he knew that just by looking at Diane's face. He went in anger out of the house.

Ros Kerr was waiting at the entrance when he arrived, wearing a tan blazer over a plaid shirt, and blue denims gashed across one thigh; she gazed steadily at him through large dark glasses as he went up the polished concrete steps out of the professionally arranged shadows into the light of the doorway.

'Inspector.'

'Ms Kerr.'

Without offering her hand or taking off her glasses, she turned and went down the hall in front of him, her movements relaxed, rhythmic, and he followed, keeping his eyes elsewhere, looking round the long, wide space, taking in the vast artworks, some of which, he belatedly realised, must have been done by her, the circle of children's handprints in mud, a wall-sized canvas of primitive blots and smears, a waist-high ceramic object with a black, warty glaze, a huge tumbleweed ball of wire mesh with something unexpected imprisoned inside it: a coloured box, some crockery? He knew very little about contemporary art; in fact, it made him feel uncomfortable.

She led him towards the living room, where he had stood before with Fothergill in front of the huge window with the classic English landscape falling away from it as if a feature of the house, and he realised how carefully it must have been arranged, like the artworks, for their contemplation.

Ros looked over her shoulder as she walked. 'Would you like a drink, Inspector?'

There was the smallest of hesitations before he answered. 'No, thank you.'

Turning to face him, she took off her dark glasses and he realised she was smiling at him. 'Are all detectives as polite as you are? I imagined you'd be more at home kicking down doors and pinning people against the wall.'

She had a light voice, careless, irreverent, and he had a sudden vision of her drunk, sarcastic and unguarded.

'Most of us are just about housebroken.'

A thought of Ryan came momentarily into his mind even as he said it. Not housebroken. He kept his eyes off her perfect mouth. There were two buttons of her plaid shirt undone and he kept his eyes off those too.

In the living room Jack Fothergill was sitting in one of the chairs, staring at his hands. As before, he was dressed in black skinny jeans and grey top. His lank black hair fell forward over his white face. He didn't look up as Ray came in. Ros had moved away towards the kitchen. Purposeful footsteps sounded in the hall.

'Jack,' Ros said lightly, 'your father needs to be in here.'

Ray happened to be looking at the boy as she spoke and saw him suddenly cringe in his seat and turn towards the hall with a look of fear. His eyes met Ray's, and, as if in shame, he turned sharply away, and the next instant had hauled himself out of his chair and disappeared through the kitchen before Fothergill appeared, striding into the room with that broad welcoming gesture and handshake of his.

They sat, as before, in the window.

'Did Ros offer you a drink?'

'I'm fine, thanks.'

Ray had forgotten how fit-looking Fothergill was, how scrubbed and stripped back, almost alarmingly open in his expressions. He wore a mustard-coloured cotton shirt with sleeves rolled to his elbows as before, to leave his strong forearms bare, and plain navy chinos with the bottoms turned up and brown leather sandals on his naked feet. He looked like a healthy, energetic, intelligent millionaire, which, of course, he was.

'It's extraordinary, isn't it?' he said. 'I called as soon as I saw the news. You could probably hear how shocked I was.'

Actually, what Ray remembered was Fothergill's characteristic directness. He thought to himself how much his frankness sounded, in retrospect, like naivety; and he wondered if he should think of Fothergill as a naive person. On the spectrum, perhaps. Taking out his phone, he placed it on the table between them to record their conversation.

'Do you mind?'

Fothergill didn't even look at it; waving the question aside, he began to talk. Shane Cobb, like Michael Dick, was someone he'd been mentoring for several months. In fact, it was because Cobb had mentioned Michael to him one day that he'd decided to take Michael on as well. In truth, Shane had proved the more difficult to find employment for, he was too keen to do his own thing; he wasn't very robust or personable either, prospective employers had seldom taken a shine to him. Though Fothergill had set up trials for him at landscaping and gardening businesses, they hadn't been successful and Cobb had fallen back on occasional agency work and the bits and pieces of what he liked to call 'facilitating'.

Ray interrupted. 'What was their relationship like, Cobb and Michael Dick?'

Fothergill thought for a moment. 'I noticed that Shane often talked about Michael, but Michael never mentioned Shane.'

Ray noted it. 'Tell me now about the day of Poppy's murder. Cobb was with you, you said.'

Fothergill explained. Over the months he had occasionally arranged for Cobb to do some casual work for him; it was a way of helping him out. That day, he'd asked him to pick up two Olympic-sized archery targets from Radley and install them in the long meadow-like garden below the house. The school was getting rid of them, partly as the result of an accident in which a boy had sadly lost an eye, and Fothergill had suggested to Jack that they take archery lessons together.

'Father–son bonding.' He paused. 'My son finds it hard to relax. He needs things he can give a lot of attention to.'

Ray thought again of the look of fear on Jack's face as he heard his father approach.

Cobb had arrived at the house in the hire van to take instruction, Fothergill went on. Then he'd driven over to Radley, about five miles away, picked up the targets, driven back and set them up as requested. He'd finished by half past twelve, when, as arranged, Fothergill had given Cobb a lift in his car down to Bagley Wood sawmill on the Oxford Road nearby, where he'd arranged with the owner, a friend, for Cobb to have a trial that afternoon.

'He needs someone in the workshop.'

'What time was that?'

'We were down there before one. The idea was that Shane would stay there until the end of the shift at six, then walk back through the woods to pick up the van. We left that here. Except for the trucks that are in and out all the time, there's not much parking at the mill.'

Fothergill explained that when he heard the news his first thought was that the police must be making a mistake: Cobb was at the mill all afternoon. 'But when I phoned my friend he told me he let Shane go almost immediately: he just wasn't strong enough to handle the work. So by two he'd left the mill.'

'Did you see him again?'

'No. I was out of town all afternoon. I didn't get home until late.'

197

'How long would it have taken Cobb to walk back here from the mill?'

'Quarter of an hour at most.'

'So he could have picked up the van by say half past two.'

'Easily. So, of course, he had plenty of time to . . .'

There was a catch in his voice, he stopped speaking for a moment to steady himself. 'Plenty of time to do what he did,' he said at last. 'Sorry. It's the thought of that little girl.'

Ray nodded, left a small diplomatic pause, said, 'Where were you that afternoon?'

'Me?' Fothergill was taken aback.

Ray waited.

'Well. After dropping Shane off, I drove to Birmingham. There was a show at the NEC I wanted to see. Classic cars. It's an interest of mine.'

'Were you there the rest of the day?'

'Yes.'

'With anyone?'

'No. I was on my own.'

He held Ray's eyes. Ray said, 'Is there anyone who could vouch for your presence there?'

Fothergill continued to look at him while he thought about it. 'There was an acquaintance I waved to,' he said at last. 'He might remember. I'll give you his number.'

'You understand why I ask these questions?'

'Of course.'

His briskness had returned and he was already waiting for Ray's next question. When Ray asked him how well he knew Cobb, he applied himself to it seriously, and, after a moment's

198

consideration, summed up his thoughts in the sort of short decisive statement that Ray could imagine him making at a board meeting. In his opinion, Cobb was an introverted, antisocial man, probably with issues of anxiety who, like so many of the men Fothergill had mentored over the years, seemed trapped by his past, not only the mistakes he had undoubtedly made but the unfortunate circumstances of his upbringing without a loving family.

'You knew he grew up in care?'

'Yes, he told me.' Fothergill gave an odd sort of smile. 'I grew up in care myself,' he said.

He began to talk about the morning of Poppy's murder. Cobb hadn't appeared any different from usual, except perhaps being a little more reticent, which Fothergill had put down to nerves before his trial at the sawmill.

'Did he ever speak to you about children?'

'Never.'

'Did he give you any reason to think he might be a paedophile?'

'I never gave it a thought.'

'Do you know where he is?'

Fothergill held his eyes, unsmiling. 'No, of course not. Obviously I would tell you.'

Now that Ray was at the end of his questions, Fothergill began to ask questions of his own. He was fascinated by Cobb's strategy. 'I suppose he thought a hire van would be more anonymous, harder to trace. But the irony is, once you were onto it, you could easily find out who had hired it. Something like that, yes?'

He wanted to know what had led the police to the van, how they could be sure that it had been used in Poppy's abduction. What had they found inside it? And where was Cobb now? Was he still in Oxford? What did Ray think? At any moment Ray expected him to start offering advice.

Fortunately, at this point, Ros Kerr appeared again. She murmured something to her husband and he got to his feet at once.

'Excuse me. A small family incident.' Then they were both gone, leaving Ray sitting alone looking out of the window at the vista of dark fields and woodland laid out so obligingly for his inspection.

The house was very quiet; it seemed to absorb all noise. Ray wondered, half seriously, if it was fitted with some special technology, like noise-cancelling headphones. All traces of Fothergill and his wife had disappeared into it. After a while, bored with waiting, Ray got up and went into the hallway to look at the art again. The giant wire-mesh tumbleweed caught his eye; he bent to see what object was inside and recognised it at once, a child's toy, a shiny plastic push-button contraption in primary colours for early years. He had two of them in boxes in his spare room at home.

Out of the silence suddenly, out of the depths of the house, came a shout of rage and an answering boyish cry of distress, and a door crashed shut; then there was silence again. Ray stood there with the hairs up on the back of his neck, listening, but there were no other sounds. A few moments later Ros Kerr came back down the hall.

'He's not coming back, I'm afraid.' She did not explain.

They stood facing each other.

'Would it be possible to ask you a few questions?'

If she was surprised, she didn't show it. 'Now?'

'Is it inconvenient?'

'I was just going out to meet a gallery owner. An after-show party. They say these things are purely social but they never really are so I really ought to show my face. Tomorrow?'

She handed him a card.

'My studio. I'm there most of the time, and, besides, it's a better place to talk. Drop in whenever you feel like it.'

She said goodbye to him at the door and he went down the steps and along the runway of sunken lights towards the darkness of the nearby woods. After a moment he looked back. She was still standing at the top of the steps, watching him go. She had put her dark glasses on again and it was impossible to read her expression. He made no gesture and neither did she; then he continued to his car, while the electronic gates ahead began to silently swing open onto empty fields.

THIRTY

The city emptied too as the hours passed and night fell, traffic drained from the roads, houses darkened, quietness filled the streets. At two o'clock in the morning there was a disturbance at Cobb's house in Cumnor which set off an immediate reaction from the surveillance team there, but it was only a break-in by a substance-confused teenager, who was freaked by the sudden appearance of an armed response unit and had to be treated for shock in the Oxford Road station at Cowley. At the respectable Sandhills house of the cab driver Ahmed el-Baz everything was quiet. Nor was there a sign of anything unusual at Van Central on the Osney industrial estate, where a new security guard sat gaming in his plastic shed. Through three o'clock and four o'clock men and women in dim offices elsewhere watched screens showing them pictures of a small, sleeping city. Only in the centre was there any activity, along the entertainment strips of George Street and Hythe Bridge Street, where police crowd control was in place. Elsewhere it was silent and still, nothing to report from the folded strips of red-brick terracing in Grandpont and Iffley Fields, the scruffy shadowlands of the Rose Hill and Blackbird Leys estates, stately Park Town, where Rachel Clarke sat in vigil, awake despite her medication, the residential park at Cuddesdon, where Mick Dick's trailer still lay ransacked, or mansion-sprinkled Boars Hill, dark under a cloud-filled sky, no movement in the streets except the cautious patter of the occasional urban fox or deer, scavenging.

No Cobb. Nothing to report as day broke and the city roused, as the streets filled up with traffic again, and Ray, awake since five, bent to his laptop in his spare room, and the Super arrived at St Aldates and stood at the window of his office contemplating the river, where the geese were announcing their torment to a new morning, and Ryan slouched in dejectedly and sat on a chair too low to the ground for comfort in a small briefing room, listening to Dr Tompkins explain, in her usual calm fashion, the mechanics of fury.

'An emotional hijack. Anger takes us over. And, in fact, people often describe it as something beyond their control, a red mist, a flood or a fire.' She paused. 'How would you describe your anger, Ryan?'

He sighed. 'Dunno, really,' he said at last.

She looked at him from under the arches of her eyebrows.

'Like, maybe . . . a dog.'

'A dog?'

'Yeah. Get my teeth out.'

She considered this. 'That sounds like it could be a frightening experience for you.'

'For me? Not really. For the other guy.'

'But afterwards? How does it make you feel afterwards, Ryan?'

He sighed again, shook his head and shrugged, and she put down her pad and took off her glasses and looked at him.

'There's something on your mind. Do you want to tell me what it is?'

It wasn't so much an invitation or an order as a sort of opening, to be taken or not, to let him speak or to keep silent, delivered so soothingly he didn't know whether to burst into tears or fall asleep; and, in fact, for a few moments he couldn't speak. What could he say anyway? His attempts to be reinstated had failed, the session was useless. He saw in his mind, in quick succession, Superintendent Wallace looking at him from his desk with that look of mingled exasperation and pity, and Carl Crapper grandstanding on the compound forecourt, signalling wildly with his underarm sweat patches, and his sister turning from him as if finally giving up, and, worst of all, Mick Dick, his stark face, terrified bloodshot eyes, running across those darkened meadows with the knowledge of what he had just done for a man who had killed a little girl.

He cleared his throat to see if his voice was still working.

'Thing about me is, I'm a bit of a dipstick. There's stuff I can do, then there's stuff I can't get the hang of at all.'

She said nothing.

'Anyway, look, point is, don't matter what report you give me. I've already blown it. Got sacked from the compound. Wallace'll hear from Crapper, and that's it, everything's fucked. 'Scuse me.'

He found her gaze restful; she had a quiet face, open, almost empty. Not kind but, as they say, non-judgemental.

'I wouldn't worry about Carl Crapper's report,' she said at last. 'The Superintendent thinks he's an absolute idiot. And you can trust me on that. I've worked with Dave a long time.'

She spoke, as usual, so quietly and calmly, it didn't register for a moment. And when she put her glasses back on and picked up her pad again, and looked at him once more with that almost demure indifference, it was as if she hadn't spoken at all, and he half wondered if he'd imagined it.

'Really?' he said, but she made no reply, and the silence grew. Her expression seemed to push it gently towards him, to let him know that it was his to deal with.

'Sister wants me to go and see Dad in prison,' he said. He hadn't planned to say it, in fact he was surprised to have said it, and sat there staring at her for a while.

'Do you want to?'

'Rather eat broken glass.'

'Will you anyway?'

'Do you think it'd be a good idea?'

'What I think doesn't matter.'

'Will it help?'

'Help who?'

'Me.'

'It might.'

'Fuck it,' he said. 'I hate things you ought to do 'cause they're good for you.'

She left another one of her silences.

'I might also be minded to put it in your report as a positive thing,' she said.

Another silence.

'If you can avoid attacking him,' she added. 'Do you think you can do that?' She wasn't being humorous.

The silence resumed.

★

On the floor above, Ray stopped off at Livvy's desk.

'Do something for me?'

'Sure.'

'Not in our direct line of enquiry.'

She looked at him steadily. He said, 'Local businessman. Thomas Fothergill.'

He wanted information, general, specific, anything at all, but in particular details of his networks, business and non-business.

'What am I looking for?'

'I just want to get a better feel for him.'

She kept her eyebrows raised but he made no further comment and five minutes later he was in a meeting room downstairs listening to Maisie Ndiaye talk about paedophile rings. Knowing that she'd worked on various national operations, he'd asked her to brief him on the way the groups operated, the sort of people involved. In fact, there was a more relevant local operation, Spire, which had been set up to investigate historic cases of abuse at the Cherry Tree School, a residential care centre for children with learning difficulties in the village of Stanton St John, five miles north of Oxford. A number of influential people had been questioned in connection with the allegations brought by six ex-pupils, though in the end only one person was convicted, the headmaster of the school, who had died while serving time at Huntercombe. Maisie showed Ray a list of the other suspects; it included a former MP for one of the shire constituencies, a prominent entrepreneur, a former Deputy Lieutenant of Oxfordshire, and an ex-priest. All were now deceased. The alleged abuse had mainly taken place at the school but occasionally at a local Travelodge or a guest house in Oxford and, once, at a hotel in Jersey where a dozen boys had been taken on holiday. Transcripts of all the interviews were on file, though – Maisie said – questions had been systematically limited in scope by the men's lawyers.

'What comes across, though, is their sense of invulnerability.'

One of the men, the Deputy Lieutenant, had been a member of the PIE, the Paedophile Information Exchange, which existed in the eighties to promote sex between adults and children. Several prominent public figures were members, including Sir Peter Hayman, Deputy Head of MI6, who campaigned to lower the age of consent to ten. Young children were often perfectly willing to have sex with men such as himself, he said, and if they later claimed to have been traumatised, it was only because bleeding hearts had told them they were.

'No one says that sort of thing out loud now, of course.'

'But there are people who think it?'

'There have been rumours of a similar group. Only rumours.'

'Here?'

'Here.'

'Gut feeling?'

Maisie opened her laptop. 'Let me play you something.'

It was an audio clip recorded secretly twenty years earlier of the ex-priest talking to one of the other men in a cafe, deemed inadmissible in court. The quality was poor; background noise had leaked into their voices.

VOICE ONE: What about Poker?

VOICE TWO: [laughter] Which one's Poker?

VOICE ONE: Blond. Very stupid.

VOICE TWO: [laughter]

VOICE ONE: [laughter] On the cusp.

VOICE TWO: [laughter] I know him. He'll be there. The waiter'll make sure.

VOICE ONE: What about the place? The usual's so dreary. It's the wallpaper, I think. Just as Wilde said, it's almost enough to put you off your stroke.

VOICE TWO: [laughter]

VOICE ONE: [unintelligible]

VOICE TWO: [unintelligible]

VOICE ONE: More poked against than poking, you might say.

VOICE TWO: [laughter]

VOICE ONE: [unintelligible]

VOICE TWO: [unintelligible]

VOICE ONE: James agrees. Nicely hung.

VOICE TWO: [unintelligible]

VOICE ONE: He would. Of course, he can afford it.

VOICE TWO: [unintelligible]

VOICE ONE: [unintelligible]

VOICE TWO: Only one of them.

VOICE ONE: But it's been resolved?

VOICE TWO: Oh God, yes, no need to worry. No need to worry at all.

Maisie said, 'Do I think there are people like this around now? I'm afraid I do. But, before you ask, we never identified James; there were five or six whose identities we never discovered, in fact.'

'Who was the waiter?'

208

'The headmaster. He procured the boys.'

Ray was silent.

'What about the boy they called Poker?'

'He killed himself.'

'And the other children?'

'Overdose. Prison. Suicide. Disappeared.'

Ray thought. He said, 'Whether he hides or runs, Cobb needs help. If such a group of paedophiles exists now and Cobb is their waiter, will they help him?'

'Almost certainly. They all have so much to lose. And the secrecy that binds them together is very powerful.' She paused. 'Do you want to tell me where you're going with this?'

Ray repeated what Sayyed had told him.

'And do you have any idea who might belong to such a circle?'

He hesitated. 'Not yet.'

'Nothing concrete?'

'No.'

'My advice to you,' Maisie said, 'while you investigate, is to keep an open mind. Don't jump to conclusions. There's nothing harder to shake than a false impression of someone. But keep it in play. Test it. Test it out with other people. We all have instincts.'

Finally Ray turned to Cobb. What was his state of mind likely to be at present?

It wasn't so obvious as it might seem, Maisie said. He would be terrified, of course, desperate not to get caught and go back to prison. Yet there might be powerful counter-feelings at work: a subconscious desire to confess and be punished. At the same time a strong sense of injustice, bitterness and a desire to prove himself cleverer than those trying to catch him. Above all, he would be agitated, probably finding it difficult to remain in control of himself. Excited even.

'Is there any danger he might attack again?'

'You asked me that before. I still think it's unlikely but he'll be more volatile now. It's much harder to predict what he'll do. What do you think?'

Ray tried to think himself into Cobb. 'He's scared,' he said at last. 'Dependent on the help of others. He knows how big the operation is to find him. I think his focus will be on escape.'

They sat in silence.

'I guess we just don't know, do we?' Maisie said.

And as she spoke, a little girl, three years old, was skipping along the railings outside St Swithun's school in Kennington. She was on her own because her cousin was staying for after-school club, as he sometimes did. She was laughing, pirouetting every so often to see if she was still being watched. Sometimes she was, sometimes she wasn't, which is why the game was such fun. Best of all, she was wearing the pirate costume which her cousin didn't want any more; she could feel the ribbons whisking her hair and her black jacket swishing round her. She was doubly excited because her secret friend hadn't been at school for a few days. And now, suddenly, here he was. With her very best jumps, she went along the railings to the end and waited there, getting her breath back, peering hard at the row of parked cars opposite, but he didn't reappear, and she was wondering if she should go just a little way across the pavement in order to have a better view when she noticed her mother standing next to her.

'Where did you get those from?' Jade said.

Mylee instinctively put the sweets behind her back. Black Jacks: her favourites. It was her experience that adults took sweets off you if they could.

'Inside,' she said, which cleverly covered a number of possibilities.

Her mother had her hard face on, but as usual she had no time to have a proper conversation, and the next moment, Mylee was being rushed along the road towards home. As she went, she twisted round to try to see her friend. But he had gone, and she would have to wait till next time.

THIRTY-ONE

At eight o'clock in the evening the phone rang and Diane answered it, thinking it would be Ray. But it was his father. As usual, he asked a few perfunctory questions about her condition before asking to speak to Ray, and, when she said that he wasn't there, rang off almost immediately; and she sat on the sofa with the phone in her hand, wondering where Ray was. He had come in from work at six, eaten a sandwich in the spare room and gone out again at about seven without saying why. She felt tired and anxious. There was a cramping pain that came and went in her belly and a weary, aching pain in her lower back and a third pain high up in her chest, slow and burning, and she sat there blaming Ray for all of them.

Five miles away, in Ros Kerr's studio, Ray accepted a drink. The studio was part of an old furniture factory in Jericho, a concrete-floored room under two high roof lanterns supported by whitewashed metal girders, lit now in the twilight by old-fashioned fluorescent tubes. The walls were whitewashed too, bare but for plumbing pipes and ventilation grilles, and at one end was a vast corrugated-metal roller door. Clutter impinged – piles of paint-stained bedsheets, a tailor's dummy, a suitcase, a rocking-horse – and at the far side, like a children's home corner, was a sofa, table and primitive cooker. What dominated the space, though, were the two industrial-scale easels under the lanterns with vast paintings standing on them, figurative designs as colourful and obvious as cartoons but dislocated in outline, broken into planes and panels to form kaleidoscopic patterns half recognisable, half impossible to make sense of, glimpses of things among the coloured shapes: a woman's face, a hand holding a snake, a shoe dangling from an elegant foot, a horned man's face thrust downwards into the folds of a toga. Behind the figures were nonsense words, jokes perhaps or unintelligible cries of pain.

'Cassandra,' Ros said. 'You're familiar?'

She was wearing loose army trousers and a khaki T-shirt. Her hair was tied up revealing the pale, erotic nape of her neck. There were smears and crumbs of paint on one of her cheeks. Ignoring the huge canvas, she moved in front of it with a carelessness that Ray tried hard not to find provocative.

'Not really. Something classical?'

She smiled. 'Very good. Princess of Troy. Cursed to speak true prophecies and have no one believe her.'

Ray looked up at the picture. A mass of flames that might be hair. A screaming mouth. An exposed breast, heavy, dark-tipped.

'What happened to her?'

She waved a hand. 'Oh, you know. Captured, enslaved and raped by Agamemnon. Killed by his wife Clytemnestra. Her children butchered. It's not Disney.'

213

She gestured at the sofa and they went to sit, and she looked at him, smiling, her head propped on one hand. 'I wasn't sure you'd come,' she said after a moment. 'Or why,' she added. Her smile lengthened and her white teeth came into view, shining.

For a moment Ray couldn't think of the answer; his mind was full of her face. Collecting his thoughts, he told her that he had a few questions.

'Am I a suspect?'

'No.'

She was still smiling. 'You're just building up a picture, is that it?' Her voice was teasing.

Some people bridle at the thought of questions, others turn nervous; he could tell by the look she gave him that she had decided to treat their conversation as a game. It made him wary. But there was something else too, a prickling excitement, something to do with the twilight, the paintings, the way she looked at him, her army trousers. A feeling he hadn't had for years.

'If you like. Our suspect was at your property for a few hours on the morning of the murder.'

She just smiled. 'Oh, I think we both know why you're really here.'

Their eyes met. 'Do we?'

'You want me to talk to you about Tom.'

Taken aback, he began to justify himself.

She interrupted. 'That's all right. I don't mind. I get it: he was this man's mentor. Perhaps,' she said, 'I'll even find it therapeutic.'

Livvy had given Ray some background on Fothergill and Baby Dynamic. The company was a tremendous success, an exemplary

214

fable of entrepreneurship: in twenty years he had transformed a failing bicycle business into the leading European manufacturer of pushchairs, regularly posting record profits. Fothergill himself had a reputation as a savvy, energetic, enterprising man, noted for his risk-taking, his philanthropy, donations to both political parties and his persistent refusal to allow his workforce to unionise.

But Ray began by asking about Cobb. Ros had never met him; she rarely met Tom's mentees.

'He's mentored a lot of men over the years.'

'If you say so. He takes that sort of thing very seriously.'

'What sort of thing?'

'You know. Doing good.' Something came across her face as she said it but it was too quick for Ray to catch.

Ray changed tack. 'He also does good in local education.'

'Yes, he's very keen on that.'

'A trustee at Magpies, and a major investor. Any other nurseries or schools he's involved in?'

'St Swithun's, our local state primary. He's a governor there.'

'Where does all this interest in education come from?'

She turned her face away and ran her fingers through her hair while she thought about it, and he watched her profile, so clear-edged and delicate, chin lifted, lips slightly parted.

'Beyond the obvious, I think it may have something to do with his own childhood. You know he was brought up in care?'

'He mentioned it. A painful experience?'

She was looking at him now with a wry smile. 'You don't know him. There are no painful experiences in Tom's life. None he'd admit to anyway. He's always made the best of everything. I

215

don't ever remember him telling me he felt unhappy.' She gave a mock sigh. 'It's very depressing.'

Ray held her eyes. 'What about your son?'

She smiled again. 'Ah, you do pay attention. Yes, that's a difficult relationship. He's not my son, by the way. His mother was Tom's first wife, who committed suicide. But Jack, yes. He's at that age, having difficulty finding himself. He has issues, actually. He's doing all right, bits of work experience here and there. He's sort of holding down a job at the moment, part-time. A barista. To be honest, I think they just let him clear the tables and sweep the floor. It's not exactly what Tom hoped he'd be doing. Not after such an expensive education. I don't get involved. Parenting is Tom's thing. But you're right, it's the one area of his life where he struggles. He can get a bit . . .'

Ray remembered the shout of fury he had heard in the house, and the cry of distress.

'Frustrated?'

'How tactful you are, Ray. Are you sure you're really a detective? What have you done with all your tough-cop brutality?' Again, that smile, that probing look.

'What makes you think I'm brutal?'

Even as he said it, he felt a little lurch in his stomach, a prickle of excitement, familiar and enticing – almost forgotten sensations coming back to him, the snap and ripple in the alert nerves, the quiet whoosh of the body coming to life. He remembered it now and relaxed into it. Handsome Ray. Perhaps, he thought, this was really why he had come. He was sick of people looking at him as if he was a failure, a disappointment. What he wanted was for someone to look at him with a little appreciation – there was

216

no harm in that – to feel that look in his gut – and elsewhere – as he could feel her looking at him now, her expression veiled, ambivalent, intriguing. He couldn't even tell what colour her eyes were; the light in them flickered and they changed.

'It's because he loves him so much,' she said and for a moment Ray wondered who she was talking about. 'He's a very protective father,' she added.

When she got up to fetch another drink he noticed again how supple she was, how carelessly she moved.

'Are you finding these questions intrusive?' he asked when she returned.

'No. I'm surprised they're not more intrusive. Frankly, there are many more intimate things I could tell you about Tom.'

She held his eyes.

'Like what?' His mouth was dry.

She left a long pause as her eyes explored his, then looked away. 'For a long time I didn't get Tom at all. Then the thought came to me: this is a man who has had to learn everything – the sorts of things that come naturally to others. How to read people, how to talk to them, and so on.'

'How to be normal?'

'More than normal. In the last few years he's learned how to shoot, how to fly. He's won medals in fifty-metre pistol competitions. He has his own plane. Perhaps you've seen pictures of it. Small thing, two-seater something or other. Has the Baby Dynamic logo all over it.'

'I'll look out for it.'

'It's the same in business. He's such a great learner. Asks lots of questions, thinks hard, works things out. Takes risks but he's always calm – and the risks always come off. He's good at com-partmentalising, keeping parts of the picture separate. It works. The thing is, Ray, he's successful at almost everything he does.'

He expected a laugh but it didn't come. In fact, she sounded weary, almost disappointed. Getting up suddenly, she walked towards one of her broken Cassandras, showing him her gym-nastic ease, her wonderful, lucid profile, and he watched her, wondering what her skin would feel like, her hair, the weight of her breasts.

He said, 'Do you know where he was during the afternoon of the day Cobb came to set up the archery targets?'

She turned. 'No.'

'But he wasn't at home.'

'If that's what he says. But I don't know. He has his own rooms at the other side of the house.' A pause. 'The truth is, Ray, we lead fairly separate lives. And I have my work.'

She walked back towards him and stood in front of him, hands on her hips, almost close enough for him to reach out and touch her, and there was a moment when Ray did not know what would happen next or what he himself might do; and then she laughed and the spell was broken.

'Do you think I'm flirting with you, Ray?'

'No.'

'How do you know?'

'You haven't asked to see my police badge or try on my Ray-Bans. That's what usually happens.'

She laughed again, suddenly girlish. 'Perhaps next time. Which picture do you prefer, by the way?'

'The one with the flames.'

'And the exposed bosom. That's the one all men choose. Perhaps you're flirting with me.'

'I don't know how to flirt any more.'

'Some people never forget.' She was escorting him out, he realised.

'Come again,' she said, 'and I'll show you some more of my paintings and you can show me your police badge.' She left him with a touch of her fingertips on his bare arm, so light and fierce it almost burned.

THIRTY-TWO

Elsewhere, Ryan was being roughly frisked.

In the flat Oxfordshire farmland, under a muddy agricultural sky, at the edge of the ordinary hamlet of Spring Hill HMP Grendon sits behind its perimeter fence like a cross between a Travelodge and a concentration camp. An unusual prison, it offers bespoke therapy to serious offenders who can't cope with the system elsewhere. A high proportion of its inmates are lifers: murderers, rapists, arsonists, child molesters. All of them have been referred from other prisons, where it seemed likely they would eventually kill someone or else themselves. For them, Grendon is their last chance.

Ryan had parked the Peugeot against the long front fence and sat there for several minutes breathing to calm himself. It would be the first time he had seen his father since his appearance in court. Flashes of the incident at the trailer park came back to him and he had to force his mind away from them, to empty himself of images, to look up at the fence and see only the fence, at the night sky, its harmless dark clouds, before he could get out of his car and walk to the entrance and give himself up to the security procedures. His was a special visit, out of hours; Dr Tompkins had set it up. It turned out she had connections.

I can do this, he said to himself. He didn't believe it.

He was escorted slowly inside, from air-lock to air-lock, through sets of metal gates and electronic doors. Under constant camera surveillance, he followed the routine. He presented his ID, and waited, and moved on. He gave up his phone and cigarettes, and waited for a receipt, and moved on.

And now, in the last holding area, he was being frisked by a guy who recognised him from school. Bullhead or Bully or something. He was short and stumpy with a large forehead. Friendly, crude, rough-handed.

'Only visiting? Used to think you was the sort of guy'd end up in a place like this.'

He had a short yelp of a laugh like a fox bark.

'Yeah, cheers. Always thought you'd end up a brain surgeon.'

There was a wait for another escort and they got talking. Bullhead remembered Mick Dick.

'Lovely guy. Real sweetie. Course, he wouldn't have been in here if there wasn't something wrong. You know, upstairs. Took out a warden at Huntercombe, broke both his arms, I heard. Self-harm, the usual. But here. Calmed down lovely. Everybody loved him here.'

'What about a guy called Cobb? Shane Cobb.'

'The nonce? Oh yes. No one liked him.'

Ryan thought about that. 'Everyone knew he was a nonce?'

'Course. Soon as he got transferred here. Had a rough time inside, I'll be honest with you. And look what he's done now.

221

How old was she? Four? You know what? Don't like saying it but. I hope someone fucking well kills him.'

He stepped away to perform the unlocking procedure. Ryan thought about Cobb. He'd read the file that Ray had let him see. A man with no friends virtually all his life.

Bullhead held open the gates for him.

Ryan said, 'Did Mick Dick get any grief for looking out for Cobb?'

The warden looked at him, puzzled. 'Don't know what you're talking about. Mick didn't like him any better than anyone else.'

Almost immediately Ryan had another surprise. His escort told him they were going over to the Acute Psychiatric Unit.

'Why?'

'That's where your dad is.'

'What for?'

'That's where all the inmates with serious mental health problems are.'

Now he noticed how like a hospital this part of the prison was, its narrow corridors, its green-washed walls and old-fashioned radiators, its neatly labelled doors, *Unfurnished Room*, *Day Centre*, *Prescriptions*. Bespectacled staff in white coats with multiple pens in their top pockets went to and fro. Men in tracksuit bottoms and knitted jumpers stood here and there gazing into the far distance. Somewhere out of sight, very badly, someone was singing 'Always Look on the Bright Side of Life'.

'What's the matter with Dad?' he asked and got no answer. He was taken through a door labelled *Visits Hall* into a small, square room filled with low tables and dining chairs, the walls

222

decorated with prisoner artworks, competent pictures of horses and cars in watercolours and oils. There was no one else there. He breathed in the antiseptic smell and sat down to wait.

After ten minutes or so the door opened again and a tiny, hunched man dressed in pyjamas came in. His monkeyish head was totally bald, his features pinched and twisted out of shape. He came slowly across the room in stiff, gristly steps and when he got close, Ryan realised with a shock that it was his father. The hulking brute of his childhood reduced to this scrap of a man old and frail.

They sat facing each other.

Ryan should have rehearsed how to begin. Faced by this stick figure with the ruined face, nothing came to mind and he sat staring.

His father moved his mouth slightly. 'One visit in all the time I been here. One lousy fucking visit. And it has to be you.'

It was the most he had said to his son for years. His voice a wet gasp.

Ryan nearly got up and left. He breathed slowly, kept his eyes on his father's face, made himself calm. 'What you doing in here?'

'Three to five.'

'I mean here, in this unit.'

His father only sneered.

'Thought you were meant to be in Huntercombe, anyway.'

He let out a short dribble of laughter. 'Those cunts,' he said and fell quiet again.

Ryan kept patient. 'What cunts?'

'At Huntercombe.'

'What happened?'

'What happened? I said I want a change of job, 'cause I wasn't feeling right. It was doing my head in. Didn't listen to me, did he? Didn't fucking listen. Only time he listened to me was when I took the stapler and stapled his nose. Cunt listened then.'

'Okay. Smooth. What next?'

'They come for me, didn't they? Twelve-handed, whatever, shields, night sticks, everything they got, throw me in the fucking strong box. Kneeling on me, on my arms, here, blowing smoke in my face. I said you can't beat me, you cunts. So they put me in a body belt. Thing down here, you know, can't move your fucking arms. I said you can't beat me, you cunts. Meds up the arse, liquid cosh, whatever. I took a shit and I spread it all over with my feet. Then it was the ankle straps. I said you can't . . .' He began to shake slightly. He gathered the last of his breath. 'Then they put me on the quarter hour watch,' he whispered and his voice went out.

'The quarter hour? Why?'

No answer.

'You telling me you tried to kill yourself?'

For a long time his father kept quiet. 'I had a modelling knife,' he said at last. There was a different note in his voice, something Ryan had never heard before, shame perhaps, or fear.

There was a long silence after that.

'Don't drink any more,' he said.

'Course you don't, you're not allowed.'

Another long silence. His father seemed to go to sleep with his eyes open, and Ryan watched him. All the long violent years shrunk down to this stick of a man, this tattered face, these skinny arms, these bony fists. Ryan remembered his childhood fear, the feeling he always had when his father got up from his chair, as he took off his belt. He didn't feel it any more. What did he feel? Slight disgust. He started to get to his feet.

His father said, 'We were all right once.' He didn't look at Ryan, didn't seem to be speaking to him. His voice a sort of slow, agitated mutter. 'First thing was the children. The boy. Ten, eleven. Couldn't do nothing with him. Then the job went. Fucked over big time. Got the Poles in, half the wages. Took drink.' Ryan made a little scoffing noise; his father corrected himself. 'Took drink worse than before. The rage got in me, see.' It was as if he was repeating something he'd said to a psychiatrist. He fell silent. 'After that? Don't know, can't remember. There are years, whole fucking years, can't remember a thing.'

Ryan had had enough.

But now his father looked at him in his old way, sharp and nasty. 'It's you should be in here, not me. Assault. Grievous bodily. You only got off 'cause of the badge.'

Ryan opened his mouth and closed it again. No point. This almost-stranger, tiny, beaten man had lost his power to frighten him.

'You abducted my son,' Ryan said calmly.

His father moved his head from side to side. 'You always were a cry-baby.'

It was such a childish thing to say, Ryan almost laughed and his father looked up and began to laugh himself.

'You're different,' he said.

'Don't be stupid.'

'How's your mother?'

'Better off without you.'

They settled into silence again, but peaceable.

'Ask you something before I go?'

His father looked at him warily.

'Was there a guy called Cobb here when you arrived?'

'The nonce? Not in the unit but out there, yeah. Didn't have nothing to do with him. No one did. Only man in the whole of the nick never had any visitors.'

'You've not had any till now.'

'Never mind that. No visitors for this Cobb. Official visits only, that's all he had.'

Ryan looked away, at the prisoner artwork, the horses galloping on the beaches, the country cottages. Faint noises came from the corridor, men talking quietly to each other. 'What official visits?' he said at last.

His father made a dismissive gesture. 'Outside guy used to come in, some scheme, I don't know. Came in for some of the others too.'

'Hear his name?'

His father thought about that. 'There was a thing about his name. What was it? He'd been given it by the state or something, and when he grew up he changed it. But some of the men here, they knew his old name, they used to tease him about it.'

'What was it?'

'Don't remember.'

'Remember anything about him?'

'No. Dressed nice. That's it.'

A man in a white coat put his head round the door. It was time to go.

226

His father began to tremble.

'What is it? Do you need your meds?'

His father's face bunched, unbunched. 'Will you come again? If I'm still here.'

'Don't know. Maybe.'

Now his father was crying, a strange sight Ryan had never seen before, his face quivering, yellow eyes leaking, and he turned away quickly and went across the room. As he reached the door his father called out, and he reluctantly turned back.

'That name,' his father said. 'I've remembered it.'

Ryan walked back into the room.

THIRTY-THREE

Another night passed, another day, without developments, the passing hours measured only by news bulletins, reliable outlets of fear, stories which, with nothing to report, turned angrily on the private lives of those involved, exclusives on the heartbreak of the father suspended from the John Radcliffe Hospital after an 'incident' with a colleague, recreational drug use of the mother who had negligently let her mind wander at the moment when her daughter needed her most, the nursery manager who, it turned out, had been dismissed from a previous post eight years earlier for poor time-keeping. There was even a story on the senior investigating officer Detective Inspector Ray Wilkins – pictured walking wearily from his car in Grove Street – shortly to become a father but racked with guilt, the writer said, by the many mistakes he had made, by his persistent failure to apprehend little Poppy's murderer.

Who sat alone and undisturbed elsewhere, waiting. He had his backpack with him; he was wearing jeans and a plain grey hooded top, to blend in, for he was nothing if not methodical. Besides, he liked to blend in. From time to time he checked his watch. He was frightened too, of course. Oxford was so small, so talkative, people noticed you, tried to look into you, to see who you really were; but he had always been good at hiding inside himself, waiting for the right moment. That was the important thing: to recognise the moment when it arrived. He had always been good at that too. Besides, he had someone to help him - someone who would not let him down.

He looked at his watch again. The afternoon was lengthening, slowing down, he could feel it softly collapsing around him; soon the playground bells of schools would ring and it would be home time, the city would forget itself, the moment would arrive and he would go. It was close already, he could feel it inside him, like a tremor or an urge. He began to check his backpack again.

Ray also sat alone, in a coffee shop at the bottom of St Aldates. He'd stepped out for a moment to clear his head, to put some space between himself and the concentrated activity in the station. Five hours earlier they'd had a sighting of Cobb: he'd been caught on camera at the Oxford Camping and Caravanning Club at the end of the Abingdon Road, grainy but intelligible footage showing him coming out of the Go Outdoors store next to the site. It was certainly Cobb. Wearing jeans and a hooded top, carrying a new backpack, which he appeared to have just purchased, he came through the door and walked quickly away from the store towards the main road. They did not know where he was now.

Ray sat with his coffee, thinking.

Although the images had been too approximate, too

pixel-watery, to convey Cobb's expression, Ray had sensed the fugitive's anxiety. He surely knew that he was running out of time. For the last few days the police had been steadily working their way through all the likely places where he might be hiding, all the houses and hostels whose addresses they had shaken out of local sex offenders in the latest round of interviews, the hotels and bed and breakfasts, the guest houses, the rooms rented by the day or hour, the safe houses and doss houses, the hideaways under bridges along the river and dens under sheets of tarpaulin sheeting strung up by vagrants at the side of the canal. The sighting of Cobb with a bag at Go Outdoors confirmed Ray's belief: he was about to run.

Manpower had been increased as a direct result of an intervention by the Home Office. In the last few hours they'd trebled the police presence in the city centre: patrols were set up everywhere. At the same time they were continuing to monitor all the rolling cameras. Above all, they were watching the public transport hubs: Gloucester Green bus station, the railway station, the taxi ranks. Any moment now, Ray thought. He should get back to the station. Finishing his coffee, he glanced round. In a place just like this, perhaps, Cobb was sitting with his bag packed, ready to make his move. He got to his feet. At the other side of the cafe a young man in an apron was wanly sweeping the floor and after a moment Ray recognised Jack Fothergill. As before, the boy was a silent, almost insubstantial presence, a sort of gloom clinging to him, his lank black hair, his pinched expression. As Ray watched, he turned briefly to empty his pan into a bin and Ray saw that the other side of his face was one long discoloured bruise from

230

eye to mouth. Then the boy turned away again and walked towards the toilets, taking off his apron.

Back at the station Ray could feel the high-wire tension. Even in his office, to which he had retreated earlier from the main incident room, F6, he could feel it. He sat at his desk, massaged his neck for a moment, took stock. In front of him were six empty plastic coffee cups from the morning; he did not remember drinking them. Updates from the surveillance teams were coming in constantly; he checked and evaluated them, adjusting the picture in his mind. In their offices along the corridor, Livvy and Nadim were also co-ordinating information flows. He was the ultimate focus, though, the pressure-point of decision-making. Occasionally, he picked up the phone and asked someone a question or told them to change what they were doing, then went back to the pictures, charts and tables on his screen. The tension of his concentration was acute – a man balancing on a wire hour after hour – and he was tired, but he felt, perhaps superstitiously, that if he could only persist without a rest for a little while longer, he would succeed.

Time passed.

Sometimes his mind wandered; he caught himself thinking about other things, that bruise on Jack Fothergill's face, for instance; he remembered the roar of his father's anger in the quiet house. What to make of the coincidence of Fothergill being with Cobb that day or his mentoring of all the other sex offenders? Earlier in the day the Super had called Ray into his office and demanded to know why Livvy was asking questions about Fothergill. Ray knew he didn't have enough to go on;

231

halfway through his explanation, Wallace had interrupted to inform him that Fothergill was the main private backer of new infrastructure of the Hub and, moreover, a personal friend of the Chief Constable. So he'd noted Ray's concerns but told him not to pursue any lines of enquiry involving Fothergill without further consultation.

To the team, Ray said only that Cobb was a loner and might need help. 'Someone to lend him a room, someone to buy him a ticket, someone to organise transport. Keep it in mind.'

From time to time, particularly as his energy levels dropped, Ray thought of his father, childish thoughts, imagining the elderly man keeping watch over him, judging him as he used to do in his childhood, giving his grudging approval or clicking his tongue with disappointment. And sometimes the image of Ros Kerr appeared to him, like a figure in a movie, playing a part, her gestures and expressions excitingly ambiguous. He did not think of Diane, though in fact it was her who rang him at a little after seven o'clock.

'Where are you?'

'Work.'

'Are you coming home?'

'No.'

It was the first time they had spoken since the previous evening when he got home from Ros Kerr's studio. He was abrupt.

'Last night, Ray.'

'I can't talk now.'

'Where were you?'

'I told you, I can't talk about the investigation.'

'Are you lying to me?'

'Diane, I can't have this conversation now.'

'Is that what you're doing, lying?'

'I can't deal with it.'

'I know you, Ray.'

'Do you?' He sounded harsher than he intended. 'Do you even know what I'm doing now, here, in the office?'

'I'm talking about *us*.'

'I'm trying to direct—'

'Us, Ray. You have to think about us too.'

'You don't understand. This is the endgame, I can't let go. I've got the Super breathing down my neck, I've got—'

'You've got us, Ray. You've got me, our babies. You have to work with us too.'

'I don't do anything but work.'

'Not just your work. *Our* work too.'

He could hear her becoming hysterical.

'In the end it's always about you, Ray. Not about me. Not about your children. We talked about this.'

'You don't even seem to realise what I'm doing.'

'I need *you*. We need you.'

'Listen, you have to—'

'When you're at home.'

'I can't be at home. This is ridiculous.'

'You have to work at your relationships too, Ray.'

'So do you.'

As soon as he said it he wished he hadn't. There was a pause in which he could hear her scratchy breathing.

She said in a rush, 'You should ask yourself why you don't have any friends.'

Then she rang off and he sat staring at his phone.

Livvy came running down the corridor and into his office.

'Got a sighting. City centre. Feed's up in F6.'

He ran back down the corridor with her.

F6, originally a kitchen and storeroom, had been converted to house the main monitoring campaigns: screens and keyboards on desks for the grunts, home-cinema-type screens mounted on the front walls for the directors. Like everything else at St Aldates, it looked improvised and temporary. In one corner was a disconnected sink. Livvy's and Nadim's teams were already there, hooked up to the on-site tech. After a moment the Super came in, a quiet but over-large presence. Ray put on headphones and took control.

On the middle giant screen was a foreshortened view from a camera at the corner of Market Street, showing Cornmarket below, one of the main pedestrianised streets in the centre of town, a bleakly featureless shopping strip. Pedestrians flowed silently in both directions in front of the stores. There were two fixed points: a man in a jacket and tie standing with a microphone in front of a poster advertising Jesus, and, opposite him, a wild-haired busker sitting on a crate with his guitar. Everyone else was moving, north or south, along the street, the ordinary, anonymous shopper flow, subdued and innocent.

'Where is he?'

'Went into the Clarendon Centre a couple of minutes ago.'

'Officers in place?'

'At the exit on Queen Street.'

'What about the other one? Shoe Lane.'

'Arriving in five.'

'Needs to be quicker.'

'On it.'

'Show me what we got.'

On one of the adjacent screens appeared a close-up image of a man in Cornmarket, recorded a few minutes earlier. He was wearing jeans and a grey hooded top and a backpack. At Ray's instruction they ran the footage backwards and forwards a few times, and as the man was crossing to the Clarendon Centre entrance he briefly turned to look back at the busker and they saw that it was unmistakably Cobb. On another screen the Go Outdoors image appeared for comparison: the match of clothing and backpack was perfect. Visuals had gone to the officers on the ground.

'He's our boy,' the Super said softly. 'But where's he gone?'

'News from Queen Street?'

'No sign of him.'

'What about Shoe Lane?'

'In position now.'

'Eyes on the target?'

'Nothing.'

Another team moved into place and Ray instructed them inside the shopping centre to sweep the shops. After a few minutes they reported no sighting.

'Looks like he got through.'

Ray swore softly.

'Where's he going, Ray?' the Super asked.

'Nadim. All cameras within two hundred yards.'

'Already up, front row.'

Camera views showed scenes of a functional modern Oxford squatting in the middle of the medieval town, an Oxford drained of heritage glamour, crowded roads, bin-lined alleys, the blank brick sides of shopping centres.

No Cobb.

Ray said, 'West out of Shoe Lane, he'll be heading through Bonn Square towards the railway station. Images.'

Nadim put up the camera views. Clumsy circle of buses and taxis; smokers sitting on steps; people flowing through ticket barriers into the stationary crowd of the concourse. No sign of Cobb. Ray alerted the officers already there.

The Super made growling noises. 'Come on, people, this is Oxford, you can't find a smaller city centre. How can we lose him? Ray! Where's he going?'

'If he turns up New Inn Hall Street, he's heading to Gloucester Green bus station.'

More images appeared: buses blocking a narrow entrance; indistinct figures queuing under fixed awnings; empty stretch of railings.

No Cobb.

Ray directed more officers into position. The room went quiet for a minute. No reports came in.

'Ray, where is he?'

Ray said in desperation, 'Give me the cameras at the railway station again. And Park End Street.'

Bare pavement, a bridge, a brick facade, a passing double-decker.

No Cobb.

'George Street,' he said.

236

Thronging passers-by, idlers in the entrance to the plaza, wheeling pigeons badly synced with their shadows below. Three officers stood watching from the doorway of the penny arcade. Nothing to report.

'We've lost him,' the Super said. 'Jesus fucking Christ.'

Silence fell in the crowded room.

Turning, he saw the police officers arriving at Shoe Lane. Luckily, he was already down the street, about to turn off, out of sight. But it frightened him. Hurrying along, not looking back, he expected to hear a shout from behind at any moment. He had a vision of himself breaking into a useless knock-kneed run, suddenly flung down onto the asphalt, all the breath thumped out of him, feebly resisting as a crowd gathered round to watch his humiliation. It would be fitting, he thought bitterly. He had known very little but humiliation; with a shudder he remembered what the men at Grendon had done to him, on the floor of his cell, a group of them standing in the doorway to listen to him plead and beg. In front of a grandiose facade he paused for breath, hands on his knees, scanning the street behind and ahead. No policemen, only some tourists sat at tables on the street, a cross-legged homeless man bundled in a blanket and, beyond, a couple browsing a cafe window. He crept along again. Up ahead people were going up and down past the end of the street. If he could get among them, he would be almost there, almost free. He felt the shudder of his heart and wondered where his pills were, but it was too late for that and, taking a breath, he slunk into the throng of people and began to work his way through them.

★

In F6 the Super said, 'Okay, okay. We're pissing in the wrong pocket here. Ray? Talk to me. If he's not going for rail or bus, where's he running?'

Ray stood there in the crowded room as everyone turned to him. For a moment there was nothing in his mind. For some terrible reason, in the hush he seemed to hear Diane's voice telling him that he had to think of others, that he had to work at relationships, that he had no friends. It came to him with horrible certainty that she was right. He glanced round and everyone was looking at him as if they had just realised it too. Then something sparked, a thought from nowhere, and he found his voice again.

'Cobb's friend,' he croaked.

The Super was staring at him. 'The kid who disappeared?'

'The cabbie.' He cleared his throat, spoke rapidly. 'Ahmed el-Baz, testified on Cobb's behalf in his trial. Is he working today? What rank does he work from?'

They scrambled. Two minutes later Nadim had pulled his cab's registration out of the DVLA database and Livvy had his usual rank from his agency. El-Baz was on shift. All eyes swivelled to St Giles, where he would be.

'Camera?'

A view of the junction at the Martyrs' Memorial sprang onto the screens: backpackers lounging with their sandwiches round the monument; a sedate stone corner of the Ashmolean, fussy brick corner of the Randolph Hotel. And, a little way up St Giles, a short line of taxis.

'There!' Ray couldn't help himself shouting.

There were four cabs. Three of the drivers were standing talking together on the strip of central reservation; the fourth, a large Arab man recognisable as Ahmed el-Baz, was taking a backpack off his new fare – a man wearing jeans and a grey hooded top.

'Bingo,' the Super said in a soft voice. 'Brief the chopper. Good work, Ray. Off you go.'

Ray had gone already, running with Livvy towards the sally port.

Now, at last, Cobb relaxed. Sitting low in his seat, he watched Oxford drift backwards against the traffic. He was on his way. The Victorian gothic villas of Banbury Road waved goodbye, the shops at Summertown wished him good luck. Soon it would be over.

They made visual contact at the roundabout at the top of the Woodstock Road, where the A40 exits the city westward through farmland towards Cheltenham. But el-Baz's cab crossed over towards the A34, the main north–south route.

Ray sat in the lead car with his driver, eyes fixed ahead, speaking continually to Livvy in the second car and the spotter in the helicopter somewhere above Kidlington, far enough away to avoid alarming the fugitive. The Super was in his ear, wanting a running commentary. They'd agreed to trail Cobb to his destination, where they might find others like el-Baz engaged in helping Cobb to escape.

At the juncture with the A34, the cab again went over the roundabout. It was a surprise.

'He's not taking the bypass. He's heading towards Woodstock.'

'Any contacts he has out there?'

'None that I know of.'

Then they were in the countryside. Driving slowly, they passed Yarnton with its fields of solar panels, haulage yards and poultry farms, and went on at a sedate pace through flat acres packed with crops. The sky opened up. Begbroke was ahead, shadowy housing behind a screen of trees, a church tower and an over-worked mini-roundabout. A hundred yards behind el-Baz's taxi, they passed over the roundabout in formation and hit the long curve of road that led to Woodstock, wide spaces now on either side of the road and, above, the big sky with nothing to be seen in it except a toylike plane coming in overhead.

'Close in a little when we get into Woodstock,' Ray told the driver. 'We don't want to lose him in the traffic.'

But they did not get to Woodstock because el-Baz's cab took the next turn.

'What's he doing?' Livvy asked. 'Is he going back to Kidlington?'

There was a short silence from Ray. A feeling grew in him. He said, 'I know where he's going and I know why.'

El-Baz's cab drove along Langford Lane across the Oxfordshire flatlands almost as far as Kidlington, then turned into a boule-vard of scrawny trees, between car parks and business premises, towards the entrance to the London Oxford Airport.

The airport was a miniature, one runway, a few sheds, a large field under the wide sky. For years a pilot-training centre, it had recently rebranded itself as the bijou airport of choice for celebrity arrivals into the UK – with a special VIP service for pets – and a base for private flyers. Beyond the sheds Ray could see the fuselage and wing tip of a plane, also miniature.

The Super's voice said, 'Ray?'

Ray said, 'Eyes out for a two-seater with the Baby Dynamic logo.'

A pause. 'Where are you going with this, Ray?'

The spotter in the helicopter came on the radio. 'Target south of the buildings. Waiting on the taxi path to the runway. Looks like it's ready to go.'

Ray said, 'It's Fothergill. He's flying Cobb out of the country.'

There was a short silence after this.

The Super said, 'Are we sure about this?'

'What else could it be?'

There was a pause, five seconds, ten. Wallace's voice came back. 'All right, then. Don't move till our man's boarding. Bring them both in.' Everyone could hear him breathing heavily. 'No fuck-ups.'

El-Baz's cab waited at a checkpoint; the barrier went up and it pulled through, beyond the last shed, out of sight. The two police vehicles quietly drew up in turn; the barrier lifted again, they went on slowly in silence, nosing round the shed, until the runway appeared in front of them. Fanned out in a row were a dozen small planes, all facing the same way, as if for a photo opportunity. Fifty metres to their left, el-Baz's cab had stopped on the tarmac. A hundred metres further on, with its door open, airstairs down already, the Baby Dynamic plane sat waiting, all logo, a giant baby's face cushioned on familiar lettering, bright against the dirty green of the long hedge beyond.

There was a sudden bird-twitter of voices on the radio: armed back-up arriving, vans being deployed to the north and south, pulling without fuss into position behind sheds and hangars.

Ray gave the instructions to wait and the radio ceased to crackle. There was silence in the car and, all around them, a waiting stillness over the whole scene, over the stationary planes, the long runway, the wide, empty field. It was a stage set before a performance begins. No one appeared on the steps of the Baby Dynamic plane, no one got out of el-Baz's cab.

Minutes passed.

'What's he doing in there? What's going on?'

Nothing was going on. They were stuck in a long moment of nothing. Ray could almost hear the faint whisper of breeze across the grass ahead. And in that quiet he was intensely aware of himself. A thought drifted into his mind: he was alone. No friends. No Diane, no twins. No Super, no Ryan. No father. Only himself in those few seconds of anticipation when, it seemed to him, his whole career was improbably balanced, like a large boulder he had seen once as a child in Nigeria balanced on a tiny stone. But he was calm. Everything was in place. Everything was going to work out.

He watched as the back door of the cab opened.

'Target on the move.'

His calm voice echoed in his head.

Cobb was holding his backpack but now he was also wearing an aviation helmet. That's what he had been doing in the cab all this time. The helmet made his large head appear even larger, like a child's. At the same moment, beyond, a figure appeared at the top of the airstairs of the small plane, Tom Fothergill, also wearing a helmet, pointing at his watch, making hurrying-up gestures, which were ignored.

Cobb dawdled at his own pace towards the plane.

242

'Not yet,' Ray said in a quiet, restraining voice. 'Not yet.'

Silently he willed Fothergill to descend the stairs to meet Cobb on the tarmac; it would give them a much cleaner strike. And, as he watched, it happened. Just as he wanted, Fothergill came down the steps and began to walk out along the tarmac. It was the second sign that it was all going to work out. The room for error was vanishing.

Now the two figures were twenty metres apart. Now ten.

Ray shouted.

The stage set buckled, its scenery came apart. Police vans crashed into it from several directions at once, tyres squealing, sirens screaming. Bulky men in black armed with submachine guns ran like quarterbacks to muscle themselves into position, kneeling, pointing. The helicopter plunged out of the sky like a fairground ride, with a high-pitched grinding of rotary blades. And through this orchestrated chaos Ray strode calmly with his loudhailer, articulating commands:

'Armed police. Hands in the air. Do not move.'

Cobb moved. He panicked. Dropping his backpack, he jerked sideways and ran, legs knocking together, clutching the sides of his helmet. A noise came from him, wailing, terror.

It was the first sign that it might not all work out as planned.

Cursing, Ray ran too, shouting at the men not to fire. Cobb had dodged away. Flinging the loudhailer aside, Ray sprinted. Cobb was at the side of the runway when something seemed to happen to him: he stumbled, now he was running like a blind person, without any rhythm or sense of direction, almost in a circle; and suddenly he fell down onto the grass and lay there, twitching.

This was the second moment in which Ray felt it might not work out. Turning, he gestured wildly at the medical team waiting by a hangar. He did not want everything ruined by the suspect's death during arrest.

Cobb was thrashing about, moaning, on the grass when Ray reached him. Was he having a heart attack? Ray willed him not to die. He began to perform the calming techniques he half remembered from his training. Flailing around, Cobb struck him twice across his face, and Ray restrained him, talking to him: 'It's okay, help is coming, it's okay, just relax, just be still, it's okay.'

Looking back over his shoulder, he saw the medical team coming towards him at last, also noticing briefly Tom Fothergill struggling against officers.

Cobb was making choking noises, clutching his helmet, trying to pull it off.

'Don't die!' Ray shouted at him. 'For Christ's sake, don't die!'

Through the tinted visor, Ray could just about make out Cobb's mouth moving wildly, pale foam frothing out of it.

'Wait!' Ray said to him. 'Wait!'

He struggled with the helmet's fastenings, his fingers clumsy and slow.

'Wait!'

He did not want it to end like this.

Finally the fastenings opened. At last he yanked the helmet off and flung it to one side, and stared down.

Face contorted in fear, Fothergill's son Jack looked up at him.

And that was the moment, finally, when Ray knew that it wasn't going to work out.

★

Five hours later, in the silvery dark of the summer night, Cobb arrived at his destination. It had been a long, draining journey. For a moment he sat in the back of the motionless cab, looking up through the window at the sky, emptying his mind, filling it again with the cloud-blurred moon, the underpowered stars, that wisp of blue haze at the horizon, allowing himself to slow down, to relax. The window was open a crack; he could smell grass and water. It was a mild world, a faded place, inconspicuous. And at last he felt safe.

He paid the driver and got out and stood on the pavement with his precious backpack, watching the cab drive away. He had been trapped but now he was free. He had been frightened but now he could breathe again. A little tremor of anger went through him. They would catch him if they could, catch him and put him away and do the things they did to him before. But they would not catch him, not now, not here.

He looked around. Everything was shut, dark; everyone was asleep except the usual night creatures, furtive and clever as him, and he put on his backpack and walked across the lawn into the safe building.

THIRTY-FOUR

Without doubt it was the biggest disaster of his career. In the toilets on the first floor at St Aldates the following morning, Ray stood looking at himself in the mirror. He looked like shit. All night he hadn't slept. Eyes bloodshot, skin greyish, mouth puffy where Jack Fothergill had struck him in his fit.

There was an ugly stain on his cream suede bomber but he hardly noticed it.

He remembered that first instant of disorientation, like walking into the edge of a door or missing a step. This boy staring up at him. Not Cobb. Then the sickening flashback as he remembered 'Cobb' getting into el-Baz's cab in St Giles, in his grey hooded top that was not quite Cobb's grey hooded top, with his backpack that was exactly the sort of backpack dozens of other people were carrying round, without ever showing the camera his face, which they had been so eager to believe was Cobb's, but which wasn't. And, out of all the not-Cobbs it could have been, it had to be Fothergill's son.

He felt sick.

At the airport he'd stood there not knowing what to say while the paramedics loaded the boy into the ambulance, Fothergill holding his son's hand but looking at him.

'I was just taking my son for a ride. My son, Ray. He's done nothing wrong. He's vulnerable. *He's not like other boys!*'

Patting his son, murmuring to him.

Then they were gone in the ambulance. It was the quick work of the paramedics, apparently, that had saved him. Twice in the ambulance he had choked on his tongue.

Ray leaned over the basin suddenly and vomited.

Most of the media outlets had carried the story, but partial and garbled: the odd photograph of a police helicopter on a runway, an ambulance outside the John Radcliffe Hospital, reports of an attempted arrest 'gone wrong', a general sense of farce. But the Fothergills had evidently not talked to the press: there was no mention of Jack. And, in fact, little mention of Ray. Criticism was reserved for the Super who had become the more visible face of 'an operation blighted by astonishing incompetence'. But the journos were digging for more; at home Diane had unplugged the landline.

It was the Super Ray had to see now. He wiped his mouth, sucked in oxygen. At moments like this he would usually smarten himself up, recall things his father would say to stiffen his resolve. Nothing came to mind now. He didn't even glance at his clothes. He closed his eyes, breathed, and went to face his punishment.

For once the geese on the river were quiet. It meant Ray could hear the Super breathing.

'I've come to offer my resignation,' he said. He hadn't known he was going to say this, and stood there surprised.

The Super said nothing, turned his back on Ray and gazed out of the window.

A minute passed.

Where are the geese? Ray thought irrelevantly.

The Super turned back to Ray, his face a greyish mauve, the colour of veins, his voice a low growl. 'Do you think I'm fucking stupid?'

Ray opened his mouth, shut it again, braced himself as the Super opened his.

'I appointed you! I doubled your manpower! I backed you! You're my man! Mine! I'm not going to let you piss off now!'

Spittle fell from the air like spindrift. Ray didn't know what to say.

'Thank you, sir.'

The Super's normally small eyes popped big. '*Thank you? For what?*'

'For . . . your faith in me.'

'*I don't have any faith in you!*'

His voice must have been heard throughout the second floor.

'Are you trying to fuck with me, son?' Now his voice was low and nasty.

'No, sir.'

'Are you playing mind games, is that it? With your Oxford University scarf and your scrapbook of photos from college dinners, and your nice little degree on parchment done up with sealing wax from the fucking twelfth century, is that what you're doing?'

'No, sir. I—'

'Shut up. You're not resigning because you're staying in post and taking the shit until you bring me that child-killer. You understand?'

'Yes, sir.'

'Where is he?'

This was the lowest moment.

'I don't know.' In the silence he risked one more unwelcome statement. 'I think he may have left Oxford by now.'

There was a longer silence then in which he was pulled into the Super's remorseless stare and twisted.

'Then get after him,' the Super said. 'Out!'

It was late when he got home. Diane didn't look up as he went in and he stood there not sure what to do or say. She was sitting on the bean bag concentrating on something in her lap. After a moment he realised what she was doing.

'I didn't know you'd started knitting.'

She gave him a brief glance. 'You obviously haven't noticed the shawls in the spare room.'

He hadn't. 'You knitted those?' He was bewildered. 'When?'

She didn't reply.

'Do you want to talk?'

'I don't think we've anything to say to each other, Ray.'

'Did you see the news?'

'Yes.'

'It was a mess.'

She didn't say anything to that, and he went up the stairs in silence to the spare room. The first thing he noticed were the knitted shawls, several of them stacked in a neat pile next to the pushchair in its box decorated all over in self-congratulatory style with Baby Dynamic logos. He knew he should work but instead slid suddenly down the wall onto the carpet, where he sat hemmed in by the educational toys, playmats, child alarms, books and clothes, staring at them vacantly without seeing them. The Super's voice was in his head, and Diane's, and Tom Fothergill's, and, fleetingly, Ros Kerr's. He shut his eyes and tried to get rid of them with the breathing techniques he had not bothered to master in the antenatal classes, but it took a long time as he drifted in and out of consciousness, and when he opened his eyes again it was past midnight, the voices were gone but the baby stuff was still there. Time got stuck, unlike his thoughts which wouldn't stay still. He angrily tried to make a mental list of all his friends. When he put his head in his hands his face felt coarse and swollen. At some point he discovered a voicemail on his phone from his father. He knew he shouldn't listen to it but out of bitterness listened anyway and heard him say, 'Ray, I don't know what's going on, they must be misreporting things, this can't be you, Ray.' He told himself again that he was going to get up and work, but he still didn't move, wasn't sure he could. His thoughts became confused. Was he still awake or was he dreaming? Occasionally quiet voices floated in from the street or burrowed through the walls but though they were in the room with him they were also far away and he couldn't make out their accusations. He felt very alone. A painful sensation began to creep through his body and after a while he understood that he was physically ceasing to be the man his father had wanted him to be, and the husband Diane had thought he was, and the DI the Superintendent had demanded him to be. He felt himself begin to go, to crumble. No more Handsome Ray ever again.

Then he woke up as his phone stopped ringing, with terrible pins and needles down the length of his left leg, listening to the unstable, aggressive silence. His face was wet and he was shaking, and he saw that it was three o'clock, and lay there on the carpet, in pain, feeling confused.

His phone rang again, and he moaned out loud, and looked at it, and moaned again, louder.

'What?' he said brokenly into it. 'What do you want now? What's wrong with you? Can't you leave me alone!'

Ryan said, 'I know where Cobb is.'

Things spun wildly in Ray's head.

'How?'

''Cause I'm looking at him right now.'

THIRTY-FIVE

They stood in darkness looking through binoculars at the back of a block of flats, a five-storey building in plain brick. Four windows to each storey, arranged in rows, like windows in a child's drawing. One of them, on the top floor, was illuminated, and a man was standing there, a dark silhouette, looking out.

Half past three. An occasional car on the nearby ring road droning by.

'It's him, isn't it?'

Ray refocused the binoculars, stared, hesitated. 'Yes,' he said at last. He didn't want to make another mistake. But there was no doubt this time: it was Cobb. As they watched, he took a packet out of his pocket and dry-swallowed a pill and rubbed his temples.

'Health issues,' Ryan said. 'He's going to have more than fucking health issues in a minute.' He glanced at Ray. 'You look like shit, by the way.'

They stood there, thinking. At their backs, behind a perimeter fence hung with warning signs, another apartment block

252

was going up, a looming dark mass of wrapped concrete and exposed cables inside its cage of scaffolding. To either side was the Rivermead Nature Park, an unkempt mess of greenery squashed between the ring road, the river and the back end of the Rose Hill estate, nothing in it of note, just common trees and undergrowth riddled with animal tracks and strewn with litter flung from passing cars. Ryan had happy memories of it, though: he'd come here one summer night to drink cider with a gang of other fourteen-year-olds and almost ended up in the river.

Another car went past. The light in the window above went out.

'Going back to bed.'

'How did you find him?'

'I'm police, Ray. I can find people.'

Ray gave him a bitter look.

'Well, I'll tell you. It's all about childhood friends. Remember them, Ray?'

'No,' Ray said bluntly. 'I don't have any.'

'Really? Me neither. But think about it. Where's Cobb going to feel safe? Who can he trust? Not one of his cronies – even if he has any, everyone's covering their own arses. Only person keep you safe no questions asked? Best mate from when you were a kid. What childhood's all about. See it every night at bath time.'

He described his visit to Grendon where he'd discovered that Cobb's only visitor had been an 'official' who had changed his name because people made fun of it, a name that Ryan's father had eventually remembered was Pigford.

'Rang a bell.'

It rang a bell with Ray too. He frowned.

'I'll give you a clue. It's in the file you give me a squint of.'

Ray remembered: the kid Cobb was in care with. Ronnie Pigford. Two vulnerable children alone together in a world of unpredictable adults.

'Pigford disappeared years ago. Portugal.'

'Changed his name, like I say. People making fun of it.'

'Changed it to what?'

'Hoggarty.'

'Hoggarty? You serious?'

'Fond of pigs, I don't know. But that's his name now. Anyway, trained as a social worker. In and out of Grendon regular for the last five, six years. One of the screws there, he was at school with me; he give me Pigford's new name, told me where he lived. Funny how easy being a detective is, eh?'

Ray stared at him bleakly.

'No need to thank me, by the way. In case you were thinking about it. Truth is, just got lucky. So. What now, big man? We could go up together, you and me, bitch-slap him out of there. Sound good?'

Ray was already making calls.

'Not keen?'

He was mobilising people, talking to Livvy, explaining, asking for checks on the tenants' database, giving instructions about surveillance, public management, armed response. Briefly, he put his hand over the phone. 'I'm not ungrateful. You've saved me, I know that. But you're insane.'

'You're going to do it by the book? Serious? It'll take for ever, man.'

Ray finished his calls. 'Ryan, listen. Did you see the news

yesterday? I'm one tiny fuck-up away from the axe. Hoggarty's probably up there with him, maybe others too. I'm not going to risk any collateral damage.'

'You're right. Shame, though.'

'And what's the Super going to say if he hears you're involved?'

'All right, point taken.'

'In fact, from now on . . .'

'What?'

'Best if you stay out of the way.'

'Oh, right. Cheers.' Ryan stayed where he was, looking round. 'You can get a camera up there, you know.' Nodding at the building site.

'I'd already worked that out.'

'I'll just disappear then.'

He stayed where he was.

'Ryan.'

'Yeah?'

'I owe you.'

Now he moved away into the trees, though his voice came back through the darkness. 'Anything for a friend. Even a stuck-up like you.'

It took for ever, as Ryan had said. Livvy arrived, small and pale in a puffer jacket, walking softly through the trees, shivering as she came. Then Surveillance in a van with their bags of tricks. A chopper lifted up over distant fields. Lights off, Armed Response slid in behind everyone else, hid themselves among scrub. Grunts took up discreet positions beyond Rivermead Road to head off civilian interruptions. And in the cool dew-slime of pre-dawn

255

darkness a night-vision camera was quietly set up in an open-air corner of concrete at the top of the half-built block.

The Super was on his way, flying in by helicopter from the Midlands. It had taken some time to persuade him that, this time, they really had eyes on Cobb.

Ray sat with Livvy in the van, headphones on.

Livvy said, 'Think we can get it wrapped up before Barko makes it?'

Ray remembered the Super shouting at him in his office, the way his spray glistened in the sunlight through the window. He looked away to face the monitors and spoke to a voice in his ear, a man known as Sticky, up with the camera at the top of the unfinished building.

'Can we get a tap in there?'

'No landline.'

'Images?'

'Here you go.'

On one screen: exterior views of the building. Five storeys, fifties build, plain brick at the back, plastered cream at the front except for a narrow strip of terracotta wall tiles above the communal entrance, where the stairwell was. A window onto the stairwell on every floor; the one on the first floor temporarily covered with an aluminium screen. It was Rose Hill, after all. Twelve apartments, two to each floor on either side of the stairwell. Each apartment had two windows at the back, looking westward onto the nature reserve, and two at the front, facing Rivermead Road. No lift. Access to the roof through the interior top-floor hallway ceiling. In the south-west corner an external door to the electrics, heating and water supply, crusted shut.

On another screen: a floorplan of Hoggarty's flat. Two bedrooms, living room, kitchen, bathroom, all around a central hallway leading to the front door.

On the third screen, the one Ray and Livvy stared at now: fizzing grey image of a room underwater. Shapes of things floated in it: a sleeping horse that could have been a sofa, a black portal that might have been a television screen.

'Quality's shit. Sorry, Ray.'

'Can't we get any better?'

The camera zoomed in, froze, clarified itself.

Living room. Door to passage ahead, door to kitchen left.

'End of the passage?'

The camera probed forward. Another door, open, into a bedroom, a zone of indistinct grey stillness.

The camera came out, tracked sideways to the other window.

Second bedroom. In the gap between badly drawn curtains, a half inch of something bulky, a length of bed. The lens strained, jumped, the picture layered and re-layered, resolving itself into something sharper, shadows streaked in contours along a duvet.

'How many in the bed?'

'Two? Or is it just one?'

'Someone with three legs.'

'Can't we do better?'

'Sorry, Ray.'

Time passed. Dawn began to come up, grey as the images on the screen, greenish at the horizon. Then yellow-beige. Slowly, as if reluctantly, the sky lightened, just a little.

The camera images did not become any clearer.

'Front bedroom. Take a look.'

Something stirring in the greyness beyond the doorway, a darker shape. It shivered, rested shimmering and came on in jerks into the living room, tall and rumpled, wearing T-shirt and boxers, stretching, looking at his wrist.

'Hoggarty.'

An ID shot came up on-screen.

'That's him.'

'Anyone else in there? Apart from our man.'

'Hoggarty's wife, maybe. Roselle. There's a daughter lives there too, twelve, thirteen. Kim.'

Hoggarty's dark grey double rippled its way out of the pale grey murk, disappeared again.

'Bathroom? Back to bed?'

They waited.

'What's the plan, Ray?'

'Don't fuck up.'

'Ambitious.'

The van door slid back and the Super hoisted himself in, immaculate despite the ungodly hour, formal in his overstuffed uniform, eyes searching for Ray, and Ray felt something inside his chest contract a little.

'Sir.'

'Is it him?'

'Yes.'

'Sure?'

'There's no doubt. This time.'

'Good to go then?'

He sat close up, peering at the screen, while Ray talked. He was

258

all over the briefing, interrupting to ask questions, demanding to know, to see everything.

'Been here before, Ray.'

'Yes, sir.'

'Different outcome this time, eh?'

'Sir.'

'Okay, carry on.'

Talking in the van ceased except for essentials. Ray willed himself to forget the Super, to be lost in the moment, to fix his mind on the screen. Almost immediately, as if he had prompted it, there was new movement in the greyness, a smaller figure pulling on a top.

'Wife, Ray?'

'Not sure. Daughter, could be.'

'Five o'clock, shouldn't she still be in bed?'

Not in bed. Standing in the living room, bag over her shoulder, doing something to her hair. Hoggarty materialising next to her. Their heads moved together; they went out and the room was empty again.

'Back bedroom!'

In the narrow gap between the curtains: a dark blur, passing to and fro. A hand rubbing an overlarge head.

'Target on the move.'

'What's going on? What are they up to? It's more or less the middle of the night.'

Ten minutes of indistinct activity, a badly edited montage of ultra-brief clips, extracts of movement too short to be intelligible. At last Cobb appeared in the living room, dressed, and stood again by the window.

'What's he got there?'

Hands behind his back under his jacket, contorting himself, positioning something.

'Firearm? Knife?'

Ray issued the warning.

Cobb was joined in the living room by Hoggarty and his daughter. They were all dressed now, as if about to leave. Their heads moved, turning to each other, turning away again. Mime of a conversation.

'Where they going, Ray? It's not even five thirty.'

He could feel the Super looking at him. He willed his mind back onto the screen.

'That bag Kim's got. The name on it. Can we get in closer?'

Lettering ballooned unintelligibly onto the screen, shrank into focus. TURNA.

'Livvy?'

'Checking now. General store at Rose Hill Oval. Bread, milk, lottery, magazines.'

It came to Ray. 'She's doing a paper round. That's why she's up so early.'

The Super considered that. 'Okay. Could be. What about the others?'

He tried to imagine. A father with his daughter and childhood friend, the child-killer. What would he do if he were Hoggarty? Keep an eye on her, never let her be alone with Cobb, never, best childhood friend or not.

'Cobb's going out for exercise. It's the perfect time. Just enough light to see where he's going, no one about. He won't risk being spotted during the day; his picture's everywhere. She's going out anyway, so she'll show him where he can go.'

'And Dad's keeping an eye on things.'

'That'd be my guess.'

'Workable hypothesis. Eyes on the entrance then. What now, Ray?'

'We can't make the arrest while they're together, too risky. Especially if he's armed.'

'Agreed. So?'

'Only other option: monitor it. Wait for Cobb to move off on his own.'

'Okay. Tricky fucking business, though, Ray. You have to be on top of it.'

'Yes, sir.'

He gave instructions, turned back to the screen.

Cobb, Hoggarty and his daughter were going through the rituals of exit, toing and froing in the living room. Then they were on their way. Ray left the van, Livvy and the Super following, and moved into position at the south-east corner of the building. The scene was deserted. Opposite the flat entrance was Mortimer Road leading to the Oval, where the newsagent's was. In a parked car at the end of it was a spotter; others were concealed round the building. Their voices were in Ray's ears, commentating on progress.

'Exiting the flat now. Top-floor landing. Three figures, two adult males, one female juvenile. Entering the stairwell. Going down together.'

They waited.

'Fourth-floor stairwell.'

It was darkish still, a heavy summer morning twilight under a clouded sky.

'Third floor now. Here they come. Still together.'

Ray issued warning instructions again. No move to apprehend until Cobb was on his own.

'Second floor. Same as before. First-floor window's screened over so next visibility's ground floor.'

The wait was longer. Very Long.

At last the spotter said, 'Here they come. Hang on.'

The main door opened and Kim walked down the path towards the road leading to the newsagent. There was no one else with her.

Ray spoke. 'What's going on?'

No one answered.

'Where's Hoggarty? Where's Cobb?'

A moment's silence.

A voice said, 'Second-floor stairwell. Here they come. They must be going back to the flat.'

'Eyes on both?'

'Eyes on Hoggarty. Wait a minute.'

'What about Cobb?'

Silence.

'*What about Cobb?*'

Another silence.

'No Cobb.'

Livvy said, 'Still on the first floor?'

The Super was saying, 'Cobb, Ray. Give me Cobb.'

Ray ran.

'Ray!'

He ran back along the south side of the building and round the corner, to the steps that led down to the basement, and peered down into the shadows, squinting. The crusted basement door was open. He thought he was going to be sick. When he spoke into his mike he was aware of the desperation in his voice.

'Target's left via the basement door, south-west exit. He must have spotted us. Repeat, target has left the building.'

Even as he spoke he was looking across the lawn at the dense screen of trees of the nature reserve behind the unfinished apartment block, where nothing moved in the darkness. There were trails in there, leading everywhere, the ring road, the river, Rose Hill shops and beyond. The Super arrived, breathing noisily, and he too stood and looked into the tangle of trees and undergrowth.

'We'll never find him in there. What happened to the fucking spotter on the basement door?'

Ray was already issuing instructions. Generic commands, just to get people going. He had no instant plan. Men and women emerged out of shadows, shifting rapidly across roads, circling round the building, spreading out across the lawn; the chopper appeared, its search-beam floodlighting the treetops, making everything else darker.

The Super was up close. 'Where's he gone, Ray?'

He didn't know. But before he could answer, there was a long, angry howl of airhorn from a truck on the ring road invisible behind the trees, and, like the Eye of Sauron, everyone's attention swivelled towards it.

'What's beyond the road, Ray?'

'Water meadows.'

'Escape route.'

263

It wasn't a question.

'I'm not sure.'

'You're not sure?'

'He's not a runner. He's a hider.'

But the Super was already giving instructions, officers moving rapidly towards the ring road, the helicopter's beam swinging up and away. A car arrived with a jolt at the kerb, Livvy got in, and it accelerated down Rivermead Road. Ray thought, *This is when I lost command, this precise moment here.* He looked the other way, towards the nature reserve, and at the same moment a figure appeared out of the trees. Not Cobb. Disgraced DI Ryan Wilkins in trackie bottoms, Loop jacket and baseball cap, who stuck two fingers in his mouth and gave a long vulgar whistle.

Under his breath the Super said, 'Please God this is a fucking dream.' But Ray was already running across the lawn.

Through the trees they ran together on an animal track, clutched at by brambles and whipped by thin branches. At one point Ryan stopped, panting, peering round.

Ray said, 'What are we doing?'

Ryan said, 'Your job, mate.'

Then they were running again. The path plunged unexpectedly and Ryan fell, pulling Ray down with him, and they rolled into bushes, and staggered to their feet and ran on again until they came suddenly to the river, its surface a flickering dazzle in the first full rays of the sun.

Ray looked up and down. 'What are we doing here?'

'Can you swim?'

'Yes, I can swim.'

'Thought so. Probably got your swimming Blue at the university, eh?'

'Boxing. It was a boxing Blue. But I can swim. Why?'

'I can't.' He waited a beat. Pointed. 'He can't either.'

Now Ray saw him, the dull shape of his big head briefly breaking the brilliant surface a hundred metres downstream, a hand waving goodbye.

The chill of the water shocked him. Ray rose gasping to the surface, looked around, saw nothing, set off anyway, thrashing badly. He could swim but he hated it. He tried the crawl, swallowed water, choked it up, carried on with breaststroke, head craned high, blinking, peering round. Cobb nowhere to be seen. Cobb gone, drowned, dead already. He refused to believe it. On the opposite bank an early-morning jogger was staring at him. Ahead, a skiff from the rowing club receded into sunlight, an Oxford idyll happening in another universe, like many Oxford idylls.

No sign of Cobb.

He went on again, stopped, spun round in a little circle, searching. Nothing but sun dazzle. How he hated water. Taking a gulp of air, he flipped over and went down. He'd seen it done on television. Underwater was all shadow and grit; it hurt to open his eyes and, when he did, all he could see were different forms of darkness moving soundlessly together. Blood thumped in his stopped-up ears. Upside down, he groped around uselessly, like a man in a child's game of blind man's bluff. Something brushed his fingertips and was gone. His lungs were hammering on the door of his chest. He swam for the surface, gulped more air and went down again.

This time he felt nothing. Saw less.

He went down five times more, then trod water, exhausted, floating blind among the bobbing bits of light. A small crowd of joggers and cyclists now stood silently on the towpath watching him. He realised then that this was the end, the final professional failure, and a failure of character, and a failure of dignity too as he huffed and gasped in front of the watching people, barely able to keep afloat. He thought of the Super, of his father's and Diane's judgement. He felt the bitterness of self-pity and understood that this is what he would feel now, perhaps permanently, and was disgusted with himself.

Then the sun disappeared, sucking the dazzle off the water's surface, and in the ordinary quiet light he saw Cobb washed up on the bank just ten metres away, quivering on the mud like a beached fish.

When they got him back through the trees to Rivermead Road the media were there in force. Cobb hadn't said anything but as soon as he saw the crowd with their lights and equipment he began to scream.

'They're going to kill me!'

The cameras flashed and whirred, the sound booms swung. The press were shouting questions as they pulled him towards the wagon.

'Why did you kill Poppy Clarke?'

'What have you got to say to Poppy's mother?'

Struggling, Cobb shouted back, 'This isn't justice! They're going to kill me, they're going to kill me just for being who I am!'

Still shouting, he was thrust into the wagon which went

forward at once, pushing past people holding up their cameras to the blacked-out windows, and accelerated down the road.

Ryan was muttering something in Ray's ear as he stood there dripping in his boxers and vest. The cameras whirred but he was too exhausted to move away. Besides, it was too late. Through the crowd the Super came towards them.

THIRTY-SIX

Mid-morning the day exploded with breaking news, filled up once again with headlines and photographs, tweets and postings, articles and opinion, with the strained, excited voices of reporters and bystanders, with savage condemnation, angry triumph, bitter relief and all the wildness of the human heart. KILLER CAUGHT IN DAWN RAID. AT LAST. GOTCHA. Originality not at a premium.

At a press conference Thames Valley Chief Superintendent Dave Wallace said that the force had delivered on its responsibilities, that the parents of Poppy Clarke could feel assured that justice would now be served. It turned out that the hapless senior investigating officer DI Raymond Wilkins, who appeared alongside Wallace, was a hero after all. There had been doubts, but in the end he had got his man, a fact corroborated by photographs of Ray in wet vest and boxers securely holding on to him. There was admiration from several quarters, especially on social media, of the detective inspector's figure. Bewilderment, too, at the person who appeared with DI Wilkins, some chav in trackies and baseball cap who had barged his way into the picture, probably high. Most attention, however, was focused on Shane Cobb. His mugshot, appearing everywhere, seemed to smirk at the thought of what he had done. Potted biographies narrated his childhood in care, his dismissal from a primary school in Aylesbury for suspicious behaviour, his prison sentence for the supply of drugs, his possession of child pornography. Contempt was given to his recent 'facilitating'. In the many accounts of his dramatic capture, outrage and disgust were expressed at his claim to be the victim, even as he had refused to deny killing Poppy. Poppy's mother made a brief, faltering statement thanking the police for their work. There was no comment from Poppy's father. Magpies nursery, though ready to make a statement, was not asked for one. Many details of the investigation remained unknown to the public, though Superintendent Wallace mentioned that further evidence had been secured as a result of Cobb's arrest, and confirmed that at least four other people were being held in custody on suspicion of perverting the course of justice. Cobb himself was in a special secure unit in HMP Bullingdon, near Bicester, where he would stay until trial. The governor commented that while he appreciated the depth of feeling against Cobb, everyone is entitled to the full protection of the law.

For Ray it was the strangest day. When he got home Diane wasn't there. She had left no note. He called friends and her family, and, at last, their midwife, who told him that she had been admitted to hospital in the early hours of the morning for tests and observation. By then it was late afternoon. Eventually he found her in a room in the antenatal suite attached to various monitors, too listless almost to turn her eyes towards him. When she spoke her voice was a whisper. Her manner was indifferent. She did not ask him about the case and he did not mention it. A paediatrician told him that she would need to be kept in overnight, and asked Ray questions about her behaviour over the last few days which he could not answer.

'You do live together, right?'

Ray said he had been busy.

Afterwards he sat with her. She didn't speak and he didn't hold her hand. Soon he realised that it wasn't tiredness that kept her from looking at him but hostility; it struck him like a heat. He was confused. What emotion should he feel? He knew enough from texts and messages to understand that he was being praised for the capture of Poppy's killer. The Super, more difficult to read in private, had publicly commended him. But the stories about the capture circulating now did not correspond to his memory. What he felt, still, was his confusion outside the apartment block when Cobb had given them the slip, his helplessness in the water, and, perhaps most unsettling of all, his grateful, irritating reliance at critical moments on Ryan. It made him uneasy. He badly wanted to feel good.

When his father called he looked at the phone doubtfully and went out into the corridor to talk to him.

'*Baba.*'

'Knew you'd do it, Ray, in the end. Always knew it.'

'Thank you.'

They're calling you man of the hour. In the papers. I have them all here.'

'Well, I wouldn't believe what—'

'Pursued him through woodland and even into the river where—'

'*Baba*. Please.'

'I know. The tabloids. But I have them all. Listen.'

The call did not make him feel better. He went back into the room but Diane was asleep or ignoring him, and he left her and went out to his car and sat there for nearly half an hour, not knowing what to do. He did not want her hostility, nor did he want the crude cheering of the tabloids, nor the ambivalent or even false commendation of the Super. Surely, he thought, there was somewhere he could find some meaningful appreciation. Finally, he put the car in gear and drove out of the car park.

In Kennington Ryan nervously endured a difficult afternoon. A copy of the *Oxford Mail* with a front-page special was on the kitchen table, but all Jade said was, 'Doesn't do you any favours, Ryan.'

'What do you mean?'

'The nose for a start.'

He had another look at the photograph.

'Just the angle of the camera.'

'Says underneath, DI Raymond Wilkins brings in the suspect despite the close attention of a hostile bystander.'

He had a go at putting a different spin on it. Big win for old-style detective work, the importance of justice being done, five-star display of general savvy and all-round smarts, no recognition required.

'Not to mention blatant interference, reckless disregard of employment prospects and utter lack of concern for household income.'

He didn't have the heart to argue. That morning a copy of Carl Crapper's final report of his employment at Van Central had arrived, containing phrases such as 'his subordination has left very much to be desired' and 'I do not think he is up to this quality role with its need for high performance', which reminded him uncomfortably of Crapper's speaking style, and on the whole he felt that he shouldn't read it. He could not escape a sense of unease. He remembered the look of disgust Wallace had given him at Rose Hill. Since then he had received a message from Dr Tompkins cancelling their final anger management session without giving a reason, and it seemed certain that his reinstatement application was now in the bin. All that remained of the process, in fact, was the final panel interview with external examiners presided over by the Superintendent, an event he thought of glumly, without hope.

He took Ryan and Mylee to the swing park. Two different people recognised him.

'You that guy on the news?'

'Thought they'd arrested you.'

He took the children down by the river instead, where they spent an hour being nervous of the geese. Retreating to a safe place, they had a polite conversation about Ryan's pirate costume, which Mylee wanted to borrow again, and Ryan listened in wonder, not knowing what made them so calm, their surprising assumption that the world, though not knowable, was manageably theirs.

His thoughts drifted to Mick Dick, unmentioned in the press. He wondered what Mick would have done to Cobb if he had made it up to Cumnor that night. Something else he would have gone down for. He tried to imagine a different life for Mick in which he didn't make mistakes, in which he worked construction sites, was one of the boys, and took little presents home to his daughter every Friday night. He couldn't. He remembered how warmly Cobb had spoken about Mick, his 'friend', and the guard saying that Mick had hated Cobb like everyone else, and he asked himself why Mick had done the favour for Cobb at the compound anyway. But he couldn't work that out either. Not that it mattered any more.

The geese had gone. The children investigated their poo. Half-heartedly and without hope he began to search for security jobs.

Two days passed. The media frenzy abated slightly. Diane returned home and perched uncomfortably on the bean bag wondering why Ray was still staying so late in the office in the evenings. Ryan received a call from Superintendent Wallace's office to ask him to pick up paperwork from St Aldates station the following day relating to his final meeting with the evaluation panel. And on the third day, a little after midnight, in his cell at Bullingdon Prison Shane Cobb killed himself.

THIRTY-SEVEN

In the conference room on the first floor they gathered at lunchtime to celebrate the end of the investigation. There would be time and opportunity later for more formal, more dignified events, black-tie award-giving ceremonies, private dinners with top brass, but this was the instinctive, spontaneous get-together for the local team who had put the most energy into the case, a chance to pat themselves on the back, have a few drinks and say the beautiful, heartfelt things to each other that they had not been able to say during the weeks of exhausting graft. They'd had enough of being vilified in the press; it was time to enjoy their moment of public acclaim.

It was a scene of shirtsleeves, crates of beer and goodwill. Pizzas, cans and bottles stood on tables. People stood in small groups talking; occasionally a group would detonate with laughter. Jacket off, face flushed, the Super went from group to group with his best loud voice, each group recoiling slightly as he approached. The noise of conversation was erratic, like traffic.

There was discussion of Cobb's unlamented death, a general

assumption that it had not been suicide. The noose he had used was made from sheets from beds in other cells. The two security guards responsible for the half-hourly suicide checks on Cobb's cell had fallen into synchronised sleep. All three cameras positioned in and outside the cell had failed. An enquiry would be held, though there was a crude and unspoken feeling that justice had been served. In any case, much less interest was shown in his death than in the continuing revelations of his depravity. Superintendent Wallace had confirmed the existence of a number of appalling drawings which Cobb had induced children at a school in Aylesbury to make many years earlier. It seemed that on the night prior to his capture he had travelled by cab to Leighton Buzzard to retrieve them from the house of his aunt, where, without her knowledge, they had been stored. News of the hi-vis jacket and workman's helmet, used by Cobb on the day of the abduction, had been leaked. The rumoured existence of a notebook was also confirmed. There was speculation that it contained descriptions of his victim, though the only sections that reached the press were of a personal nature. *All my life I have had to hide* was a typical entry. *But what if I hide myself too well and can't find myself again?* And, more strangely, *What if I am outside?* This sort of self-indulgent thing naturally caused more outrage.

Ray stood in a corner of the room surrounded by people. His hand was shaken, his arm mock-punched, the arms of others were put round his shoulders. He had perfected a semi-funny story about not being able to swim. From time to time he glanced quickly at his watch, as if wanting to get away, though there was no getting away, everyone demanded their right to congratulate him.

★

It was the noise that attracted Ryan's attention, he heard the hubbub as he walked along the corridor towards HR. It was the first time he had been at the station since the night of Cobb's capture and he had a bad feeling. The message telling him to pick up the paperwork had been brief and unfriendly. The Super hadn't been in touch at all; Ryan remembered the way he had looked at him as he had stood with Ray and Cobb in front of the reporters that night. He didn't feel up to seeing him now; he feared what he might say. Nevertheless, curious, he went over to the conference room. He thought he would just peek through the glass panels in the doors – but as he got there the doors opened and Nadim came out and told him he was late.

He looked warily beyond her into the room.

'Not invited.'

'Don't suppose that ever stopped you before.'

'I only come in to pick up some stuff.'

As he spoke he spotted the Super standing in the centre of the room, casually intimidating three newly qualified officers, and turned to leave but the doors had already swung shut behind him, and at that moment the Super clinked a knife against a bottle and barked for quiet, instigating a ripple of voices calling for speeches and asking where the strippers were. Ryan hid himself behind a group of tall lady officers.

The Super soon held them all in his gaze.

'Best speech I have ever heard, the guy just raised a glass.'

He turned to Ray and tipped his bottle towards him and stood back. There was confusion, relief, and some sporadic applause.

'Your turn now,' the Super said, unsmiling.

Some chanting of Ray's name took place.

As at last he stepped forward his phone went and he killed it and put it in his pocket. There were cries of 'Tell her to wait!' and, even funnier, 'Tell her there's a queue!', to which Ray didn't respond; then he began to speak.

'Early on, someone told me they thought Cobb was a rat.'

Supportive noises: 'Too right!', 'He *was* a rat!', et cetera.

'I thought he was a rat too.'

More of the same, some of it humorous: 'Takes one to know one!'

'I didn't expect him to be *a water rat*.'

Laughter.

'I would have worn my inflatable armbands.'

More laughter, slightly forced, fading quickly to empty smiles and mild distractedness, enquiring nods towards the crates of beer, furtive glances at watches, and so on, and Ray moved on, a little stiffly, to more serious sentiments, shared values of hard work, the desire to see justice done, fellowship. Ryan watched him, noticing things, the way Ray's face gradually took on a dull shine, his evasive focus, as if he were speaking to the far wall of the room, the hesitations whenever he had to refer to Cobb, unable to settle on the right term, calling him 'the perp' and then 'that man' and finally just 'Cobb'. He watched the Super too who kept his expressionless gaze on Ray throughout. As Ray wound down his speech, thanking people, Livvy, Nadim, the Super, his focus wavered, slid off the wall, and his eyes briefly met Ryan's before flicking nervously away.

'In the end,' he said, 'this was never about Cobb, it was about Poppy Clarke. It was about making a world that's safe for children.'

The speech was over; there was a general, relieved tendency of bodies towards the tables of refreshment.

Nadim said quietly, 'He doesn't like it that Cobb killed himself.'

Ryan said nothing.

'He's been uneasy all day. It's odd. It's like he feels guilty.'

Together, they watched Ray politely fending people off, edging away, eventually moving out of sight.

'This is big for him, though.'

'Yeah?'

'Massive. Don't you go on social media?'

'For kids, isn't it?'

They watched Ray disengage himself from a group with a quick smile. For a moment he seemed to look in their direction, then he turned the other way.

'They'll give him some sort of gong for sure.'

'Not surprised. Taught him everything I know.'

They watched Ray pause to joke with Livvy, their arms briefly round each other, quickly removed. As she turned away his face went blank.

'They're a good team.'

Ryan blew out his cheeks. 'Yeah.'

As Nadim talked, Ryan kept an eye on Wallace moving restlessly between knots of people, causing a drop in conviviality wherever he went. Ryan didn't think Wallace had spotted him yet but he wasn't sure. He was waiting for an opportunity to slip away.

Nadim said, 'That other case is coming to trial next week. The one about your friend, Michael.'

That got his attention.

'Charges?'

'Death by dangerous driving.'

'Hard to make stick. No witnesses, no evidence. Secondaries?'

'Perverting the course of justice.'

'Yeah. Suspended sentence, maybe.'

She nodded. 'That's what they're saying. It's not much, I know. I'm sorry, Ryan.'

He shrugged. 'He was used to shit deals. Anyway, won't make any difference to his little girl.'

He remembered Ashleigh sitting at the table, popping Smarties in her mouth and forgetting to close it, staring at him from under her floppy hair. What about the ribbons? he wondered. By now they would have been taken away by the forensics guys. But would she remember, when she was grown-up, that she had worn a murdered girl's ribbons in her hair? Or would she bury the memory, as we often bury the memories of things that happened to us as children?

He'd drifted off for a moment. Looked about him vaguely. By now Ray had worked his way towards the other doors on the far side of the room. Wallace had disappeared.

'Can't see Barko. Has he gone? Can you see him lurking anywhere?'

Turning to Nadim, he found himself looking at Wallace, standing next to him, who stared at him for a long, painful moment before saying, 'He's still here, bright boy. He's going back to his office now but he expects to see you later. Not much to say but we might as well get it over with.'

Some delicate, minor organ shrivelled inside him.

The doors shut on Wallace's abrupt departure. He looked around for consolation. Ray was over at the far side and he began to make his way past groups of people towards him.

THIRTY-EIGHT

In Grove Street, Diane watched the midday news. Rachel Clarke, mother of Poppy, was giving a statement about the death of the alleged murderer Shane Cobb. Her face was an alarming shade of orange, a sign of desperation in the make-up room. Her eyes flickered, wandered. In a voice slowed and thickened by Nitrazepam, she said she felt nothing about Cobb's death. 'I think about my daughter,' she said. And, after a long pause: 'I don't think about anything else.'

Diane sat on the bean bag in pain. She asked herself why she was bringing children into this world. Growing up comfortable in Richmond, she'd never been aware of danger. Money had pushed it away, into other neighbourhoods. But money gave no guarantees, vigilance and deceit would be necessary, she would have to hide things from her children, as her parents had hidden them from her. She was aware how alarmist these thoughts were, how unreasoning. But fear is not a matter of reason. The improbable is a matter of fact, as Rachel Clarke understood.

She called Ray – the fourth time – and listened to his answer-phone and left a message. He was avoiding her. On the bean bag, she shifted, and shifted again, trying to find a comfortable position. For a while she drifted into a trance-like semi-sleep in which she saw images of Rachel Clarke's orange face. Time passed, she grew stiff and wakeful. Hearing a noise from the back of the house, she turned, yawning and wincing, to find a man coming through the French windows, and was so shocked she forgot to find it frightening, and the moment to scream passed as he came in and closed the windows behind him.

'You shouldn't leave your garden gate unlocked,' he said. 'Anyone could just walk in.'

He was early middle-aged, blandly good-looking, dressed in smart casual clothes, blue jeans, T-shirt and linen jacket and expensive shoes, and he looked fit and well-groomed. He peered around the room as if appraising it.

'I knocked at the front door,' he said, 'but you didn't answer.'

Diane found her voice. 'Who are you?'

'My name's Tom Fothergill.'

He seemed relaxed, not like he had just walked uninvited into her house. The thought came to her that he was a madman.

'I know Ray,' he added.

'What do you want?'

Instead of answering, he took a sudden interest in her.

'Twins, isn't it?' he said, coming closer. 'How are you feeling? Ray said you were having a bad time of it.'

As if on cue, a spasm went through her and for a moment the pain was so acute she couldn't answer.

'Straighten your back. That's it. Draw in your bump.'

281

Suddenly she felt his hands on her, in the small of her back, pressing her belly – and the pain passed. He behaved as if touching her was normal, a purely practical matter.

'Imogen, my first wife, suffered during her pregnancy. Back. Pelvic girdle. Have you been sick? Bad?'

She nodded. 'Hyperemesis gravidarum.'

'Really? In your second trimester? Have you tried steroids? Prednisolone, it's a corticosteroid. Doctors here say they don't like to prescribe it but the truth is, they can't get hold of it very easily. Listen. I've got a friend runs a pharmaceutical. Let me have a word with him.'

He asked questions about her preparations for motherhood, living arrangements and schooling, listening, nodding, making practical suggestions. All the time he watched her, it should have made her embarrassed but his manner was so open and unguarded she forgot it. It was several minutes before she asked him again why he had come.

'To return these.' He took something out of his jacket pocket and put it on the coffee table. It was a pair of Ray-Bans. 'They're Ray's.'

In the silence that followed they looked at each other.

Diane said, 'I don't understand.'

Fothergill began to walk round the room, peering at things. 'I liked him,' he said after a moment. 'He's a good detective, asks the right questions. Doesn't allow himself to be deflected. Nice dress sense. I'm sure he's popular with the ladies. And he has manners too. I'm sure he's going to be a good father.'

He walked at ease around the room. It was strange how easy he was. Unless he was pretending.

Diane said quietly, 'Why do you have his Ray-Bans?'

'He left them behind in my wife's studio.' He gave her a sympathetic look. 'Did he tell you anything about me?'

'No.' She remembered how she had argued with Ray about Ros Kerr. 'He doesn't talk about his cases.'

'I respect that.'

He paused at the kitchen end of the room. 'I like the cherry-wood, by the way. And the granite. Italian, isn't it?'

Once again it came to her that he was mad. He sat down on the arm of the sofa and looked at her for a long moment before beginning to speak in a quiet, confidential tone. 'I grew up in care. Boys' homes at first, then foster parents. Fothergill's not my real name. They were decent people, or they thought they were. They beat me sometimes but I don't think it did me any harm. I had difficulties, it must have been frustrating for them. I had to learn things before I could do them, even little things, normal things, things people usually do instinctively. I even had to learn how to be a child. I think that's why I mentor criminals now. They have to learn, things don't come naturally to them.' Without taking his eyes off her, he smiled. 'I'm good at it, learning. I started running businesses when I was eleven years old, buying and selling sweets at school. Other things later. When I was twenty-three, when I knew what I was doing, I bought a bicycle company that was going bust and started to make pushchairs. Do you know what the global pushchair market is worth?'

'No.'

'Two billion dollars. Growing at about two and a half per cent a year. The childhood market in general is very lucrative.

283

Children mean money. Parents spend big. They love their kids, of course.'

Diane thought of the Baby Dynamic pushchair upstairs in its box.

'Some companies take advantage of that. I went the other way, spent a lot, produced something really worth the cost. People respond to that, in my experience. It's about honesty, really. Love deserves honesty, don't you think? It's simple, like an equation.'

Diane said, 'He's been with your wife, that's what you've come here to tell me?'

With the slightest hesitation, Fothergill went on. 'My son has some of the same difficulties I had. But he won't learn, I'm afraid. And I'm not very patient with him.'

This was a different mood. They were silent.

'He's not very happy,' Fothergill said.

Another silence. He was gazing at his hands in his lap. Diane felt suddenly that she had never seen anyone so lonely, a man completely apart, inaccessible.

'That must make you unhappy too.'

He didn't look up. He sighed. 'I don't really know. I've never really understood unhappiness. Or love, for that matter. The thing is, I've always tried to be a good man. A good father.'

She realised he was crying. Perhaps not mad, she thought, but lost. She felt frightened again; the lost are dangerous, they have nothing more to lose. The tone of Fothergill's voice didn't change and his bland expression didn't change but tears overflowed his underlids and ran quickly down his cheeks, as he carried on talking.

'I'm the only one who can help him,' he said. He looked up. 'You can understand that, can't you?'

When he looked at her his face was hard with anger. 'Can't you?' he repeated aggressively.

'What do you want?' she replied in alarm.

He stood up and took a step towards her.

THIRTY-NINE

In the conference room at St Aldates the lunchtime party had begun to thin out. Twenty or so people remained, nursing the last of the beer, talking in low voices about drifting off-site to continue drinking at The Old Tom pub up the road. Ray was no longer with them, he had slipped away long before, and Ryan, who had failed to catch him, stood alone, putting off the moment of going up to the Super's office. As he hesitated, Nadim came back into the room, peering round in an agitated way.

'Seen Ray?'

'Went.'

'I need him. He's not in his office. Not answering his phone either.'

'With Barko maybe, getting his shoulders chewed off.'

She shook her head.

'Tried his teammate, his trusty DS?'

'On a train going north.' She looked at him strangely. 'You might do.'

'Do what?'

'Come with me.'

'Yeah, but—'

'No time to argue.'

They stood together outside C3, looking through the mirror at the man sitting at the table inside. He was a spare, strong-looking man with dark skin and thick black hair, and he was wearing a pair of green overalls.

'Tariq Sayyed,' Nadim said. She explained who he was. 'Turned up half an hour ago wanting to speak urgently to Ray. Says it's important.'

'What's it got to do with me?'

'He won't talk to any other officer. But I think he might just talk to you.'

'Why would he do that?'

'Because you met Cobb. It's Cobb he wants to talk about.'

'I dunno, Nadim. If the Super finds out—'

'What difference will it make? You're cooked already.'

'Fair point.'

'He might even know something about your friend.'

They looked again into the interview room. Sayyed was fidgeting in his seat, looking about the empty room. Ryan sighed a long sigh.

'Fuck it,' he said.

LOCATION: C3: ugly, airless, bare, dim, small.

INTERVIEWER: DI Wilkins in trackies and Loop jacket and plaid baseball cap.

INTERVIEWEE: Tariq Sayyed in polycotton green gardening overalls.

DI WILKINS: How's it going, Tariq? Don't suppose you know how these things work, do you? I can never . . . Hang on, I think that's . . .

TARIQ SAYYED: Who the fuck are you?

DI WILKINS: I think that's it. Fingers crossed, eh? Used to work with Ray. Got involved in this case. Didn't mean to. Friend of mine got killed. Mick Dick. Heard of him?

TARIQ SAYYED: He the guy helped Shane inside?

DI WILKINS: That's Mick, yeah. Lent him.

TARIQ SAYYED: I remember Shane mentioning you now. You went up to Dean Court to talk to him about your friend.

DI WILKINS: That's it. Sat in a room full of junk.

TARIQ SAYYED: Been there years that stuff. Listen, I got to speak to DI Wilkins.

DI WILKINS: You can tell me. I'm also DI Wilkins.

TARIQ SAYYED: What? I don't know. Maybe I can come back.

DI WILKINS: All right, Tariq. Listen, this is what I think's going on. What you want to tell me, it's not something easy to say. Otherwise, you know, you would have told Ray before. I mean, look at yourself. Shaking like a fucking junkie, man. Must have taken a fair bit of courage just to come in. So, if you walk out now, chances are you change your mind, don't come back.

TARIQ SAYYED: Yeah, but . . . I don't know, man.

DI WILKINS: Up to you. Do the right thing, do the wrong thing. Your call.

TARIQ SAYYED: Fuck.

DI WILKINS: Something for Shane, is it?

TARIQ SAYYED: Yeah. Yeah, it is.

288

DI WILKINS: Something important?

TARIQ SAYYED: Yeah.

DI WILKINS: Going to get you in trouble?

TARIQ SAYYED: It might, yeah.

DI WILKINS: Well. Have a think about it.

TARIQ SAYYED: Look. He were my friend. I owe him. What they're saying about him, it's not true. I can't have it.

DI WILKINS: What's not true?

TARIQ SAYYED: He didn't take that little girl.

DI WILKINS: How do you know?

TARIQ SAYYED: 'Cause I were with him.

DI WILKINS: [silence]

TARIQ SAYYED: It's true.

DI WILKINS: I believe you. Why didn't you say before?

TARIQ SAYYED: 'Cause we were . . . 'Cause we were . . . we were somewhere we shouldn't have been.

DI WILKINS: Where's that, Tariq?

TARIQ SAYYED: A place in Abingdon. There's boys there.

DI WILKINS: Times?

TARIQ SAYYED: We got there about half four, stayed while six. I weren't up at Binsey, I got a friend to lie for me. I'm in trouble now, aren't I?

DI WILKINS: Probably. But you just done the right thing. Worth something, isn't it?

TARIQ SAYYED: Maybe.

DI WILKINS: Ask you something else. Shane talk about Mick much?

TARIQ SAYYED: Just, he were good to him inside. Shane had a rough ride there. I know what it's like.

289

DI WILKINS: And after they came out?

TARIQ SAYYED: No. Didn't see each other. Lending Shane money were just an inside thing. He must have felt sorry for him. Outside, your friend didn't want owt to do with Shane. Avoided him. He wouldn't even take back the money. Happens like that. I know.

DI WILKINS: Interesting. Cheers. Tell you what, I'll get someone to bring you a cup of tea.

He stood outside.

'Well, that's a pisser. Not so massive for Ray after all. Interesting, though.'

Nadim was on the phone, trying to get Ray, trying to get Livvy.

'I've sent him a text,' she said. 'But he's not picking up.'

Standing there watching her dial and redial, Ryan drifted off, thinking about Mick Dick. He remembered the guard at Grendon telling him that Mick Dick didn't like Cobb better than anyone else, and Charlene telling him that Mick never returned Cobb's calls, and Fothergill telling Ray that though Cobb talked about Mick Dick, Mick never mentioned Cobb at all. And he asked himself why then would Mick Dick do a favour for Cobb at the compound? And he told himself that he wouldn't.

So was he doing a favour for someone else?

Someone who knew Mick had the skills. Someone who'd told him it wasn't a big deal, just an in-and-out. Someone Mick had really wanted to help out. Someone who was still out there.

He closed his eyes and saw again Mick's face big with shock and terror, saw him running across the water meadows in the dark. What was he thinking? He saw him clambering out of the bushes, heading somewhere. One hand up to his ear. Up to his ear . . . The thought snagged again, the way it had snagged before. A gap into which something fitted which oddly wasn't there.

He looked at his watch. Nadim was still talking. 'Ray Wilkins,' she was saying. 'I have to get hold of Ray. Yes, it's important. Yes, it has to be now.'

Ryan edged past her, miming urgency and went quickly down the corridor.

FORTY

He looked round as he stood at the door, asking himself what he was doing there, though, of course, he knew, or half knew. He was glad to have left the party. It was a warm afternoon, lazily shining, sunlight glinting off glazed timber and plate glass, soaking into the glowing lawn, the air still with an almost pointed stillness, as if it were holding its breath, as Ray realised he was holding his. He breathed out. Without thinking, he fussed with the waistband of his jeans, adjusted the hang of his tee. Breathed out again. And then she answered the door and stood looking at him.

They were standing in the living room before they spoke.

'He's not here.'

'Back soon?'

'Don't know.'

He looked at her then, and she glanced at him, half smiling, and looked away, out of the window where the Oxfordshire countryside performed for their contemplation. He felt again the little jolt of excitement. She was wearing a grey wrap dress which clung, wrinkling, to her body. Once he started to look at her he couldn't stop. Her body seemed unnaturally vivid to him, every detail, the finely boned face with its erotic mouth and amused eyes, her smooth bare arms and lightly shining bare shoulders. He noticed how tight her thin skin was across her collarbone, the way her hair hung in a glossy, jagged curve against her cheek, the pale gleam of neck beneath it. He noticed the exact distribution of the weight of her body as she shifted position, how her hip moved, how her calf muscle flexed, how the clinging dress wrinkled on her thigh, and knew these symptoms for what they were. In a very real, physical sense, he felt magnetised to her. *This* was why he had come. She looked at him again, the way she had in her studio the previous evening, and the evening before that. He saw the interest in her eyes, and he felt again the almost sickening lurch and pluck of the urge, and the guilt. He moistened his dry lips. He remembered how they had talked as she showed him her pictures, how he didn't know what to say, how she gently mocked but all the time with that careless, inviting humour, and looked at him.

He had showed her his police badge and she had laughed at him.

'Why have you come?' she said.

For a moment he said nothing. He saw himself stepping towards her, taking hold of her face in his hands, pressing his mouth on hers; he imagined her mouth smiling under his kiss.

He cleared his throat, said carefully, 'I wanted to talk to Tom.'

'Why?'

He remembered the last time he had seen Fothergill, at the Oxford airport, holding his son's hand as they loaded him on a stretcher into the ambulance.

'To apologise.'

'He won't know what to do with your apology. He's not that sort of person.' She didn't explain what she meant by that. 'Anyway,' she said lightly, 'he's not here. Only me.'

She faced him, looked at him, smiled. It was too much. Some sort of heat seemed to come off her, he could feel it on his face. And felt again the lurch somewhere in the pit of his stomach; his body seemed to move by itself. He was stepping towards her, leaning forward with his face; he was pressing his mouth to hers, and felt her lips under his, frozen. Discouraged, he stepped back and stood there, as she shook her head.

'Ray,' she said. 'Ray.'

'I thought—'

'You've misunderstood. I'm sorry. We can't do this. You know we can't.'

She was speaking to him gently, as if he were a child.

'But—'

'Flirting. But not kissing. Not touching. Not getting involved.'

He stood there foolishly.

'We're not children, Ray.'

His silence acknowledged it.

'Not at the mercy of our instincts. You know this, Ray. Our lives have grown up round us. We've got marriages, kids. Kids on the way.' She put her hand on his arm. 'I like you, Ray. I like flirting with you. You're a good man. Stay like that.' She smiled. 'I'll make some coffee.'

It was over. This was the real conclusion to the investigation, not the arrest of Cobb, not the media acclaim, not the stale party in the station conference room, but this, a small humiliation

294

dealt to him by a woman he didn't know, as if he had tried to be someone he wasn't and had been gently found out. He felt stupid.

They sat at the end of the enormous dining table.

'How is he?'

'Tom? I never really know.'

'He was upset about what happened at the airport.'

'Yes. Yes, he was. It's the only time he gets upset, when Jack's involved.'

He watched her as she sat there, holding her mug in both hands, sipping. Beautiful and desirable still.

'And you?' he said.

'Was I upset? Not about that.'

'About everything else. Poppy Clarke. The questioning.'

Her eyes laughed at him. 'Still probing, DI Wilkins? The investigation's over, surely.'

He acknowledged it.

She thought for a moment. 'I push things away. That's my style. I think about other things.'

'Your work.'

'Not just that. No.' She became thoughtful. 'I've tried hard all my life to be an unserious person, dismissive. I'd rather treat it all as a game. Well, the world is so fucking awful. I don't need to tell you. It's your job to be in that world. My habit is to stay out of it.'

He thought about that. 'Your work,' he said at last, 'is full of the horror of the world.'

'But my work is also a game. It makes the horror manageable.'

They drank coffee. She went on again, as if talking to herself.

'It's true, though, I didn't push all this away as well as I usually do. I tried, I didn't follow the news reports, for instance. But I felt it all the same. It pressed in on me.'

'Tom was caught up in it.'

'It wasn't him, it wasn't you coming round with your questions. It was that man. Knowing that he was here. That day, the day he killed her. Here.'

'Cobb.'

'In his van. I felt the physical closeness of it. That's what I remember now.'

'I understand.'

She went on. 'It's not as if I saw him much. I saw him only twice, in fact, once when he arrived in the morning, and once when he drove away again in the evening. That was all. But, looking back, it's as if I felt his presence all day. I still feel it.'

They sat drinking coffee.

'You,' she said. 'You do this for a living. God knows what it does to you.'

He ignored her, pulled his mind away. He felt a sort of sluggishness as he began to think.

'In the evening,' he said slowly. 'You saw him drive away in the evening.'

'Yes.'

'What time?'

'A little before seven. Why, what's the matter?'

'The van wasn't here in the evening.'

'It was. I saw it. I saw him.'

'I don't understand.'

296

His mind worked so slowly. Cobb had been dismissed at the sawmill at two o'clock. He'd come back to the house to pick up the van. By two thirty he'd driven it away, first down to Garford Road, then out to the Elsfield woods, finally back to the compound at Osney. He had no reason to drive back to Fothergill's. Why would the van be here at seven o'clock?

'It doesn't make sense,' Ray said.

'What doesn't?'

But before he could reply there was a sound from down the hallway, the front door opening and shutting.

FORTY-ONE

The ditch was full of weeds: nettles, cow parsley, hemlock, straggly stuff like green spaghetti coiling out of the earth, all scratchy and tangling, smelling oddly of mice and saliva. They burned his hands and arms as he groped among them. His fingers were thick with mud. He straightened, looked round, thought about giving up, carried on instead. As he worked he held an image in his mind, a big man in full flight across water meadows dark as a cellar in the moonless, drizzly summer night, an ungainly man stumbling through goose grass, up and down the unpredictable corrugations of the ground, fighting for breath but forcing himself on, powered by fury and humiliation, with a hand up to the side of his head. Why? Because he wanted an explanation. Because he had to talk or that fury would choke him. So he ran, repeat-dialling as he went. *Pick up, you fucker, if you want to save yourself.*

But there was no phone. Only a gap where it should have been. Everyone said he'd probably lost it. Ryan wasn't sure he believed it any more. The police said they had swept the area at the time. But Ryan knew what that meant. Who wants to wade through a ditch more than once?

Ryan reached the end of the allotted length of ditch and turned and went back the other way, more slowly; and pulled himself out at last, his trousers soaked to the knees. Frowning, he glanced across the meadow, calculating the likely route taken by Mick Dick that night. Taking sightings against features of the road, he went out onto the marshy grass and began to slowly sweep up and down.

Ray had once told him to be methodical. He remembered his exasperated tone of voice when he'd said it, sounding less like advice and more like judgement, but he hadn't minded. Ray was a snob, of course, but only because he'd grown up rich; he didn't actually think he was superior, like so many of them did. So, as per Ray's advice, he went methodically through the grass, and in this way found a kitchen knife, a glasses case, an empty shotgun cartridge and a good deal of litter.

An hour passed.

Other people would have given up but Ryan disliked giving up, it made him feel as if someone had got one over on him. He got back into the ditch and, beginning at the opposite end, began to work his way through the weeds again. As he went along, stooping and rummaging, his mind wandered. He thought about children, the way they grew in whatever space they were given, it didn't seem to matter, a deluxe apartment in Park Town, a small room in a pebbledash semi in scruffy New Marston, a fixed caravan in a trailer park. He thought of his own son with his usual bewilderment. Ever since little Ryan had been born, even at first sight in the hospital as he lay in the plastic crib, no more than a damp mess of bruises, a misshapen head, face scrunched up in sleep, he had never seemed anything other than a complete and separate person. There was nothing of his father in him. Ryan felt as if he had no natural rights over him. If he'd been told that he wasn't the father at all, he would have believed it except for one thing: the physical sensation of his feelings, those indescribable moments of secret communion, as when he stood in the darkened bedroom watching his son sleep and his breathing slowed down and he felt his face shift as he began to smile. He didn't have any plan or ambition for little Ryan and knew that was wrong. If someone had asked him what children are for, he would have said they are here to save us.

He reached the end of the ditch and pulled himself out and sat at the side of the road, feeling crap.

No phone found. The other people must be right, after all. Mick had lost it, like he always did. Ryan's mental image of a man holding a hand up to his ear began to fade. It was hot, a haze destabilising the far green edge of meadow; a buzzard drifted overhead, crying, as if for all lost things. Sweating badly, he had wiped mud across much of his face, he could feel it pulling at his skin as it dried. He looked at his watch: he should go back to St Aldates now, listen to Wallace tell him that his application to be reinstated had failed. He really didn't want to.

With a sigh, he lay back on the grass and gazed upwards. The alder tree above him was a mesh of spindly grey branches and dusty leaves already crisping at the edges, a gently tilting mass of broken light and shade. A bird flew in and out. A butterfly lurched haphazardly through the leaves. He rested his eyes in the greenness of it, let his mind drain itself empty and fill up again with green shapes, details without meaning, a patch of sunlight peeling slowly off a branch, a strip of lichen yellow as mustard, a cluster of small brown cones. He gazed at it all listlessly. His eyes drifted over a pale gash in the bark of the trunk, and a broken stump higher up, and, above that, stuck in the cleft of two smaller branches as if defying probability, a black oblong shape that would not resolve itself into any part of the tree no matter how long he gazed at it, something unnatural, something that had no business being there.

'Fuck-a-doodle-do,' he said under his breath, almost in admiration.

He had no idea if she would be home but he was in luck, she'd just got in from her shift. She led him into the small, bright back room, where Ashleigh was sitting at the table as before, staring at him curiously over a large beaker of milk.

Ryan handed Charlene the phone. She turned it over, gave it a glance, handed it back.

'Yeah. That's Mick's. Cracked screen. He could never look after anything. Where did you find it?'

'Up a tree. Impact creates unpredictable patterns of fallout.'

'Sounds like the story of Mick's life.'

'Police'll want it.'

She shrugged.

'Don't suppose you know his security code?'

She shrugged again, gave him a number.

'Charger?'

He plugged it in while Charlene went in and out of the room

301

collecting items of Ashleigh's clothing. The black screen turned into a picture taken at a funfair of a man holding a child holding candy floss. He'd seen it before but it caught his attention again, he was held by the expression on their faces, the same solemn look, almost severe, as if the moment of candy floss was a serious thing not to be trivialised by smiles. Then he checked numbers dialled and sent text messages.

Charlene said, 'Are you done? I've got to go out with Ash now.'

He sat in the car with the phone in his pocket, thinking. Between two fifteen, when he'd left the van compound, and two thirty, when he was struck by the car, Mick Dick had made eight calls and sent three text messages all to the same number, all the texts saying more or less the same thing.

Ryan leaned back, breathed out, closed his eyes. One last time he imagined Mick Dick running across the water meadows towards North Hinksey Lane and the subway under the ring road. It was the middle of the night, the number Mick was calling rang and rang, he sent text after text, but if he didn't get an answer, it didn't matter because he was on his way, fixed on what was ahead of him, the lumpy meadows, the lane with its ditch and fringe of scrub, the path between the houses to the underpass, and the rise beyond, in one direction the townhouses of Cumnor and the Dean Court estate, where Cobb had lived, and in the other the dark bare lump of Boars Hill – and the mansions of the millionaires.

He called Ray. No answer. He called Nadim. Not available. Called the St Aldates switchboard and was put through to voice-mail. He called Ray again, and again. Sat there.

At last he phoned Ray's home, something he'd never done before.

It rang and rang, and finally it was answered. There were a few muffled crackles.

'Hello?' he said. 'Diane? How's tricks? This is a bit of a long shot but . . .'

He hesitated. On the other end there was nothing but some laboured breathing. And then a long scream of pain.

FORTY-TWO

Tom Fothergill came down the hall and stood in the doorway of the living room and looked at them. For a second he stared blankly, then smiled, lifted his arms.

'Ray.'

Ray had instinctively taken a step away from Ros. Now he stepped forward, towards Fothergill.

'Tom.' He made efforts to put an appropriate expression on his face. 'I was hoping to catch you. To say how sorry I—'

Fothergill waved away his apology. 'No need. What about a drink?'

Ros had already moved away. They were alone, the two of them. Fothergill went past Ray, into the kitchen, already talking. He was going to insist that this time Ray try the fig cordial – it was the perfect day for it, in fact, he said, smiling encouragement. Why not take their drinks outside, where they could enjoy the sun?

'I want to show you our meadow.'

Fothergill talked as easily as ever, this time polite, empty chatter, and Ray listened, making inane comments of his own, feeling the unreality of the situation, its necessary fiction. It was all so strange. Everything they were saying to each other sounded like script; they were hiding themselves in it, Ray thought, hoping not to be found out, while trying to find out what the other had done. What did it mean that Cobb's van was still at Fothergill's house at seven o'clock? He tried to focus but his brain worked slowly, clouded by those other thoughts, other disorientating images, his mouth on Ros's mouth, the look on her face, things he must keep hidden from Fothergill.

With his drink, he followed him outside to an enclosed patio of smooth blue flagstones which descended between high walls of weathered steel and timber down several levels towards a lower tier of pale cream stone in which a swimming pool was set, a crisp shape of water like a screen showing a colour image of sky and cloud. They went down the steps, still talking fictions, past ornamental trees, smaller sunken squares of mirror-like water and tropical plants frothing out of cool geometries of marble, all the way down to the pool, where Fothergill showed Ray the firepit and hot tub, and invited him to admire the trim acre of lawn below, as closely shaved as a football pitch, before they went on further, along a path of clean white gravel, to a rotunda standing above the valley, as funkily modernist as the house, all curves and sharp contrasts in polished granite, steel and timber.

'I come here to relax,' Fothergill said, 'when things get too much.'

It was cool inside, in the shade. They looked out through a wide unglazed window at the fields and meadows falling towards Oxford in rucks and seams and ripples, like a vast green rug shaken out carelessly and left there for someone else to tidy up. Ray tried to focus on what was necessary.

'Do things get too much for you often?'

'Not too often.' Fothergill smiled, holding Ray's eyes, as if inviting him to admire the difference between what was being said and what was being concealed.

The interior of the rotunda was covered in strange wall paintings, vaguely classical figures at odds with the ultra-modern architecture.

'I commissioned these,' Fothergill said. 'Ros can't bear them.' He smiled again. 'She gets to choose what goes in the house. But here, this is my domain.'

So the dream continued. Painted figures swirled up the walls. Some of them were children, Ray noticed, peeping out from hiding places, their faces shining, innocent or not so innocent. Some were naked.

'And here,' Fothergill said, going over to a wall cabinet, 'is where I keep my sports pistols. Did Ros tell you I compete?' He unlocked the doors and they appeared, rack after rack of them, hanging obliquely, bat-like.

'Fifty-metre pistols, small bore, O-two-two. The Pardini Bullseye is the best. I practise in the meadow,' he said with a nod towards the window.

Leaving the cabinet doors open, he returned to his seat.

'What do you think of my wife?' he asked.

He had stopped smiling. Taken by surprise, Ray hesitated. 'As an artist?'

'Of course not. As a woman.'

As Ray hesitated again, Fothergill continued: 'She's very

306

beautiful, isn't she?'

Ray warily murmured his agreement.

'Men can't keep their hands off her. It's not just her beauty. She's got something else, it might be her manner, the way she looks at men, or perhaps it's just the way she walks. What do you think? I'm not very good at understanding these things.'

As he spoke, he watched Ray intently, and Ray, saying nothing, turned to the view, afraid his face would give him away. He felt an accusation but couldn't tell from Fothergill's tone what he actually knew, what he might only suspect. He could feel Fothergill willing him to speak, and he instinctively resisted it, still trying to separate what was being said from what he was thinking. He had to keep focused on the van. What had Fothergill told him about the day of Poppy's murder? He had dropped Cobb off at the sawmill then driven to Birmingham, where he had spent the afternoon alone at a motor show. But had he?

'Your wife is very beautiful too, of course,' Fothergill said.

Ray's thoughts jolted away again. '*What?*'

'I met her this afternoon.'

Ray stared at him. His first thought was that this was part of the false script, the dialogue that had no meaning.

'Where?'

'At your house. Nice place. I liked it.'

'What were you doing there?'

'Returning your Ray-Bans.'

Ray stared at him.

'You left them at Ros's studio. Ros gave them to me.'

For a moment Ray's thoughts seemed to carry him away from what was being said.

'Artists, Ray. Complicated people.' Fothergill's expression hardened. 'What do you think of that?'

Ray turned from him once more, not only to hide his confusion but in a last desperate attempt to shut him out. Instinctively he took out his phone to call Diane, but he couldn't concentrate on even the simplest things. His mind was all questions without answers. Had he really left his Ray-Bans behind? Why had Ros given them to Fothergill? Why was Cobb's van still at Fothergill's at seven o'clock? All the time he was gazing, almost hypnotised, at the nude children with old, knowing expressions swimming round and round in spirals up the wall.

His phone gave a beep. A text from Nadim.

It read: *Call me. Sayyed here. Cobb had alibi!*

It was as if someone had slapped him in the face. His mind lurched, he gave a croak and said, 'The van. Cobb didn't pick it up at two thirty. He picked it up at seven.'

For a moment Fothergill didn't react. 'The case is over, Ray,' he said at last.

But Ray persisted. 'The van was here. On your driveway. For someone else to use.'

Now Fothergill reacted; his face grew heavy, his shoulders fell. It happened quickly, a sort of deflation. He got to his feet, a little clumsily, and stood by the window, looking at the gorgeous vista. When he spoke his voice was soft and conciliatory.

'I've always known I wasn't like other people, Ray. Not quote normal unquote. My foster parents told me, insisted on it. They made it worse, of course. I was only a child. Unformed, like other children. Not fixed. Still possible. That's where the beauty of children is, in their promise. Don't you think?'

He turned, gestured at the pictures on the wall, the peering children with their knowing faces, in his own face now a tremendous sadness.

Ray went on. 'You told me you were at a motor fair in Birmingham. But the friend you said saw you there never got back to us. We didn't pursue it, we were too fixated on Cobb.'

'Poor Cobb,' Fothergill said.

His eyes met Ray's, then flicked away towards the gun cabinet.

'I don't say children are innocent, Ray. I wasn't innocent as a child. There were things I knew that most adults never learn. Children watch, they know. Very soon they begin to understand.'

Ray was determined to ignore him. He said, 'Cobb didn't drive down to Garford Road in that van, you did. You're a trustee at Magpies, you take an interest, you help out. You had opportunity to get friendly with Poppy.'

Now Fothergill was murmuring incoherently to himself.

'It was you,' Ray said. 'You drove out to the Elsfield woods with her, didn't you, and you killed her and drove back here and left the van on the driveway for Cobb to pick up later, thinking it had been here all afternoon, and drive it back to the compound? You'd thought it through, worked it out, calculated the risks, like you always do.'

'Ray, Ray,' Fothergill murmured. He began to pace about in agitation. 'Please,' he said. 'Please.'

Ray said, 'Move away from the cabinet.'

'Ray,' he pleaded, moving towards it.

Too late Ray understood his intention and leaped forward.

The Peugeot banged like beaten metal as Ryan accelerated along the eastern bypass, keeping an eye out for patrol cars. He went at speed past the car plant shining in its hollow, whipped round the Littlemore roundabout, took a risk with a red light by the big Sainsbury's and headed west. Diane hadn't said much before they gave her oxygen but she'd said enough for Ryan to suspect where Ray was.

He went over Hinksey roundabout and up the steep wooded slope towards Boars Hill, engine banging.

Leaving the Peugeot in front of the gates that wouldn't open to people of the wrong sort, he ran along the wall through knee-high nettles and thistles. Unlike the house itself, the wall was made of traditional rubble stone, presumably a condition for planning permission. Not that Ryan had a view on regulations. But it made the wall easier to climb.

Then he was banging on the door.

Then he was shouting.

Then he was looking at the babe he'd seen before, standing there, hardly surprised at all, composed in fact, looking at him coolly. He liked that, he almost gave her some old chat but stopped himself.

She said, 'Yes, I think he's still here, talking to my husband. But I don't know where they are. Is there a problem?'

'Kiddie got killed. That's a problem.'

'You mean Poppy Clarke? I thought that case was solved.'

'Just got unsolved.'

Before she could reply there was the short crack of a gunshot somewhere in the distance.

She pointed.

He ran.

★

Ray and Fothergill sat side by side on the stone floor of the rotunda. A Pardini Bullseye pistol lay where it had come to rest a few yards away from them.

'That was silly, Ray,' Fothergill said. 'I wasn't going to harm you.'

Ray got to his feet and stood over him, shaky. He felt the oddity of the moment, the ultra-stylish rotunda, the creepy wall paintings, the multi-millionaire owner of Baby Dynamic slumped at his feet. 'Thomas Fothergill, I'm arresting you for the—'

'Not my name.'

'What?'

'Fothergill's not my name.'

'What is your name?'

'I've never known.' Wearily he got to his feet.

Ray began again. 'Thomas Fothergill—'

'Stop, you fool. Look.' Fothergill was holding out his phone. 'Go on, take it.'

On the phone there was a video playing. It showed an auditorium, rows of seated people with their backs to the camera, looking towards the stage in front of them, where a man in a white shirt was sitting in front of a giant image of a car on a screen, talking about carburettors.

'The fabled Lamborghini Miura,' Fothergill said. 'Regularly voted the sexiest car ever made. It was an interesting talk.'

Ray looked at him blankly.

'Watch,' Fothergill said. 'You'll see.'

Ray watched the video. The man on stage continued to talk.

311

After a few seconds someone in the nearest row turned round in his seat. It was unmistakably Fothergill.

'My friend sent it to me when I asked him to corroborate what I told you about the motor fair. It's time-stamped. You'll be able to identify the location as the main auditorium at the National Exhibition Centre in Birmingham. I was there all afternoon.'

Ray stood there confused. The video was plain enough but he couldn't make sense of it. He tried to concentrate, he needed time to work it out. But he didn't get it. There was a noise outside the rotunda, rapid, erratic footsteps grating on gravel, and Ryan came skidding through the doorway, a startling, indeed alarming, figure, and – seeing the gun lying on the ground – he stepped over it smartly and backed Fothergill against the wall. He was in a rage.

'Move, and I'll kill you with my fucking thumb. Ray? Ray, mate? Speak to me. You all right?'

Fothergill said bewildered, 'Is this police procedure?'

Ryan said, 'Dunno. You should ask a fucking policeman. Me, I'm a friend of Mick Dick and I've just failed an anger management course so you can draw your own fucking conclusions.'

Ray got hold of Ryan's arm and Ryan flung it off, hands flexing, head twitching, eyeballing Fothergill, who had by now drawn his conclusions and was pale and quiet. Ray argued with Ryan furiously, trying to draw him away.

'Christ's sake, Ryan.'

'Move,' Ryan said to Fothergill. 'Go on, breathe, give me an excuse.'

'Ryan! Listen!'

'I'll slap your expensive nose right off your fucking face. Think

I won't?'

'Ryan!'

'I'll give you something to spend your money on. How about twenty grand's worth of completely necessary cosmetic surgery?'

'*Ryan!*'

Ray finally succeeded in dragging Ryan back from Fothergill, who slowly slid down the wall until he was sitting forlornly on the stone-flagged floor under a painting of a fetching boy with an unforgiving look on his pretty young face.

'He's got an alibi,' Ray said finally.

There was a moment when they both just stood there, panting lightly. Then Ryan tossed him a phone.

'What's this?'

'Mick Dick's. Take a look.'

There was a text on it sent to Fothergill at 2.15 a.m. the night of Poppy's murder.

You never said it was that girls ribbons what have you done.

'It was Fothergill asked Mick Dick to retrieve the ribbons from the van, not Cobb. So what's that about?'

They looked at Fothergill crouched against the wall, his face clenched shut.

Ray said slowly, 'The van was here . . . but he was in Birmingham.'

Ryan said, 'Who else was here then? Who else could have used the van?'

They looked at Fothergill. His face collapsed. 'Please,' he said. 'Please don't judge him. He's just a child.'

Jack Fothergill had his own rooms on the opposite side of the house. He wasn't there. The rooms were a mess, teenage chaos of clothes, equipment, bedding, unwashed crockery.

'Where is he?'

Fothergill didn't know, or wouldn't say. He was no longer the talkative, confident millionaire, no longer tanned and fit-looking; he stood contorted and shivering in the doorway, his expression so strained it was as if he were only just holding the parts of his face together.

'He's vulnerable,' he managed to say at last.

Ray said, 'He did work experience at Magpies. Where else?'

Fothergill shook his head. 'I made him give it up.'

'Where?'

'The school down the hill, in Kennington. St Swithun's.'

Ryan gave a twitch.

'He's not capable,' Fothergill said. 'I didn't know what to do. I had to protect him. He's my son!' he shouted. 'It's what parents do!'

Ros Kerr appeared behind him and seemed to take everything in at once.

'My car's gone,' she said to Fothergill, who looked at her in fear.

Ray looked at his watch. Four thirty. Kids would be leaving after-school clubs. 'How far is St Swithun's?'

But Ryan was already out of the door.

The school was almost deserted; most children had already been picked up. Mylee was the only one still waiting at the entrance of the short driveway at the side of the school buildings. She was wearing her cousin's pirate costume, and she was waiting to see if her friend would appear. He didn't always, which was confusing but also exciting. Her mother was inside, signing some forms with her teacher, and Mylee had quietly slipped out into the warm afternoon, the sky blue all over, sunshine lighting up the ground, the walls, the wheelie bins.

She heard him before she saw him, she was clever like that. He made a special whistling noise, like a bird, to let her know the game was beginning, and she put her hands over her eyes, counted, snatched her hands away and looked round, so quick she saw the edge of his shadow sliding behind the furthest bin; and she laughed, and heard him laugh too from his hiding place. He had a nice laugh, not like an adult's laugh at all but free and a little wild, the sort of noise you make when you can't help yourself.

She had never known if he was a proper teacher or a helper teacher; he hadn't been in school for days, but it didn't make any difference. In fact, it was more exciting not knowing.

She could feel her heart beating.

She closed her eyes again, and heard rustling noises, and opened them suddenly but he had hidden himself too quickly this time, behind the nearest wheelie bin. He was making excited half-smothered little noises now. She could imagine his face as he hid, a nice face, funny with all that hair hanging round it. Next time he would catch her, or she would see him. Either way it was the best, most hilarious bit of the game, the bit when they laughed together, and he gave her the sweets, always Black Jacks, her favourites. She hoped it would happen before her mum came out. They never played the game if her mother was there; it was a rule.

She closed her eyes.

And heard him creeping towards her, but kept her eyes closed, trying not to giggle, because she wanted to be caught, wanted to scream with laughter.

Then there were other footsteps, an intrusion, and she crossly opened her eyes.

Jack stood on the driveway, a long-haired adult-boy in *Jesus is My Homeboy* tee and black jeans and trainers, suddenly lost. His father held out his arms to him. Behind his father were two other men, both looking at him. The little girl was saying something but he just handed her the sweets and stepped away, walking solemnly without speaking towards his father.

Ryan and Ray stood a little way off at the side of the road, waiting for back-up to arrive. Mylee was inside the school with Jade. Fothergill stayed locked silently in an embrace with his son by the wheelie bins.

'How old do you think he is?'

'Older than he looks. Twenty-three, if I remember. He's got issues.'

'What issues?'

'Schizophrenia.'

'On meds?'

'His father wouldn't allow it.'

'How do you know all this?'

Ray thought of Ros talking in her studio. He said nothing. Patrol cars drew up.

'Thought at first he'd shot you.'

'Don't know what he was trying to do. Don't think he knew either.'

A black Range Rover also drew up and a familiar figure got out, tight-suited as usual, and began to walk towards them.

'All we need's fucking Barko.'

'How's your niece?'

'Yeah. Don't even want to think about it.' He lit up, blew out smoke. 'Funny how things work out, eh?'

'Hilarious.'

'Got there in the end, though. Always an upside, Ray.'

Ray didn't reply. The Super approached.

'Fuck!' Ryan said suddenly. 'Forgot to say. Diane.'

'What about her?'

'She had to go into hospital. Her waters broke.'

Ray stared at him. 'Don't be stupid. She's only six months.'

'Mate.'

There must have been something in his face. Ray ran. He went at speed past the Super, who turned to stare impassively at him before continuing towards Ryan, waiting for him fatalistically on the pavement.

FORTY-THREE

The rooms in the new maternity ward at the John Radcliffe Hospital are artificially bright and scrupulously bare except for essential things, bed, bath, washbasin, chair. There is a green curtain on a curving runner set into the ceiling if privacy is needed. Calm rooms, but a little cold. Efficient rooms. Rooms with amnesia, always forgetting the mess and emotion of the births that have taken place in them.

When Ray ran in, Diane was lying awkwardly on a bean bag, legs apart, head lolling like a despot, being examined by a midwife. As he appeared, she let out a sob.

'Three centimetres,' the midwife said. 'That's good.'

'Only three?' Diane cried in horror. A contraction came and she made a noise, the like of which Ray had never heard, an animal growl deep in her throat, then she turned her head and stared speechlessly at him.

'Breathe,' he said, alarmed, using the calmest voice available to him. 'Breathe as if you're blowing out a—'

'Don't fucking patronise me,' she said in one long, quick gasp. 'You did this to me.'

With another growl she turned her face away, grimacing, arching her back. In horror, Ray looked at the midwife – a young woman, slim, probably childless – who indicated the door with a nod of her head.

In the corridor they spoke.

'Who are you?'

'What do you mean? I'm the father.'

'Oh. Not the guy who brought her in?'

'Of course not. He's just a . . . No. Not him. Me.'

'Okay. Listen. Six months, obviously not normal.'

'Then why?'

She shrugged. 'Could be a number of things, high blood pressure, problems with the uterus, infection. Stress is the commonest cause of premature birth. Has something stressful happened?'

He left a gap where his answer should be. 'Is she going to be okay?'

'She's had tests, no major problems. She's been in the theatre, nothing's happening, she's back out here. So. We wait, monitor, see what happens.'

Ray was aghast. 'Wait? Just wait? Can't you . . .'

'Can't we what?'

'I don't know. Operate?'

She gave him a long, cool look. 'First time for you, is it?'

He swallowed, nodded.

'It's not science. It's nature. You'll see plenty of science later if we need it.'

She went back into the room and left him there.

★

319

After an hour Diane went into the bath. She lay against the side of the tub, eyes tight shut, face flushed and swollen, mouth open, saying nothing. Occasionally she convulsed with a contraction, the rest of the time she lay completely still, as if her body didn't dare move, her distorted outline under water very clear and very wrong. It came to Ray that she was going to die, that the babies were going to die too; it seemed to him that everyone else was merely pretending they weren't. It also came to him that it was his fault, and that this was his punishment. He watched the surface of her face, slack and exhausted, shaken by sudden wrinkles of pain. As he remembered kissing Ros in Fothergill's kitchen, he felt the guilt of it in his stomach like nausea. He'd thought the story was elsewhere, over now, but it was here, still going on, still unbearably unfinished, unsolved, and he was stuck in it.

Several specialists came and went but the babies would not be born.

'Isn't it time to intervene?' Ray said.

They were courteous, serious, calm, telling him nothing.

Very little happened very slowly.

Almost imperceptibly the room filled up with extra equipment.

An anaesthetist attempted four times to administer an epidural. It did not take.

Other medical staff appeared, they stood around talking, looking interested, called their friends, chatted, drifted away without taking notice of Ray's panicky questions. Helpless, he sat in a corner of the room fixated on Diane. He was responsible for what was happening to her, and not in a vague metaphorical way.

A specialist came in, examined the monitor, looked puzzled, went away again without speaking to anyone.

A second midwife arrived. Diane was conscious again but barely responsive. With her feet on the hips of the two midwives, she tried to ride each contraction, arching her back, tucking her head into her chest, gulping down huge breaths, heaving downwards in agony. But the babies still did not come.

The specialist who appeared now was chubby and unshaven with a curved fleshy nose, glasses and tousled hair. He was a surgeon. Over his smock he wore a gold chain. His voice, when he finally spoke, was very quiet and heartbreakingly sincere. There was an issue with delivery, he said. There were three choices. A top-up of epidural and continued pushing. A drip to speed up contractions. A spinal block and into the operating theatre. Ray began to answer but it became clear that the surgeon had actually been talking to Diane, who asked in a gasp to be taken to the operating theatre.

The consultant anaesthetist arrived, a huge Indian man, chewing gum, and they all moved at a brisk pace down the corridor.

In the theatre there was more equipment and brighter light from a bank of mobile lamps suspended watchfully over the operating table. In plastic smock and elasticated papery shoes, Ray took up his privileged and useless place at Diane's head. A wet flannel, which he had thoughtlessly brought with him like a security blanket, drooled in his pocket. By now he had stopped asking questions and no longer listened to what people said to him. He began to pray. He made a solemn vow that if only Diane and the babies lived, he would atone, he would be different.

The spinal block was administered by the gum-chewing anaesthetist and his assistant. It didn't work and everyone was puzzled.

Every few minutes Diane was seized by another contraction. A baby doctor came in to check the new-borns and was surprised to find that they had not yet been born. Another anaesthetist arrived. Ray became alarmed by the increase in headcount; there were ten people in the theatre now and a new sense of urgency seemed to move through them. The surgeon himself showed signs of wanting to get things going. The anaesthetist repeated again that he wouldn't hurt Diane, who let out another scream as he spoke.

Ray prayed out loud, not caring if anyone heard him.

The surgeon crouched between Diane's legs pondering the situation. At her next contraction he reached in and turned the baby's head with his hand, and she screamed again.

It was obvious now that something radically different was needed. Ray waited impatiently for the decision to be taken, for the hi-tech equipment to be put in place, for science to finally take over, for a proper controlled operation to begin, but instead, to his horror, the surgeon took up a rudimentary metal contraption like a clamp and began to adjust it, like a plumber his spanner. And as Diane pushed again, her face flushed and bloated, he rudely pushed the thing into her and tugged, grunting. Others suddenly crowded round, a rugby scrum of specialists. Diane was yelling continuously now, and someone else standing too close was making loud, stupid noises, who, Ray realised at last, was himself. There was going to be no calm and sophisticated procedure. The surgeon rolled his sleeves up and had another go with the forceps. He put his foot up against the end of the table, braced himself, took a breath. He reached in, tugged hard and staggered backwards, dragging something with him, a baby's head, black and hard like an elongated stone, an outcrop of rock drenched in rain. He manhandled it crudely, pulling this way and that, and the baby's body came free, and he slapped it down on Diane's belly, a tiny, curled, clenched, live thing the colour of dark shale out of rich soil, slimed with blood, ruddy black, the umbilical cord, thick as a hosepipe, trailing behind it. The baby doctor cut and clamped the cord with a hiss of escaping air, and the new creature made a noise through its mouth.

Ray chewed his knuckles, aghast.

'A beautiful boy,' the surgeon said without looking or apparently caring. He was already manhandling the baby's twin.

Ray felt dizzy and, suddenly, overwhelmingly upset. Someone was asking him if he was all right. He seemed to be weightless, insubstantial. Briefly he was on the floor, then for some reason he couldn't speak. And at last he was aware of being led away, into the corridor, where he sat on a hard chair with his head on his knees, sobbing.

Someone pressed a mug of tea into his hands, milky, sugary stuff, the worst tea he had ever tasted, and he drank it thoughtlessly, hunched over, staring at his feet, which were still clad in the papery hospital shoes.

'Hits you, don't it?' Ryan said.

He was sitting on a chair next to him.

'I remember Ry being born,' he went on. 'Started in the car park. You think it's going to be some sort of safe hospital thing and instead it's like this fucking mud-wrestle.'

'I didn't know,' Ray said. 'I had no idea.'

'Guess it's not always like that. Just for a lucky few, eh? Still, children, Ray. What they go through just getting out into the world.'

'What I went through just watching it.'

Ryan was contemplative. 'Never felt I meant anything before Ry was born, know what I mean?'

But Ray just looked away, blinking. They sat in silence for a while, patients shuffling past in slippers. An elderly lady patted Ray on the head as she passed.

Ryan said, 'Fothergills went off all right.'

For a moment Ray didn't know what he was talking about; when he realised, he found he didn't care.

'Heard from Nadim. Forensics found a kiddie's pirate eye-patch in the kid's room. Bound to be a match. Anyway, don't think there's going to be an argument about it. They've all been giving statements. Sayyed says Cobb called him from the brothel in Abingdon and he went out to join him and they stayed there the rest of the afternoon. Cobb was depressed at being let go so quick by the sawmill, needed something take his mind off it, he said. About seven, Sayyed drove him back to Fothergill's to pick up the van, making it look like he'd been at the mill all the time.'

'Ros saw him drive away in it.'

'The kid had been helping with the archery targets earlier. He'd heard that Cobb was going to be at the sawmill till seven. Van was on the driveway. Cobb had left the keys under the seat. Hi-vis jacket and helmet in the back.'

They sat again in silence.

'Not a kid,' Ray said. 'Twenty-three.'

'Not anything. They'll rule him incapable, my guess.'

More silence.

324

Ray said, 'Fothergill thought you were going to kill him, I think.'

'Considered it.'

'Might not have been the best thing reinstatement-wise.'

Ryan made a noise.

'What?'

'Didn't work out, reinstatement.'

'What happened?'

'Usual bollocks, lack of discipline, disobedience, uncontrolled temper. Other stuff, I don't know. Barko give me a heads-up. Get told formally tomorrow.'

'I'm really sorry.'

'My own fault. Anyway, you get on well with what's-her-name.'

'Livvy. She's good. She's not like you, though.'

'You're just trying to make me feel better.'

'Not gobby and awkward, I mean.'

'Well, there you go.'

'Or brilliant.'

Ryan gave a laugh. 'That's it. I'm going to be the most brilliant night security guard of my generation.'

He got up.

'See you around, mate. Enjoy being a father.'

FORTY-FOUR

He had borrowed a suit, an overbright blue polyester blend three sizes too big for him; the crotch hung down halfway to his knees, the sleeves covered his knuckles. He looked at himself in the mirror. Narrow face, grease-smear of scar tissue, big bony nose, all as familiar to him as his own smell. But plastering down his hair with eau de cologne had been a mistake.

Little Ryan stood behind him.

'Daddy?'

'Yeah?'

'Why do you look like that?'

'Wish I knew, mate.'

For some reason one of the photographs Mick Dick's mother had shown him came into his mind, a little boy in football kit crouching over a ball, fingertips touching the turf, his smile a little blast of pure happiness, and he looked down at his son, still examining with interest the material of his overlong trousers, and thought wonderingly how children find happiness anywhere, and what a gift that was.

Jade came into the room, Mylee creeping in quietly behind her. Mylee had been quiet, in fact, since a long talk with her mother the day before.

'How do I look?'

She shrugged. 'They already know you're a knobhead.'

Breaking news overnight had been vague and partial, the police had not yet made a statement, and the media were wary of publishing stories too soon about the family of a millionaire entrepreneur able to afford punitive lawyers to fight his corner. There were rumours, social media gossip, anticipation that a sensational announcement was imminent.

'Bit of luck it won't happen before they're done with you. It'd only give them something else to hit you with.'

He shrugged. 'Think they've lost interest, to be honest. Worst they could do is charge me with obstruction. I reckon they'll just terminate the process and get me out of the building quick as they can.'

'What about after? What time's your interview? Will you have time to change?'

Ryan was going for a night security gig at a cement works out at Bicester.

'Don't think dress code's a significant feature of the job, to be fair.'

'Yeah, well, don't be late back. Your turn to pick them up.'

'All right.'

She hesitated. 'Good luck.'

Ryan stooped to his son who pouted his lips and lifted his face to be kissed.

'Be good, Daddy,' he said conversationally, and Ryan laughed and went out of the house feeling lucky.

At one end of the conference room on the first floor of St Aldates, Superintendent Wallace was addressing members of the evaluation panel gathered to formally hand down the ruling in the Wilkins reinstatement application process. There were five of them altogether: Tisi Phou, director of people, who had chaired the previous disciplinary enquiry resulting in Wilkins' dishonourable discharge; senior solicitor Meg Ayers, who had also been a part of that enquiry; Mr Raminder Khan, legally qualified chair; Ms Becky Sherlaw-Higgins, headteacher, selected from an approved list of lay people; and Superintendent Wallace himself. They had been discussing the case for the past hour and now it was time to sum up and confirm their decision. Mr Khan was nominally the chair but Superintendent Wallace was by common consent the real decision-maker, and he had a firm and settled view.

In the few minutes before Wilkins was brought in to hear the verdict, Wallace stood summing up.

'Leaving aside examples of general poor behaviour, the many instances of manner and attitude falling far below acceptable standards, I'll just recap the key items of material obstructions, interferences and mistakes perpetrated by the subject of this reinstatement process.

'He covertly, and knowingly, subverted police processes by soliciting confidential information pertaining to an ongoing case, namely the investigation into the death of Michael Dick, continuing to do so after multiple verbal warnings to desist.

'He incited a senior officer to break police codes of conduct by interviewing a witness unrelated to any investigation being undertaken by that officer.

'He took evidence without authorisation from a crime scene at the Van Central compound.

'He led a warrantless forced entry into a private property at Dean Court containing further evidence.

'He made an unauthorised entry into a secure area of ongoing police activity at Rivermead Road in Rose Hill, leading the senior investigating officer away from potential lines of enquiry.

'He intervened in a situation in the grounds of a private residence at Boars Hill, confronting a private individual in a manner that can only be described as violent and threatening.'

Wallace took the spectacles off his nose, and gazed at them all with the look of disgust still on his face.

'All of which demonstrably led to the apprehension of those who had acted unlawfully, with expected successful judicial outcomes to follow. Which no one else had been able to achieve.'

Shifting parts of his bulky body inside his cramping uniform, he left a long pause as he regarded them with a vague air of menace. 'Kid got no manners,' he said. 'I don't give a shit. He gets results. The public's safer. Reinstatement upheld. Any questions?'

No one spoke.

He pressed a button on the intercom on the table in front of him.

There were footsteps outside and after a moment the former DI Ryan Wilkins came in, tugging irritably at the crotch of his overlong trousers, looking about him with the wary, exposed expression of a child.

329

Read on for the next instalment
in the DI Wilkins Mysteries

LOST AND NEVER FOUND

I

The illegal car wash on the southbound road out of Oxford is the cheapest in the city, a makeshift compound of oily puddles and streams, slick and black under dripping awnings. Here, hour after hour, cars shunt slowly across the concrete, while dozens of men and women in waterproofs and goloshes crowd round them with hoses and sponges, soaping, spraying, wiping, rinsing. Occasionally these people speak to each other, brief asides in a language that might be Russian or perhaps Albanian. Mostly they are quiet. They are tired, bending and reaching in unvarying routine as the cars creep past: the saloons, the four-by-fours, the station wagons, hatchbacks, mini vans, coupés, sedans. They know them all, these cars, all the brands and models, they have seen them all many times.

But they have never seen a Rolls Royce Phantom. Here it comes now, on this slush-coloured February morning, enormous and otherworldly, gliding onto the splintered, streaming forecourt, one hundred per cent out of place, a visitation from another dimension; and the men and women stop to look. They have never seen anything so strange, that huge boat-like hull, that unearthly colour, crystal over Salamanca blue, the whole flowing technology uncannily natural, like the movement of blossom in a breeze or waves on the surface of the sea. They are seeing these things for the first time, vividly, and will remember them later, when the police arrive to take their statements, as they will remember the driver, a woman of complete self-possession, who sits behind the wheel ignoring everything, obliviously performing neck exercises. Though they never look at her directly, the car wash men and women take in everything about her too, her elfin face, ragged-chic blonde hair, blue, distant eyes, small, pointed chin. A young face, though she is not young; she looks like a child left in charge of the family car. They watch her out of the corners of their eyes when she gets out of the car and walks slowly over to the picnic tables set up at the edge of the compound to wait for the interior cleaning to be done, standing there in a pool of greasy water, wearing elegantly tight-fitting olive green pants and expensively simple blue sweater and a touch, here and there, of bespoke jewellery, slim, modest, remote, her eyes strangely vacant, as if her mind were fixed on something else entirely, as if she existed without any connection to the current moment; until, at last, a man detaches himself from a little group of workers and walks across the wet compound towards her.

2

That evening, in the famous auditorium of Oxford's town hall, the Thames Valley Police gala dinner was taking place. At ten o'clock it had been proceeding, in formal mode, for more than three hours, and now, in the unstructured gap between meal and speeches, it was starting to lose its shape. While the stage was being prepared for the award-giving, the diners, sitting twenty to a table under the intricately decorated ceiling, removed their jackets, undid their waistcoats, discretely adjusted their ball-gowns and gave rise to an impressive babble. People wandered about; some had to go outside. Liqueurs were served; the room was warm and dimly lit and loud.

At a table almost in the middle of the crowded floor, DIs Ryan and Ray Wilkins (no relation) sat with their partners trying to keep a conversation going with Detective Superintendent Dave 'Barko' Wallace. Wallace was a copper of the old school, a wide man with a thick neck, outspread thighs and seal-like body not shaped for tuxedos. He sweated steadily from his shorn head down, his small eyes angry and vigilant, as if intent on catching someone out. He was a bore. Ryan noticed his apparent inability to blink and wondered if it was a Govan thing, like his gargling accent or intimidating silences.

Ryan was good at noticing things: he looked at them quickly along a jabbing length of bony nose and the details stuck to his eyes. He sat contentedly with a can of energy drink, which he'd had to bribe a waiter to bring him, idly scratching, noticing his girlfriend Carol's left thigh, suddenly pale and bare where her dress had fallen to one side, the result of a nervous restlessness. He noticed movement at the back of the stage, and nodded towards it.

'Wonderwoman flown in.'

Ray released his wife's hand and turned in his seat. Both he and Diane were London-Nigerian, highly educated and elegant with it; Ray in particular was a stylish dresser, wearing tonight a silk tuxedo with blue and maroon floral patterns and black satin lapels. He had one of those handsome faces in which all the features seem to come together in a common purpose, the boy-hero jaw, the shapely mouth, intelligent eyes. By contrast, Ryan looked like the trailer park kid he was, badly finished off about the chin and ears. He had a sort of borrowed look about him. His suit, rented of course, was slightly big and itchy around the groin.

Barko said, unblinking, 'You referring to Deputy Chief Constable Lynch?'

On stage there were two people. One was the Lord Lieutenant of Oxfordshire, a former banker now carnivalized in eighteenth-century tunic complete with cap, sash and ceremonial sword. The other was the guest speaker of the evening, a shortish, powerful-looking woman dressed in black leather jacket and jeans, strikingly at odds with the evening dresses on display everywhere else. She was listening, or perhaps not, to the Lord Lieutenant, her face impassive behind Aviators.

Barko said, 'Son, that lady's had more commendations than any other serving officer in this force. Big ones. Silver Medal, Bravery Award.'

'CBE,' Ray said.

Ryan shrugged, peered into his can, tilted it far back, swallowed, gave a little grimace.

Perhaps Barko would have said more, he leaned towards Ryan with sudden intent, but at that moment the on-stage microphone came to life with a screech, like a hideous malfunction of the pleasant hubbub, and everyone turned again, wincing, towards the stage and the legendary figure of Chester Lynch, standing there alone now, relaxed in the limelight of their attention. She was still wearing her Aviators. Ryan remembered then that Barko had long ago served with Lynch's unit, perhaps even before the creation of the Chester Lynch legend, when Lynch was not yet the gloried maverick she would become; and he wondered what their relationship had been like. Carol turned to him and as she smiled with that dazzling mouth he saw in her eyes something else, some strangeness, mild panic almost, or judgment. Then Lynch began her address.

'Didn't want to come here, do this.'

Her voice was the well-known gravel-chewing Cockney drawl, her face the familiar carved oddity, all planes and angles, not so much handsome as riveting. Riveting was the quality she cultivated. Her skin was so black it was almost purple.

'Make a little speech, hand out an award. Didn't want to do it.'

She left long pauses between her sentences, silences which no one disturbed.

'They said, come on Chester. You'll see all these beautiful people. The young men, they said. The women. The whole force has got good-looking, they said. It's true, by the way. But that's not why I come.'

She shook her head slightly, looking down at them.

'They said it'll be a spectacle. Spectacle's actually the word they used.' She snorted lightly. 'They talked about the meal, the braised beef cheek, sautéed whatevers, the canapés, the Krug, don't know what else, candied fruits is it, snuff? They said it'll be elegant. Do I look like I'm interested in elegant?'

She gestured slightly, contemptuously, at her clothes.

'They told me they'd make everything easy, send a limo. You know the sort of thing, champagne on ice in a little silver bucket, peanuts in one of them lead crystal tumblers weigh a tonne in your hand.'

She took off her Aviators, slowly folded them and put them carefully into the inside pocket of her jacket. 'Well. I didn't come for the ride. I didn't come for the nibbles. No.' She lowered her voice. 'I'll tell you why I come.'

She looked round the auditorium. Thirty seconds seemed to pass. No one breathed.

'I come because you're fucking brilliant people. My people. That's why I come.'

There was applause then, a lot, and she stood drenched in it.

'Alright, alright,' she said. 'Calm the fuck down.'

Laughter. The laughter of the willing.

'It's not about me,' she said. 'But they told me I got to say something about myself anyway. You know, by way of introduction. A few words. It's nonsense, I know that, stupid, you don't need to tell me, no one needs my story, you've all got your own. Still. They did ask. And I can do it in three minutes.'

She took a breath, looked round.

'Grew up in Walthamstow. Scholarship girl at the university here. Wanted to be a copper, became a copper. Came to serve here in, I think, early 2002, worked the beat four, five years. Did some training, got some skills. Same as you. Did a little time in Violent Crime, got moved on, some of you heard about that. Ups and downs. Had some ideas, about street crime, vagrancy, so on. Put them into action, got some results. Got kicked in the coccyx by austerity like everyone else. Then they put me in charge of this National Uplift thing. Well, I'm a black woman, aren't I? See me on television, in between the sit-coms and the documentaries about endangered types of moth.'

She looked at them with what seemed like the purest anger.

'Best years of my life? No question: working the beat up at Rose Hill. Learned all the important stuff then. Make the tough choices. Take the difficult decisions. Why? They're the ones get results. Don't matter what they call you, and I've been called some things, on the street, in the boardrooms, I know that, I got the nicknames. Don't matter. Don't even matter if there's truth in the nicknames. Results, that's the thing. That's what I'm about.'

She shrugged modestly, buttoned her leather jacket.

'End of speech.'

Her watch was a heavy metal thing chunky on her wrist, it caught the light as she lifted it.

'Two and a half minutes. Result, right there.'

More laughter, a murmuring of appreciation.

'Anyway,' she said, picking up the trophy that had been at her feet and casually waving it to and fro, 'speaking of results, there's a young man here tonight . . .'

Ryan stopped listening, went back to noticing Carol, who sat vividly next to him in her evening dress of electric-blue silk. She'd relaxed a little. They'd been seeing each other only a few months and they were still in the first phase of their relationship: he was living in a state of constant sexual emergency. God, she was built. Nine years older than him, thirty seven, with one ex-husband and two kids, sharp-faced, alarmingly erotic, shockingly straightforward. She liked to shock, in fact. It was part of her attraction. She'd grown up wild in Didcot and other places, messed about, missed a lot of school, but now she owned four florists and lived in a converted farmhouse on the edge of Kennington. She had the business smarts big time, and the things that go with it, organisation, toughness, energy, a little bit of aggression. All in all, Ryan wasn't at all sure why she'd picked him out. They'd met one morning outside the infant school, where he was waiting with little Ryan to pick up his niece Mylee. He hadn't even given her some old chat, they just talked about the kids, and something clicked, some weird mechanism pulled them together, set them going, all the way from St Swithuns Primary School to the fifty fourth Thames Valley Police Gala at the town hall.

Chester Lynch was still talking but Ray was getting to his feet, which Ryan thought was pretty uncool, a very un-Ray-like thing to do in the middle of a speech; and it was a moment before

340

he took in the general applause, noticed people at nearby tables congratulating him. As Ryan watched, Ray leaned over and kissed Diane, buttoned his shimmering tuxedo, and began to make his way towards the stage.

Fuck me, Ryan thought in shock. *He's fucking well won something.* Perhaps he actually said it out loud because Carol turned to him with that look of hers that he didn't yet understand, hard-eyed and startled, as if she too was transfixed by the action on the stage, by Chester Lynch greeting Ray with a fist bump. And the next moment he was on his feet, fingers in his mouth, whistling and stomping his feet, while Barko sat immobile, staring at him in scorn.

They drove back to Kennington in her Range Rover. His Peugeot was still in the garage. For a while she didn't say anything, and he watched her as they went quietly through the hush of Oxford at one o'clock in the morning, past the cathedral, down the long stretch of road where the college playing fields are laid out like art works on the carefully curated green of the water-meadows.

'Just taken by surprise is all,' he said at last.

She gave a brief smiling pout of disbelief, looking at the road ahead.

'Alright. Jealous, then. A bit.'

The smile played at the edges of her mouth. The urge came on him, very strong, to kiss her, touch her, put out his hand and feel the thin silk of her dress slide over her leg, he almost groaned with the force of it. But it also seemed a truth-telling urge, and he said, 'A bit, I don't know, pissed off. I mean, I did actually do quite a lot of the leg-work.'

She drove on.

'This is after your discharge,' she said after a while. 'So you weren't actually a policeman.'

'Just suspended,' he said defensively. 'Working my way back, fast track.'

They drove past the Premier Inn.

'Fastish,' he said.

They went over the railway tracks and turned towards Kennington.

'What's your problem with the lady giving out the prizes?' she asked after a while, in a different tone.

'Lynch? She's alright. Just like, everything's exaggerated with her. Toughest cop ever. Smartest cop ever. Coolest cop. It's like this whole Chester Lynch legend.'

He looked at her sideways, her profile.

'People got a crush on her. Ray's got a crush. Maybe it's a black thing.'

'Not allowed to say that, Ryan.'

They drove on.

'What did she get her CBE for?'

'Street vagrancy policy, I think. Sort of a clean-up. Move them on, basically.'

'And she got results?'

'If you look at the stats, yeah. Crime down, anti-social down, drug trade down. But police complaints went up big time, and if you talk to any of the homeless, fuck. They hate her. Call her the Mover.'

They drove under the by-pass, quiet now.

'Got moved on herself from Violent Crime, she said.'

'Yeah, all the way up to DCC.'

'But moved on, why?'

'Well, that's something else. Scandal, controversy, whatever. Shot some local gangster in a lock-up. Rumour was she just took him down, personal thing. Don't believe it. Maybe even put it about herself, for the, you know, what's the word?'

'Notoriety?'

'That's the one. Worse thing, I think's, stuff with the homeless. I mean, they might be losers but still.'

He shifted uncomfortably in his seat; it wasn't clear if it was the thought of Chester Lynch or his scratchy dress trousers that chafed him.

'Know any homeless, Ryan?'

Briefly he thought of his old schoolmate Mick Dick. Homeless, then dead. He sighed. 'Not any more.'

They went slowly up the long road with its street bumps until they came to Kenville Road, where Ryan lived with his sister, Jade. Little Ryan would be there, asleep in his bed in the room he shared with his father, and Ryan thought of his son with the total abandonment of love. He looked at his watch: going on one thirty.

Carol slowed, came to a stop, looked at him. There was a moment's silence between them. 'Do you want to come back to mine?' Her dress had fallen off her thigh again and he stared at it, mesmerised, swallowed. She knew he didn't like missing breakfast with his son, especially not after missing bedtime reading the night before.

'He had a tummy upset,' Ryan said.

She nodded. 'I'll get you up early, drive you back in time for breakfast. Or maybe,' she said softly, 'I'll just keep you up all night.'

He looked at her. They drove on.

So Oxford settled into sleep. A small city, damp, unconscious under February cloud, its clustered monuments making their familiar iconic gestures against the dim sky, here the Radcliffe Camera's fat dome, there the sharp tack of St Mary's spire, their outlines crisp as cardboard cut-outs. And in the shadows of these buildings, on pavements slick with condensation, the homeless lay, silently outlasting the cold in their bags and tents. In Blue Boar Street, in Cornmarket, at Blackfriars, St Aldates, St Ebbes, outside the Odeon in Gloucester Green and in other haunts, they crouched hunched under fire escapes or in doorways. In the shadows of the great colleges, wrapped in layers, wearing scavenged boots that didn't fit, they lay prone on cardboards beds rimmed with the day's detritus, invisible under piles of clothing. They persisted, getting through the night, alone, or in twos or threes, or in larger groups, not sleeping but sometimes no longer conscious, left out in the open like so much litter, lost things. But at the makeshift camp in the graveyard of St Thomas the Martyr, at three o'clock in the morning, there was no one. It was deserted, they'd vanished in haste, leaving everything behind them, their tents and boxes, rags and empties, abandoning the graveyard with its tilting tombstones and dripping yew, putting distance between themselves and silent, dirty Becket Street, darkest and dirtiest street in town, where a Rolls Royce Phantom lay buckled and wedged in the entrance to the rail station car park.

344

ACKNOWLEDGMENTS

It's a pleasure, as always, to note the help I've received. I am indebted to the Royal Literary Fund for financial assistance. Then there are the usual suspects. My agent, Anthony Goff (thank you and I'm sorry). My publisher, Jon Riley (for making the critical difference); editor, Jasmine Palmer (for making things so much easier); copy-editor, Lorraine Green (for saving me from myself); publicist, Katya Ellis (for making the unlikely happen); and the rest of the team at riverrun and Quercus, who show such remarkable professionalism.

I must also thank my daughter Eleri and son Gwilym both for their instructive comments on the text and for continually showing me the world in a new light. And, once more, thanks and love to my wife Eluned, whose help is too large and various to be defined.